Bombay Baby

Leela Soma

First published 2011 by Dahlia Publishing Ltd
6 Samphire Close Hamilton
Leicester LE5 1RW

ISBN 978-0-9566967-1-7

Printed and bound by Good News Digital Books

Acknowledgements

I am grateful to all my friends and family who have supported me and kept me going when I needed to. To Frances for being patient with me and for being the first reader, a very special thanks. I am indeed indebted to my nephew Karthik and his wife Vidya who have helped me enormously at every stage of the book and in getting my website to speed. A special thank you to my publisher and editor Farhana who helped get this book to the public. Last but not least, I couldn't have written this book without support from Som and Nita.

Chapter 1

Her life was a jigsaw puzzle with a single piece missing. She had to find that missing piece. She was Scottish but there was the *other*. It was a tiny void that kept resurfacing; despite herself, it was something she could not ignore. Tina watched the deep, dark waves, of Loch Lomond, crested white with bubbly foam as they lashed wildly on the shore. She dug her shoe into the pebbly sand and the crumbling mass gave her a sense of comfort.

Amongst the lush green of the trees she noticed the lone copper beech tree. Its reddish maroon leaves flamboyantly swayed against the peridot swathes of lush vegetation. The serenity of the Loch soothed her for a moment, but as she looked down at the brown earth, it unsettled her. Nature continues in an ever ending cycle, undergoing little change except when man interferes, she thought.

Tina rubbed her hands together to warm them; she held them up, examining them as if for the first time. Brown hands, different to her parents.

The mist-laden Campsie Fells loomed in the distance, portent of a rainy afternoon. She walked on close to the loch; the quartzite curving wall looked like an artist's work, dividing the land from the water. She picked up a pebble and threw it in and watched as the water rippled, unsettling the calm of the loch.

The niggling awareness of not knowing who she really was, ever present.

Must see how Jenny can help me again, she thought to herself.

After an hour she took the bus, it was weaving its way on the busy Great Western Road. Tina was making the first tentative step on her long road of discovery. The bus was crowded. The cacophony of sounds around her, the ring tones of mobiles, and bits of conversations helped to drown her thoughts. The loud engine noise and the traffic distracted her. The woman in the seat across from her shouted above the din, into her mobile phone.

"Aye, I'm oan the bus. Aye, see you in a bit. Naw, she's not coming back. Aye, she said she's had enough of them. You better not leave, stay in the hoose till I get back."

I don't know who I am.

Tina's mind darted between the snippets of conversations on the bus and her own thoughts. She drummed her fingers nervously. Her mind wandered, she thought of Jenny to focus her thoughts.

I don't know who I am.

Someone rang the bell for the next stop. The electronic tickertape on the monitor on the bus read "Next stop Kelvinbridge." The driver applied the break suddenly and a few people jerked. Tina felt her body lurching forward. The young man, who was holding onto his eco-friendly jute bag strained with groceries, grabbed the seat frame in front to steady himself. Jolted out of her thoughts the frayed edges of her angst drew her back to the bus once again.

A handful of schoolchildren got on the bus, shot Tina a quick glance and then turned away.

No I'm not like you, safe in your own identities, she thought as she watched the swarm of school kids laughing and messing about with each other.

She was a brown girl born to white parents.

Like a cuckoo in a reed warbler's nest.

An old woman had whispered those words such a long time ago. Even though she had not understood the meaning of the phrase at the time it had stuck in her mind. She wished her life wasn't so complicated.

Tina looked out of the window and saw a haze of purple; schoolchildren in their blazers cross the road. Some walked into *Philadelphia*, others headed for *Roots and Fruits* whilst the rest huddled themselves around *Costa*.

Smug in their own skins.

The bus moved again. Tina reached for the iPod. The large sheaf of notes rustled as she twiddled the white cord, and the thin sliver of musical wizardry appeared from her bag. She plugged in the earphones, pressed menu and selected shuffle. The swathe of music relaxed her. She could have been in her own room, away from the crowd, with her thoughts. Her mind escaped to another world made up of her own space and thoughts despite the noise around her.

She was heading towards another counselling session with Jenny, which made her feel better. She didn't have the answers yet but she was sure to find them by exploring, Jenny had told her. At last she had taken the courage to follow her heart and find answers.

Tina's parents had tried to explain the paradox that was her life, a brown girl born to white parents. She had been very young when they sat her down and told her in simple terms. She had not really understood what it meant. As a child aged four, she found it difficult to grasp the meaning of embryo donation or adoption, words that were long and alien sounding to her. She had turned away from them and played with her toys. It had been such a difficult concept to her that she had swept it aside preferring to leave it in the background. It was only much later that vague doubt appeared, and remained close behind her, like a shadow. Now at the cusp of her adulthood she felt the need, a real urgency to find out who she really was.

Jenny would help her. That incessant voice, urging her to find out, had finally risen up and she could not ignore it any longer.

*

Jenny looked out of the window. The girl was not walking up the road yet. Tina, next on her list, was the most intriguing of her clients. She had pondered over her case so many times. Jenny had dealt with several cases of adopted people. She relished the fact that she could help them overcome their angst as they searched and found their long lost birth parents. Some found closure. Others had to be helped to come to terms with their unsuccessful search. Jenny specialised in this field. Having been adopted herself, she had a deeper understanding of their feelings, the confusion, and the desperate search for belonging. She read over Tina's notes again.

Tina was different. She had registered for counselling herself, seeking help without her parents knowing. She had a real passion for finding out where she came from but confusion and feelings of guilt were obstacles that could jeopardise her search.

At their first few meetings, Jenny did very little probing, she let the young woman talk. She admired the fact that Tina had come to her of her own accord, had asked her doctor for a referral. Jenny established a good rapport with her, and won her trust, she hoped.

The bell rang. Tina stood at the door; she was a pretty girl in jeans and a t-shirt that hugged her curvaceous figure. She held herself well and there was a determined thrust to her jaw. Framing her eyes were long lashes. They swept over her wide brown eyes, making her an attractive young woman. Her deep dark brown eyes revealed an entirely different story.

"Come in Tina,"

Jenny closed the door behind her. They entered the consulting room. Jenny moved behind the wide desk to retrieve her notes then settled into her chair. Tina sat at the chair opposite, the space between them well measured so that it was intimate enough to talk in a low voice but not too close. Tina glanced at the desk and saw the striking colour of a fresh posy of pinks in a tiny vase. It lifted her spirit.

"So, how have you been, Tina?" Jenny smiled, encouragingly.

"I'm fine." Tina said, allowing her eyes to meet Jenny's for the first time. She gave a hesitant smile before rubbing her fingers together.

The sound of the ticking clock reassured her. Tick. Tock. Jenny was reluctant to fill in the silence with another question so they both sat still.

After a moment's pause Tina sighed, a frown flitted across her face and then she straightened her back as though she had resolved to move on. With a determined look, she pulled out the papers from her bag. She'd spent hours downloading the information and had read it several times, highlighting relevant bits with a bright orange pen.

"Tina, did you find anything interesting from the internet? Are you any further forward?" Jenny probed.

Tick. Tock.

"No, erm yes…"

Tina's brows knitted for a second. She looked vulnerable, pained.

Jenny made a note in her notepad. *Not yet sure about her research? Confused.*

Jenny looked up and nodded for Tina to continue.

"Yeah, I got some info on a clinic in India. The clinic has a website that gives all the information on the procedure." Tina flicked through the pages and stopped at the third page. She hesitated, waved the sheets impatiently.

Jenny raised her eyebrows, questioning silently.

Tina shrugged and then continued.

"I tried to get information on patients." She shook her head. "Oh, it's useless!"

"Why? Didn't you get anything that you were looking for?"

"No, but I was surprised to read testimonies from patients from all over the world. People from USA, UK and many local people have used the clinic. I thought there would be patient confidentiality but some of the testimonies are from people so happy with their babies that they have given some of their details, even photographs of their babies."

Tina stopped, blinked as if trying to stop her tears flowing.

"It's okay, just take your time," said Jenny softly.

Tick. Tock.

"I…couldn't find, I mean…there was…no testimony from… that lady donor…my mum or dad. No photos." Tina drummed her fingers lightly on the sheaf of papers. A tear rolled silently down her face.

Jenny busied herself by scribbling notes on her pad. *A long summary of her finds. Meticulous.*

"So have the testimonies helped you in any way?"

"Yeah, they looked so happy to be holding a child. Some of them spent so many years trying alternatives but it came to nothing. They seemed so desperate. This was their only hope. Their only chance, in a way, to have a family of their own."

Jenny observed Tina's feet tapping nervously,

"What do you think is the best way forward from this?"

"Do you think I could write to one of the clinics and ask them for information? Maybe they might know the woman who donated the egg?"

"Do you want to do that, Tina? Do you know if that is the right clinic?"

"Yeah, I suppose I need to find that out too. The whole point of my delving into all this is to get as much information as possible, surely?"

"Has the clinic mentioned the names of donors? That information is likely to be under lock and key."

"The website is more about the success rate of the embryo transfers, photos of the happy families with their babies. Most donors aren't part of the happy ending. They're invisible."

Tina's voice rose sharply. She checked herself and the tears at the corner of her eyes glinted. She looked down and her lashes provided a veil from her emotions.

Tick. Tock.

Jenny was silent.

After a pause, she cleared her throat gently. Tina looked up and continued. "Maybe they don't give out the donor information," she almost whispered.

"You need to be prepared for that fact. Also you have to remember this might not be the clinic where your parents were treated," Jenny replied.

"I could ask my mum. Maybe she would know who the lady was, she would remember the clinic, surely? But I don't want to hurt her."

Her fingers ran a brief tap on the papers again.

"Why do you think you'll hurt her?"

There was another pause.

Tina looked out of the window. The rain had started. It lashed on the panes and the glassy droplets began to pattern the window.

Tick. Tock.

"She'll think I don't love her enough, that I'm looking for a woman who has nothing to do with my life except…"

Tina twisted the sheaf of paper on her lap. Tears again threatened to fall from the edge of her eyelashes. Jenny passed her a tissue but said nothing.

"But she is part of me and I'm part of her without her even knowing. I am her flesh and blood. Oh this is so hard."

The tears started again. The drops fell silently dampening her T-shirt. Tina used the tissues to wipe away the agony of the emotions twisting her heart, finding the words to express them, was so much harder.

"I know you said that I should tell them I'm seeing you, but I haven't. Not yet" Tina added.

"Why is that? I'm sure they must know something."

Jenny swept her hair from her face and tucked it behind her ear.

"I don't know. Where would I start? How would I even bring it up? I'm not sure what I want or where this is going, it would only hurt them if I choose to do…"

Jenny nodded and smiled.

"You are helping me, just talking with you is…good."

Tina looked at her, gratitude laced her eyes. She wriggled in her chair. Her handbag slid off her shoulder and her purse fell on the floor. A photo of a white couple, much like the ones Tina had seen on the clinic's website, with a toddler perched on their lap, fell at Jenny's feet. She glanced at it before handing it back to Tina.

Tina looked at the photo.

"That's me on my first birthday with my mum and dad posing for my grandma. It's been in my purse for ages." She explained.

"They got their happy ending too." She shoved the purse back into her bag closing the clasp.

"I'll write to the clinic, that's what I'll do. I've got to, really." She said firmly.

"If you're sure that's what you want to do." Jenny nodded in approval.

Their meetings always had this pattern. Tina arrived in an indecisive, confused state, but talking out her thoughts made her feel better. She just needed somebody to listen. She felt clearer about her next course of action and left Jenny in a happier state of mind. She was spurred into action.

Just voicing her innermost thoughts helped her enormously something that she could not do even with her closest confidante, Keisha. In her own mind she was determined to send an email to the clinic that very evening.

*

On the bus home, Tina put her iPod back on. She selected the track. It was almost an automatic action. The music in her ears soothed her. It was not long before her mind was filled with thoughts. It was as though something had come to a close. Finally she'd made a decision to email this clinic. What had become an obsession about finding the woman who had donated the embryo was becoming a reality.

There was a loud scream. Tina turned to see what all the noise was about.

"Get aff. Mum look, he's annoying me."

There were two children squabbling and a harassed mother sat beside them trying to control them. They looked very different but were obviously brother and sister. The girl had dark hair and fine features, the boy had ginger hair and green eyes.

Why do I notice these things, Tina wondered.

The boy had driven his toy car on the girl's head and it was now tangled in her hair. The mum pulled the boy to her side and told him to stop the nonsense. As an only child Tina often thought about what it would be like to have a sister of her own. She wished she could share her feelings with someone.

As if by telepathy her mobile phone rang.

"Tina, what's up? Not heard from you since last night?"

It was Keisha.

"Been busy…"

"Is that you on the road or sumthin' rattlin', on a bus? Where are you goin'?"

"Just running an errand for mum." The passing of a lie easily slipped from her tongue. Even to her best friend.

"I'm coming round later. We need to suss out that new club, are you up for it?"

"I'll think about it. I've got to finish that dreadful coursework for English. I'll call you later K."

Tina walked slowly towards her house. Margaret, her mum was in the garden in her wellies, deadheading some roses. Her old jeans were tight around her big thighs, her bright red neck showed above the faded t-shirt and the big bosom was covered with an old cardigan. She brushed her dark hair with her garden-gloved hand, her blue eyes twinkling under her glasses. She had a friendly, kind face, an open smile that endeared her to all.

Margaret turned as she heard Tina's footsteps, and smiled broadly, obviously glad to see her.

"Tina, where have you been? Want a snack? I'm starving I'll make a sandwich, just give me a minute."

"I'll make it myself." She was just about to rush back in before she stopped and turned back, "Do you want one?"

"That'll be nice Tina. There's some ham and cheese in the fridge. I'll tidy up and join you."

Tina made the sandwiches. She got the seeded batch loaf, put a light spread of butter on the slices, laid the ham and cheese slices carefully, cut them diagonally and put them on plates. She switched the kettle on. She heard her mum prising her wellies off near the back door, thumping them down.

"Just coming love. Start yours." She shouted over the sound of gushing water in the utility room,

They sat at the kitchen table, the wear and tear over the years were gouged into the table. Margaret often looked at them with pleasure and pointed them out with pride. Tina had fulfilled her barren life and given her some meaning. There were dents she'd made with a fork as an impatient toddler; the ink marks that had dyed into the tiny holes from her primary years and love for crayons and felt tips as well as the tired rings from her cups of tea in her teenage years. The stains surfaced deep into the solid oak, perhaps it was possible to remove them at first but now they sat embedded within the grains, impossible to remove. Margaret held on to them, admiring them, a tribute to her little miracle.

Margaret looked at the surface of the battered table and then at Tina. She removed her glasses and wiped her eyes.

She's showing her age, thought Tina, as she saw the glint of grey in her hair. *She's old enough to be my grandma.*

"So were you in town shopping? Find anything nice?" Margaret asked. *When did it become so difficult to talk to her?*

Tina answered in monosyllables trying hard not to expand too much on the lies she'd told. The less she said the better. She'd thought about telling the truth, she'd even rehearsed the scenes out with Jenny, but it was too difficult. She could never find the right time or the right words. She loved her too much. Her mum had been the most important person in her life and meant everything to her. And yet she felt so different. She wasn't at one with her. She wondered what this other person must be like, the one that had donated her eggs to the clinic. The woman whose genes had made her what she was.

11

Tina looked down at her plate and then took out her mobile. "I need to text Keisha about this evening," she said loudly signalling the end of the conversation.

She slid out of her chair and headed for the door.

"I'll clear this away love. You just get on with what you need to," Margaret called after her.

She busied herself with washing the plates and mugs, humming a tune. *Need to tidy up the flower bed*, she thought to herself noticing the rose bush through the kitchen window.

The garden was her hobby, a love that she had nurtured from her youth. She tended it with loving care. The perfect lawn, the beautiful flowerbeds and the colours throughout the year revealed at every season, reflected her hard work.

"I'm meeting Keisha at seven so I'd better finish my school work," Tina called out rushing up the stairs.

Margaret watched her walk away, with an unexpected lump in her throat. Suddenly it hit her. Her only daughter would be leaving soon. She cast her mind back to the trials and tribulations that she had gone through to have her.

Chapter 2

She felt it, the dreaded damp between her legs. Not again! She slipped out of bed, heart thumping, careful not to disturb Tony. She looked at the red patch, knowing what it meant but not wanting to accept it. This was their third IVF attempt in the last eight years. Sobs pulsed up, sickening and deep, clinging to the back of her throat. She stuffed a towel in her mouth to silence herself. She tiptoed out to the hall into the spare bedroom. Her legs gave way and she fell on the floor.

Doubled up in despair, she lay on the floor unable to stem the numbness spreading over her. Tears rolled down and dampened her cotton nightdress. It was late. Way past midnight. Time had ticked away her future. She had so little time left she thought. Her hopes of becoming a mother were being snatched out of her bosom. Hours later she woke to find herself still lying on the floor, her eyes opened as the dawn crept into the room. She stifled her pain in the best way she knew by massaging her neck and arms, and picking up the pieces of her shattered self pretending everything was okay. Trying to act normal and putting on a brave front.

Motherhood. Was it too much to ask? Was it selfish to want a baby so badly? In the world teeming with six billion people all she wanted was a family, the chance to hold an infant in her arms. A baby she could call her own. She got up and lay on the bed, a stiff painful back ache slowly added to her discomfort. The void in her life that she had tried to fulfil for almost a decade now was sapping all her being.

Tears flowed again, she wiped them, sobbing softly into the pillow. Tony walked in and cuddled her; his warm, sleep-filled body comforted her. She could not stop despite herself. Her sobs grew louder

"I can't face the world. I'm a mess. I'm not going into work."

His arms tightened around her.

"I'll call and let them know you're not well," he said.

He lay beside her for a while then got ready for work.

"Where are you going?"

She sipped the hot sweet tea he brought her and looked around the room. Her eyes landed on the family photo of herself, her sister Brenda, her mum Betty and Amy her niece. Family: the word pierced her heart like a sharp knife.

Her sister, she thought, *always smug. Always the blue eyed blonde who could do no wrong.*

Family, that was what she was yearning for now. Margaret got up and looked out of the window, another grey dull day. The garden was sparse; the winter froze the ground to an almost barren wilderness. She sighed; all her months of work in nourishing the soil, protecting the young plants, taking some to the green house had little effect this year. She closed her eyes and imagined a lush garden filled with exotic flowers, imported orchids, a trailing bougainvillea, and frangipani. The image made her give out a dry laugh. Such wild thoughts on such a dreich day still did not make her feel any better.

Why me, why does Brenda have such a plain sailing life, gets all she wants. It's not fair. She lay back on the bed not wanting to move.

The trilling phone woke her up.

"Feeling any better? Have some rest, I'll be there soon." Tony's voice had a weary edge to it. He had tossed and turned in the early hours.

She got washed and switched the TV on.

Later she heard the rattle of the key turning in the front door and Tony bounded in looking anxious and concerned. It broke his heart to see that she was becoming obsessed with being a mother. They both hoped vainly that she would be pregnant. They tried everything that doctors advised. She took her temperature to ensure it was the right time of the month.

The worst part of Margaret's obsession to become a mother was the awful sobs that rent the house every month. The charts were strewn over the bedroom as she sobbed her heart out when she found that she was not pregnant. Tony found that having sex on the right night became a chore and the romance and fun went out of the relationship but he loved her so much and he was clear from the start that he would support her. He wanted more than anything to give her that child she craved for. He had never thought that it was going to overwhelm their lives.

He picked up the letters and opened them, reading them as he walked up the stairs. He steeled himself as he saw her and gave a smile.

"Hey, look you've won that trip to the Chelsea flower show for us in spring," he placed the letter beside her and took her in his arms. She buried her face in him as he hugged her tight. Her sobs felt like arrows blitzing his heart.

"Green fingers and nothing more, I...can't even conceive...I'm nothing'

He lifted her face towards him, "We can try again."

"Tony, I can't do it anymore...not another IVF attempt...all those Clomid injections...rushing to the doc in the morning before work. No! I just can't."

"I know I know...shush." he stroked and kissed her hair and let her cry.

The adoption process had not been successful either. Being at the top end of the age range meant their chance of getting a baby was ruled out straight away. The only offer was a vague possibility of older children with special needs, even that was not an assurance. Margaret found the whole procedure with social workers prodding into every bit of their lives an enormous strain. The pain was getting deeper. Margaret wondered how much longer this torture was to continue. Watching Amy grow up and helping out with babysitting her was pleasurable but made her own need for a baby even greater. The dark grey jumper that she wore reflected her mood.

The pebbles from the shores of Loch Lomond that Tony and Margaret had collected lay in the corner of the garden. Smooth flattened by years of water flowing over them, imperfectly round, pink and brown, flecked or plain they gave a shape to the tiny rockery that she had designed. The pale sun glinted on the pebbles and rocks that she placed along with the alpines, the heathers, carefully placing the lime-haters on the top and the Aubretias and Dianthus at the bottom. The white, pink and purple colours contrast against the green conifers that stood proud at the top. Each time she planted a young plant her desire, her need for a child rose up from within her like a flame.

Wanting a child never left her. In the deep recesses of her mind she kept that hope burning bright. A child is like stardust from God and I'm going to have one, come what may, she told herself. She looked up at the apricot skies with grey clouds that seemed to endorse her deep need.

Margaret found it hard to ward off the depression that was imminent. When one of her colleagues, Fiona left for maternity leave she came home and cried her eyes out. She was bereft. Her behaviour changed. She seemed to close in on herself.

When Tony joined her in town after a Saturday afternoon football at school, he found her in Mothercare.

"Are you buying something for Fiona's baby? I thought the school secretary was organising it," he commented. The baby blue and pink clothes and toys surrounding them were like pinpricks to him. *Why was she in this shop?* he wondered. *Why is she torturing herself? I just can't understand her behaviour any more*

"No," she said her eyes glazed, not following what he was saying. Margaret had a shopping basket full of baby clothes. Her eyes were intent on a young couple, choosing some clothes for their soon-to-be born baby. The woman's bump was huge. She kept rubbing it unconsciously as she picked out some booties and hats. Margaret heard Tony's voice.

"No, you're not buying for Fiona's baby?" Tony asked, gently placing his hand on Margaret's as she clutched a baby grow.

"Just leave me alone," she hissed, darting an angry stare at him. She left the basket on the floor and walked out of the shop. Tony felt the gaze of an astonished shop assistant burning his back as he quickly followed her.

Days later he found her sitting with catalogues of baby toys, reading magazine articles on motherhood. She wanted so much to be a mother. It was like a seeping wound that never healed. A wound that was so deep that Tony was afraid it would eventually form a chasm between them. The rows got worse; Margaret reacted by sulking or clamming up.

"I am not finding this easy either," Tony shouted at her. "For God's sake, pull yourself together. There are plenty of people with no kids. What's the big deal? I'm sick of this."

Her eyes said it all. Dead like the plants outside, withering, a brown leafless mass that stood like lifeless skeletons, etched on the dull green of a moss filled lawn. She barely functioned.

He went and fetched a glass for his whiskey.

Tony banged the door as he came in.

"Get to the bloody doctor and get yourself sorted. Are you taking the Valium he gave you?"

She turned away from him.

"The head teacher spoke to me today and has warned that either you get back to work or it will be your P45 soon. Margaret, are you listening?" he shouted and threw a card at her.

She turned her face to him slowly and picked up the card. It was a get well card from the pupils, signed by all the pupils in her sixth form class.

Dear Mrs Wilson

We wish you speedy recovery and hope you'll be here to help with our exams. The prelims are on next month. Please come back.

"They don't deserve you," Tony walked away and poured himself a big measure of the whisky bottle.

He looked at her properly for the first time in months. Wan and pale, she sat motionless. His anger dissipated, his heart went out to her. He sat beside her.

"Margaret, please, for the kids sake why don't you get back to work? They need you. The supply teacher they have is hellish."

Work may be the solution to this, he thought to himself as he cuddled her.

Slowly she recovered.

The schoolwork got her out of bed and helped shake off the depression.

*

Margaret stood back and looked on with pride at her handiwork in the garden. The shrubs were doing well. The front garden was a picture. The lawn was accentuated by the flowerbeds in glorious colour. The beds were like a necklace adorning the emerald green lawn. Amethyst and pale colours were interspersed with bright pinks. Life sprouting in the ground after the bare winter lifted her spirits. The garden was her passion. Tending the plants, seeing them grow from tiny seedlings to flowering bushes was fulfilling. She brushed the dirt from her hands, and then walked to the back garden. A frown creased her brow. The rhododendron bush had taken over the rockery and spread into her favourite azalea. It looked cowed, failing to flourish however hard she had tried. She set about pruning the rhododendron. Margaret was brutal with the plant.

"I should've waited till the autumn," she told herself.

She worked solidly for another hour till the azalea had more room and the sun was able to reach its weak branches. She put all the garden tools away and washed her hands in the kitchen sink. The phone rang.

"So what are you doing for mum's fiftieth birthday?" It was Brenda.

"I'll call you at the weekend and we can discuss it then, Brenda."

Margaret's tired face, reflected in the hall mirror, stared back at her. The wrinkles at her eyes furrowed as she heard that rasping voice.

"I knew you'd say that, so as usual I've organised it all," Brenda tutted.

"Fine, so why did you bother calling me then?"

Margaret could feel her head throbbing.

"Fuck's sake, I do everything and you can't even talk to me properly," Brenda screeched down the phone.

The party was to be held at the Grosvenor Hotel in the West End. Margaret was angry that Brenda had chosen such a grand venue.

"I've told her hundreds of times, not to book a costly restaurant," Margaret complained to Tony.

"What are you on about now?" Tony asked as he polished his shoes.

"Brenda! She's booked the *Grosvenor*. Tony, how many times have I told her not to book an expensive place? I want to pay for mum's celebrations too."

"Margaret, let her do what she wants. Let's go and enjoy it. Don't spoil your mum's special day with a row." Tony looked himself in the hall mirror, ready to leave for work.

The Grosvenor Hotel on Great Western Road was a stunning Victorian building with rows of arched windows. It had been built in the 1800s. The hotel faced the Botanic gardens and was an unpretentious yet grand place that people frequented for special occasions. Brenda and James were standing at the function suite door to receive the guests, looking resplendent in their new clothes. Tony and Margaret nodded a hello and walked past them to Betty.

"Happy birthday, mum."

Margaret gave her a kiss and handed her a present, a brooch with an Edwardian design. They helped themselves to the drink that the waiter brought and Margaret took an extra glass for Betty.

"Mum, here have a drink. Would you like to sit down?"

Margaret asked her as she gave her a glass of champagne.

"You both take such good care of me," said Betty, happy to see Tony and Margaret. "Brenda is too excited and has already had a bit too much to drink," she whispered.

"She's just enjoying herself," said Margaret, not very convincingly, having seen the high colour on Brenda's cheeks. Once all the guests had arrived and were seated, Brenda came over to Margaret and Tony.

Brenda looked Margaret up and down.

"Oh Margaret, that beige dress does nothing for you. I told you to get the red one," she said.

"It's okay. I liked this better." Margaret smiled through gritted teeth.

At dinner, Brenda drank a bit more wine and was garrulous, laughing and talking loudly. Later she stood up and made a speech about her mum and wished her a happy birthday. She giggled as she asked Margaret to say a few words. James looked at her sternly but Brenda was too busy having another drink. Margaret wished her mum happy birthday and thanked all the friends who had come and joined in the celebrations. Brenda stopped her mid-sentence.

"Look what I've got for mum," she announced triumphantly at the table, giving her mum a beautiful wrapped gift and a big kiss.

"Happy birthday mum, from your favourite daughter."

She tried to hug her and stumbled a bit.

"Mum!" exclaimed Amy, her face blushing as she saw the glass in hand nearly tipping the drink on to the table. Everyone laughed.

"Open it, please. Go on. Show it to everyone!" Brenda shouted. Amy opened the gift for Betty. A lovely bejewelled watch blinked at her.

"Thank you so much dear, it's lovely," said her Betty.

Brenda clapped her hands and shouted "So it should, it cost me a bloody fortune, three thousand quid."

James took her aside and hushed her.

As the watch was passed around for people to admire, Margaret heard one of her mum's old friends mumbling, " For all that it cost, she probably can't see the bloody time on it," peering at the tiny dial.

"Margaret!" Brenda shouted over the din of the people's chatter, "you really need to start a family, I would have done that by now, slowcoach," she leered.

Margaret walked out of the party and sobbed in the car as Tony tried to placate her.

"No one understands that doctors have found nothing wrong with either of us, so why can't I conceive?" Her voice broke as the sobs became louder. He held her tightly till she calmed down. Then he drove on slowly to their house. They had gone through this so many times over the years. Doctors could give no reason at all. Every test they both had undergone gave them no answers.

"Six percent of all couples who don't conceive have no reasons for their infertility," the specialist had explained.

"At least if they said there was something wrong we could have found a way," cried Margaret. "Years of these checkups and tests, three attempts at IVF and no real chance of adoption. It's hopeless. I can't bear it Tony. I can't take it anymore."

She clung to him as he drove home. They talked long into the night. Tony suggested they needed to distance themselves from the family. Stop being second parents to Amy and give themselves a bit of space away from Brenda. The long six-week summer holiday was just round the corner. Perhaps they could go away? Tony planned a surprised escape to show Margaret that life, with just the two of them, could be fulfilling. *Perhaps it could be just like old times?*

He booked a holiday to Goa in India, a country that had fascinated them both and one that they had always planned to go before all of this. The brochure promised blue skies, sandy beaches and an all-inclusive package which sounded like a bit of heaven on Earth. Margaret was thrilled but decided it was best to keep quiet about their plans just in case Brenda thought of coming along for the ride!

Chapter 3

'The eighteenth birthday is the passport to adulthood.
One can be enfranchised, not just politically but
have the right to make one's choices in life.
It is a momentous change from that of a reluctant teen to
becoming a responsible adult.
Different pathways open up and offer a delicious new freedom
that has evaded your life so far.
You can shrug free of your parents influence if you want.
Some slip into this stage in life without
any change at all,
some, like me, crash into mistakes
that colour all our lives.
I know you will make the right choices.
I wish you a wonderful birthday and a great future.'

James had given Tina the book earlier saying, "I know Brenda
has bought you something, but this is something from me to my
favourite niece."

Tina's eighteenth birthday loomed on the horizon. She
pondered over the words inscribed on the book. In a few weeks
time she could take decisions that would help answer the
question that niggled at her for most of her life. *Who am I?*
As far as she could remember her existence had been difficult to
fathom understand.

She picked up the birthday cards that were lying on the
doormat and wandered into the kitchen. Margaret was pouring a
mug of tea for her.

"Is that one from Amy?" she asked noticing the Canadian stamp on the card. "Ah, that's nice of her. She always posts early to make sure it gets here on time."

"Yeah," said Tina as she put the cards on the table. "Thanks for the tea, mum."

"Now, Tina about your party." Margaret started and stopped.

Tina was glowering at her.

"No mum, I don't want to celebrate."

The table shook and the tea sloshed around the mug as Tina placed the mug down with force.

"Tina, it's your eighteenth, it's important," Margaret tried, surprised at Tina's reluctance to have a party.

"I don't want a party. I don't think I could sit through another one of those family parties. I'll just take a couple of my friends out."

"How about inviting your friends for a big bash then we oldies could leave when you have your disco. We want to mark this for you, love."

"Oh please." Tina rolled her eyes, an expression which drove Margaret crazy when she was teaching.

"Tina, I'm sorry but I insist. Both dad and I were looking forward to the celebration. Maybe on your twenty-first birthday, you can have your own way."

Margaret put the kettle on again for another mug of tea for herself.

"Why can't you understand? I don't want a fuss. We're all busy with our Advanced Highers and no one really has a *big bash*."

Margaret tried to laugh it off but she was becoming increasingly annoyed by her daughter's stubbornness.

"Big bash! I'm not really au fait with the current teen lingo am I? I've asked Keisha to come around and she'll give me a good idea of what you'd like. I never thought you'd be so awkward about this whole thing!"

Margaret came over to Tina and offered her a cuddle, to tease and annoy her more. Tina resisted, her body language said, *hey keep off me!*

"Keisha hasn't a clue," Tina frowned into her mug of tea.

The door bell rang.

Keisha waltzed in. Her dress sense was certainly unique. She was no follower of fashion but oozed personal style. A mass of curly hair was tamed into a high ponytail, a colourful orange scarf hung across her shoulders and trailed over a multicoloured T-shirt which she had obviously designed herself. "Me on my ain" was splashed across the front. A pair of black jeans with rips all over and doc martins finished the look.

Margaret shook her head, a smile crossed her lips, crinkled her eyes, the crow's feet in deep lines visible under her glasses.

"Come in Keisha, we were just talking about you."

"All good I hope, Mrs. W."

Her cheeky grin showed her high cheekbones, the ever so faint touch of blusher added a touch of glamour to her flawless, honey-toned skin.

"Tina is refusing a party. Can you believe it? It's as if she doesn't want to celebrate her eighteenth?"

"Leave her to me Mrs. W, I'll sort her," said Keisha slapping Tina affectionately on her back.

The two girls left the kitchen and walked up to Tina's room upstairs.

"Shall I get you a wee cup of tea dear, or something to eat?" Margaret called after them,

"No thanks Mrs. W. I'm fine," Keisha shouted from the top of the stairs.

Tina straightened her window curtain as Keisha fell on her bed and lay spread-eagled without a care in the world.

"So what's this? Doing me outa a party? Why, Tina? Out with it."

She rested on her elbow, eyebrow raised.

"Nothing, I just don't feel like it."

Tina sat beside her, smoothing the duvet cover.

"Come on there must be a reason, even I had a family party, naff I know but it was fun in the end. When the oldies left we danced the night away, you remember?" Keisha's eyes sparkled mischievously.

"I know, Keisha but I've too much on, the exams for a start, then."

"Exams! We've spilled our guts last year and we've both got unconditional offers at the uni so what's the big deal?"

"I still want to do well in these exams."

Tina fidgeted with her hair.

"I know, so do I but come on, how about a party first? Your mum seems quite upset."

Keisha got up, opened a tiny pot containing blusher that was on the dressing table and dabbed a bit on her hand, checking the shade by moving her hand to catch the light from the window.

"It's just Aunty Brenda and the rest of the family. They do my head in, fussing over everything, comparing me to Amy."

"Not good enough I'm afraid. I don't buy that excuse." Keisha hoisted herself on the bed and sat cross-legged, facing Tina, and showed her the blusher. "Is this new?"

"Yeah. I got it from town last week the lady said it was perfect for Asian skin tones," she said taking it out of Keisha's hand and dabbing some across her cheekbones.

"What do you think?" She said pouting at Keisha.

"Naomi Campbell, eat your heart out!" She teased.

Tina smiled.

"Now that wasn't so hard – was it?" she said. "I can't remember the last time I saw you smile."

Keisha stared at Tina.

Tina said nothing.

"Well I'm waiting! Why don't you want to celebrate your birthday? It's a big one."

There was a time when we could share everything. Now it's all changing. Tina got up and switched on her iPod on the dock. Amy Winehouse's gravely tones of *Black on Black* blasted through the small speakers. They both sat listening to the lyrics for several minutes.

"I need a party, I've even got your present and don't you dare do me out of one. It'll be like our chance to say goodbye – none of us know where we'll be next year." Keisha threw the little teddy, Mr. B at her. Tina caught it and held it tight as the angry expression on her face changed to a smile. She could never be angry with Keisha for long. She was her mate, an optimist who could tease out the tension in her. Tina looked at her, thought for sometime and then shrugged,

"Well, okay, if you insist."

Keisha jumped off the bed, her ponytail swinging and her scarf trailing behind her. "That's more like it."

The next hour was spent planning the party, Keisha and Margaret kept getting carried away and Tina had to keep them in check, to tone down the plans to what she would feel comfortable with. An excited Keisha waved goodbye, adjusted her earphones and skipped down the driveway. Margaret was pleased and filled her evening with fine tuning the details of the party, the guest list and making a list of suppliers from the Yellow Pages. Tina had other things on her mind.

The party was in full swing. Brenda arrived first, dressed in her usual designer gear and holding a parcel which was slightly too large and overdressed for the occasion. It was sure to make a spectacle of itself, wrapped in handmade paper and tied with an enormous pink bow.

"Happy birthday, darling!" She said giving Tina a peck on her cheek. "You still look like a wee schoolgirl. My Amy looked so grown up at eighteen." She handed her the enormous gift, Tina was annoyed by her comment but politely thanked her and said nothing.

"So what did mum and dad give you for your eighteenth Tina?" Brenda pressed, without so much care for the answer.

"Just a minute Aunty, there's Keisha; I need to get her to do something for me. I'll be back." She quickly ran to Keisha's side.

Brenda ran an eye over the room. Nothing pleased her. She tutted with disapproval, at the decorations that were not colour coordinated and at the table laden with food that was not to her liking.

"Hope you gave her something useful like driving lessons, not some sentimental guff." She said finally noticing Margaret who had been standing by her side for some time.

Margaret had spent over a month making a CD for Tina. It was full of snapshots of old home movies, and photos from her birth till the present day. She had collected beautiful poems that she had found on the internet and copied them onto handmade paper and stitched them into a booklet. Tony had taken digital photos of the poems and included them in the CD.

Margaret didn't answer.

"I've given her the most gorgeous dress that she can wear to her prom and some money, of course," Brenda said.

29

"Yes, we gave her some money too." Margaret said turning to face Brenda for the first time since her arrival. "This music is not really for us is it?" she moved away slowly.

Keisha had turned the volume right up and the younger guests danced and chatted happily. Margaret was pleased to see that Tina was enjoying the party especially after all the fuss she had made about having one.

"We'll get Tina to cut the cake, make a toast and then we'll leave these youngsters alone," Margaret said, not realising that Keisha had organised to go clubbing after.

Once the group of friends left Margaret poured her sister another glass of wine.

Brenda downed the wine disappointed that it didn't offer her any solace.

"So, what did you get Tina for her eighteenth?" She asked again not remembering if she had forgotten the answer to her question or whether Margaret had not told her.

The doorbell rang. It was a neighbour from across the street.

"Saved by the bell," muttered Margaret to herself as she opened the door.

"Just a wee minding for young Tina; Where is the birthday girl?" asked the old lady.

"Oh how kind of you Mrs. G. She's just this minute away with her friends. Do come in and have some cake," said Margaret.

Brenda left the party disappointed that she had not got more gossip about Tina. It would give her something to talk about to Amy in their next Skype chat. She wanted to share all the detail with Amy. She was lonely and it made her feel as if they weren't so far apart. Amy often remarked that she and Tina were so different it was hard to believe they were cousins at all.

Tina lay on her bed after the celebrations. She played the CD on her computer. She read each poem in the handmade booklet.

She was touched by her parent's gift. Emotions were running away with her. She felt so loved, it touched her heart and she wept. Her mind and her gaze cast across the envelope with an 'I owe you.' How could she forget about the money? Would accepting it for your own pursuits be such a bad thing? Three thousand pounds could buy driving lessons, a car, or fund a gap year. She wept at their kindness but the money had her mind making wild plans to travel to India. Her heart rippled with guilt and excitement now that she had actually got the money for her trip. What had once just been crazy ramblings of her mind could soon become a reality.

Was eighteen not a kind of rite of passage that made it okay to break off from the family and spread one's wings? Was it society giving a nudge as if to say, "You are an adult now, you can make you own decisions, vote, get married, drink, move away, fend for yourself?"

Her mind obsessed about making that trip to India. She wanted to find out more about her background. She was scared, worried, and guilt enveloped her like a cloud. She did not want her parents to find out. She felt she was letting them down in some way. Who would understand her predicament?

Every time people assumed she was adopted, her mum had to explain. She had read all the newspaper articles about Louise Brown, the first test tube baby. Prised out, as a group of cells, fished out of a Petri dish and inserted into a womb, her life transplanted. The first test-tube baby was at least not different from her own two parents. There was no mystery to her origins. This was different. Tina was not even the same colour as her parents; it was obvious for all to see. *Why did she feel so different?*

Tina spent a restless night with dreams and ideas intermingling, confusing her more than ever. Her parents had mentioned India when they explained to her about her birth.

Tina had to go. She could not give up this chance and then live in regret. She made her mind up. She would do all in her power to find that missing piece.

*

Meanwhile Margaret got into bed grateful that the birthday party had gone well. She hugged Tony and whispered "Aren't we lucky? Tina is a beautiful young lady, I feel so blessed." He gave her a kiss and rolled over. She lay wide awake thinking of their first trip to India.

Chapter 4

Tony and Margaret lay on their deck chairs, sipping cool drinks, reading their books under the parasol. The heat and humidity was unbearable. They realised that it was the wrong time to visit Goa, but with school holidays this was the only time that they could afford to get away. Tony was reading descriptions of the place and was chuckling at some of the hyperbolic words used.

"What's so funny?" asked Margaret, applying some sun tan lotion liberally to her arms.

"We're in paradise, according to this book."

"Huh?" she was not paying much attention. The sun was blazing, despite lying in the shade she could feel the heat seeping in. She closed her eyes behind her dark shades and lay down on the chair.

"There are lots of legends pertaining to this veritable paradise. Lord Vishnu aimed seven arrows and created this incredible beautiful beach. Lord Shiva used this whenever he had a tiff with his consort Parvati. Maybe that is why holidays in Goa are so out of this world." Tony read out aloud from the book he was reading.

"Paradise! I'm not sure but the beach and the hotel is certainly beautiful," agreed Margaret, "though the poverty here is shocking. Nothing prepares you for it."

Tony continued reading quietly. Margaret made herself comfortable to read her book.

"Wow, ain't it hot out here?" A woman's voice shrilled.

They heard her before she came and sat beside them. The American accent, loud, and brash was hard to miss. She drew up her deck chair and waved to them.

"Hi, I'm Barbara, call me Babs and this is my man, Chuck." She laughed aloud. Chuck said a quiet "Hi" and waved.

"Isn't it awful, the heat I mean?"

"Yes, I'm Margaret and this is my husband, Tony." Margaret laughed too, then turned away to get back to her book.

"I love the hotel. The beach is great and the people here are so friendly and warm don't you think?"

"Yes, true," Margaret agreed.

"Are you guys, taking any of the tours of the Old Portuguese sights that the hotel is arranging?"

"Not sure yet," said Margaret, "we've just arrived."

"You must come along. It would be good to have company," she insisted. "We could go halves?"

"I'll let you know," said Margaret, opening her book again.

"Okay, see you guys later."

Barbara jumped into the pool to cool off. The water splashed all over Margaret. She sighed but said nothing. She looked over at Tony but he was still reading his book.

They could not avoid them at meal times or around the pool.

The hotel had few other guests and they were glad to accept the American couple's company.

"Scotland! Wow! Chuck's family are from out there, well generations ago I mean. I have some Italian and European ancestry, as far as I know. Isn't it fascinating? Now tell me about Scotland."

Within a week they had become good friends. Chuck was happy to share a beer or whisky with Tony. The women even hired a taxi to do some shopping together.

"Hey how about taking one of the tours?" Barbara suggested and booked one for a day tour.

They set off in the cool of the morning.

Mascarenas, the guide, stood with his arms akimbo. The tourists gathered round him.

"Welcome to Goa, the Pearl of the East. Perfect beaches, great food, nightlife and today its heritage," he said with a flourish.

He gave the usual instructions about staying together, and details of the trip. His mannerism, his charm was heightened with his skill of sprinkling words with humour.

"Let's go, gang," he urged.

"Goa's history goes back to the third century BC when it was part of the Mauryan Empire. It was part of the glorious Vijayanagar Empire till the 14th C. But we're concentrating on the Portuguese heritage so we'll skip a few centuries," he joked.

"Wow, ancient huh?" Barbara rolled her eyes and pulled her sunhat over her forehead.

"It was to control the eastern spice routes, as well as to spread Christianity that the Portuguese came to India in 1498. They found the natural harbours in Goa ideal for their purpose, and stayed on. Gradually Goa became the seat of the Portuguese empire in the East and remained under Portuguese rule till 1961."

"I think we're lucky to get this guy," said Tony sarcastically, as they listened to his spiel in the air-conditioned coach. The first stop was the The Basilica of Bom Jesus which was designated a World Heritage site. The oldest in Goa, the baroque church had marble floors inlaid with precious stones. The altars were elaborately gilded but the rest of the church was simple. The pews were hewn out of simple local wood, there were no other examples, no gaudy coloured paintings or statues. An elegant old church that held its history in its simplicity. There was a silver casket with the body of St. Francis Xavier.

"Preserved since 1555 when he died," said Mascarenas, "and still fresh as the day it was buried."

"Aye that'll be right," said Tony under his breath. But Barbara was impressed.

Mascarenas's grasp of history and willingness to answer any questions made it memorable. "This is amazing, sure blows my mind away," said a wide-eyed Barbara.

The coach moved on. Mascarenas offered more details. The Portuguese heritage in Goa was distinctive and exotic. The churches, the white washed mansions that still remained after hundred years were a contrast to the rest of the buildings around.

The Portuguese dance, was the corredinho, which some Goans performed wearing beautiful red skirts, red scarves, white blouses and heavily embroidered waistcoats reminiscent of typical Mediterranean dances. The sounds and some of the culture linked to the enforced conversion from Hindu to Roman Catholic were retained. There was even the nostalgic idea of reviving the Portuguese heritage in some areas. Some locals were re-learning the Portuguese language.

"Thousands of years of Hindu-Muslim rule and then the four hundred year Portuguese rule has made Goa unrivalled in its history," explained Mascarenas. "Now my stomach says I'm hungry. Yes, we head for a delicious lunch break."

"Four hundred years being ruled by Portuguese? I thought us Brits staying for over two hundred years was bad enough," said Tony, intrigued with the history. He bought a book to delve into the rich cultural past.

"There is so much to see, so much to do in India; I love the colours, the sounds, the smells, the food, and the ancient culture, hey guys, what about you?" Barbara looked at Tony.

"I agree, I do like the ancient culture but it has been subsumed with all the Bollywood posters and tourist tat they are selling. At times I find it over-powering and the poverty is…shocking." He shook his head.

They passed some shacks and slum dwellings that were insubstantial and looked so precarious the way they were put together with plastic sheets and odd building materials. Pungent smells of cooking and incense from temples wafted over when they walked in the streets. Little urchin children followed them, hassling for change or with bright smiles asking to carry their bags or help with shopping. Dogs and cows roamed the streets. There was little civic sense; people spat on the streets, threw litter everywhere and there was a general feeling of chaos. Despite that, Chuck pointed out that they could not miss the exuberance, the positive and sunny disposition of the people.

"If you can see past the dire poverty and appreciate the friendliness of the people, India is fascinating." He said.

Margaret and Barbara decided to go to church on Sunday whilst the men stayed back to watch a local cricket match.

"I'll try and teach him the rules of the game. A Scotsman teaching cricket to an American! Now that should be fun," said Tony, as the women left dressed in their fine cotton dresses.

The old cathedral gave them goose bumps. The mass that they witnessed was a curious mixture of Indian hymns and Catholic rituals. Both women felt a strange surge of emotion. Was it being in a completely different culture they whispered to each other?

They were participating in a service that was familiar and yet unfamiliar. When the service was over they both sighed.

"I feel like this service has refreshed me, even brought a bond between us," said Margaret. Barbara nodded and closed her eyes. *The sun is strong* thought Margaret.

"Come let's have a break, you look a bit pale" said Margaret.

Barbara was strangely quiet.

They sat in the café nearby to have an iced coffee. Margaret went in to order.

"Hope they hurry, I'm parched," said Margaret as she slid into the seat. The service was quick. They know how to look after tourists in Goa, she thought to herself.

The waiter brought the iced coffees almost immediately. The tiny wafer with it was crunchy and delicious. Margaret nibbled on hers. Barbara hardly looked at hers. Margaret sipped the cold coffee. The brown liquid soothed her throat. Margaret was startled to see Barbara wiping her eyes and sobbing quietly.

"Are you okay? What's wrong, is it the heat?" She touched her arm lightly.

"Our stay in India. It's not just a holiday." Barbara confided. "I, we don't have kids and…" the sobs caught at her throat. "I've spent years on infertility treatments and even tried IVF treatments but nothing's worked. No one tells you about that, only twenty-five percent of the IVF treatments are successful. All you see are lots of babies smiling out of papers since the Louise Brown's case."

Margaret nodded.

"I have…we have the same problem. We've been trying to have a baby for years. I know exactly what you mean."

"Oh my God, I can't believe this. No one understands, but you you'll know." Barbara smiled nervously. "Oh hope you don't mind. I need to talk to someone about it. We're so excited. We're here for an embryo transfer." She hesitated before blurting out. "It's our last chance."

"What?" Margaret could not believe what she was hearing.

"What like surrogacy?" Margaret asked, amazed and pleased that they were talking about such intimate things with each other.

"I know it's confusing," said Barbara. "We went through years of not conceiving. I did a whole lot of reading and research on the alternatives. Surrogacy is great if you can get an embryo made up of your own sperm and egg but it didn't happen with us."

"I don't understand" Margaret's heart was beating quickly.

This was too much for her to take in, she felt bewildered.

"Well, they offer an embryo that is genetically not yours and if you carry the pregnancy to full term you deliver your own baby."

"But will the baby not look Indian?" the colour deepened on Margaret's cheeks.

"Yep, sure but that's fine. We've had a lot of sessions with my therapist. We're more than a hundred percent sure that this is what we want. Mags, I want so much to feel my baby in my womb. Can you imagine how that would feel?"

"Sorry I can't get my head around this. You mean that you're going to have a baby that is not yours genetically but carry it and..." Margaret stared at Barbara, reached out her arm, but said nothing.

"I know it sounds strange. People have artificial insemination with a donor's sperm, have eggs that are donated so why not the next best thing?" Barbara was so passionate and happy that she was given a chance at something that seemed unattainable. "I'm sure I'll love my baby because I would be physically carrying the baby for nine months and giving birth to it. He or she will be nurtured by me, how much closer can one get than that? Margaret you'll know what I'm talking about."

Hours passed as they discussed it thoroughly. Margaret's disbelief changed slowly to one of intense curiosity and then suddenly a voracious appetite to find out all that she could about the procedure.

"Please Barbara. You need to tell me all about it. I'm like you, I'm desperate for a baby too. You don't know how much I'd got my hopes up since the Alastair MacDonald case. He was born so close to home."

From being a holiday acquaintance, Barbara now became an intimate friend with whom she could share her deepest thoughts.

They ordered a light lunch and continued. There were many questions that Margaret needed the answers to.

"You know, I feel so good after telling you about this Margaret. There is something deeply spiritual here, earlier in the church I felt a kind of stirring, I can't explain, I just know it is going to be right for us. Thank the Lord you are here to share this with me." Barbara's held Margaret's hand tightly.

A group of children ran down the pavement with marbles in their hands, the colours glinted in the sun. A small girl in a red dress ran into Margaret's chair as a marble rolled out of her hand. Margaret bent down and picked it up and handed it to the child, who gave her a dazzling smile. The two women smiled at each other, eyes expressing the words that were left unsaid.

When they got back to the hotel, the men were still at the cricket match. It gave Margaret time to think. The church and the information from Barbara, too many things had happened in those few hours. It was as if God had answered her prayers.

Margaret wanted to tell Tony right away but changed her mind. This was a huge possibility, an embryo that genetically belonged to neither her nor Tony, yet she would carry the baby.

Margaret found the whole thing exciting and bizarre. Questions ran through her mind. Would it work? Would she be capable physically of a successful pregnancy? She was confused. Then the smile of the little girl in the red dress made her shudder with excitement. She waited till they had their dinner, a nail bitingly slow one for her. Finally, she decided to talk to Tony about it.

"It's science fiction. You're not serious," was Tony's first reaction.

He was stunned.

"Well if Barbara could go through with it, surely I stand a chance. Tony please hear me out."

"Sounds bizarre to me," Tony rubbed his chin.

"Look she told me it is possible. If the clinic agrees to take us on then it is a question of following through. The donor embryo will be inserted when I'm ready and…"

"Wait a minute; you are way ahead of me." Tony interrupted. "How much will it cost? Is it safe? I mean we know nothing about this."

"Tony please, listen to me. It is not very different to Louise Brown and the first IVF baby. We went through three attempts at it didn't we? " Margaret gave him the brochure that she picked up from Barbara's room. She stayed silent as he read it, more than once.

"Well?" she asked expectantly.

"Let's find out more eh?"

They both spent the next day talking with Barbara and Chuck to understand the procedure in more detail.

"Are you sure you want to go through with this?" asked Tony.

"We must try everything. Tony you know how much this means to both of us," Margaret beseeched him.

"It's such a big step."

He rubbed his chin, hesitating.

41

"It's our last chance. Tony at least we could find out if it is a possibility."

Margaret's voice dipped in disappointment. Her heart reached for the words hope. Wasn't hope the child of the unborn future, it seemed to ask her. He saw that her face was wreathed with sadness.

"You're right," he said. "We shouldn't head back home then regret that we've missed out on a life changing opportunity forever.

Tony called the clinic and booked an appointment. "Yes, yes, yes, no problem at all sir, just come, I'll put date in diary," said the cheerful secretary.

Chapter 5

The morning was perfect, dry with the sun peeking out making the garden look colourful, the flowerbeds bursting with annuals and perennials, the pinks, and mauves of the pansies vying for attention with the bright orange marigolds. The rose bushes had arrived in a big package from the online nursery. Margaret had wanted the fully-scented Floribunda rose bushes in yellow but there had been none in her local nursery. She chose the bed carefully, made sure that she nourished the soil with the right nutrients and planted them.

Life was kind. Tina was blossoming into a lovely young lady and working hard for her exams. She had already been offered a place at the prestigious Business School at Strathclyde University to read Information Technology. Margaret brushed the peat from her gardening gloves, put them into the shed, and cleaned up in the sink in the utility room. She took the chicken out of the oven and glazed it with fat, it was nearly ready. She put the potatoes on and started to peel the carrots.

Tina walked in and stood beside her.

"Give you a hand, mum?"

"Could you set the table for me, love?"

Margaret gave the carrots a wash as she peeled each one and put them into the pan.

"Oh, and get a bottle of white wine would you? Put out three glasses now that you can have a wee glass with us," she added.

Tina laid the table.

"I'm planning to go to India for my gap year. I was looking on the internet," she said casually.

The peeler from Margaret's hand fell, and the metal hit the tiled floor, clattering. Tina picked it up and gave it to her. She heard her mum's sharp intake of breath, then a sigh.

"Tina, why? It's so far away. What about Europe? Keisha and you could have a great time together," said Margaret holding the peeler, her knuckles showing white.

"No, I'm not going with Keisha. This is something that I want to do…"

Tina stood her ground, but glanced anxiously at her mum. They heard the key in the front door and Tony came in and put his jacket on one of the chairs. "Mmm…smells good…," he said and picking the wine bottle, opened the screw top lid and poured some into a glass. There was a silence that made him look up.

"Mum, I've always wanted to see India. Dad and you've talked so much about it."

"Dad," Tina turned to Tony, "I'm thinking it's about time I went to India."

"What this all about? A holiday?" Tony asked, then seeing Margaret's face he put the glass down. Her eyes were bright.

"You want to find her, am I right? Your real…" she began to say.

Margaret's words were muffled, tears started to roll down. She wiped them with her hands, leaving little bits of carrots on her cheeks.

"Mum no…I just wanted to…" Tina's voice trailed as she saw her mum's shoulders heave. Margaret sobbed uncontrollably.

The sounds shocked Tina. She made a gesture to reach out to her mum, and then hesitated.

"I don't want to hurt you…If you're going to get upset then I won't go, I'll stay…I love you."

The shadow of a cloud moved hiding the sun for a few minutes making the room dark. The sound of silence hung heavy as they all stood transfixed. Tony comforted Margaret and held her in his arms. Her sobs subsided slowly and she wiped her eyes and sat looking down. A deep red covered her neck and arms. The timer pinged and they moved around the table as though they were in a tableau. Tony took the chicken out of the oven, carved slices and placed the potatoes on the table. Tina and Margaret joined him at the table but said nothing. The evening news played on in the background. The carrots lay in the pan uncooked.

*

The barn owl hooted on the tree outside her bedroom window. It was a sound that Tina was used to hearing in the dead of night. She stretched her arms above her head, tired after hours of work at her desk. She was studying for her exams. The most stressful period of her young life, the Advanced Higher exams were the first set of qualifications and she wanted to get good grades. She glanced at the desk; she had doodled on the page in front of her, her concentration briefly disturbed. The desk was littered with foolscap sheets of paper scrawled with notes. A mug of cold tea lay beside the heaps of books that the angle poise lamp illustrated. She got up and looked out of the window. It was a clear night; the crescent moon cast a pale light on the dawn sky. It was three-thirty in the morning. No wonder she was so exhausted! She fell onto the bed and snuggled under the duvet.
The sounds of the morning routine assailed as she pulled the duvet over her head.

"Tina, come down. I've made a fresh pot of tea."

The smell of freshly baked bread wafted in the room. Tina took in a deep breath but her eyes were heavy and she struggled to open them. Today was the last exam and then she could relax and enjoy her free time.

She could hear her mum moving around in the kitchen. The delicious aroma enticed her to go down and eat but the thought of seeing her mum after last night was too much.

"Tina. Come down."

Margaret stood at the bottom of the stairs as Tina walked down.

"Ta mum, smells super. Almost makes me forget about the exam this afternoon."

They sat at the table and Margaret watched as Tina ate her brunch, a few rashers of bacon, and a fried egg on a fresh piece of bread. Another loaf was in the oven filling the room with warmth.

"Are you going out with Keisha after the exam?" Margaret asked.

"No, I'm exhausted. I might just come back and have a kip. We're meeting on Friday when she finishes her last exam. Then we'll celebrate together."

"Of course, I forgot that her last exam isn't till Friday. Well, dad and I are away to a concert this evening so you have yourself a quiet evening in. You've worked so hard Tina, you deserve a good rest."

After the concert, Margaret and Tony lay in bed. They both knew what each other was thinking. They knew that one day this day would come, and now it had they felt totally unprepared. Tony suggested that they broach the topic with Tina again. Tell her the truth. Margaret was reluctant but in the end agreed. It was the only way their daughter could ever appreciate what they'd gone through to have her.

*

Bombay was an hour's flight from Goa. The Wilsons sat holding their hands in the cramped space on board the local flight. Hopes rose as they neared the metropolis. A baby in the bassinet in the front row cried loudly, the mother searched for something in her bag. The plane took a downward plunge, the engines switched on and the 'seat belts on' sign flashed above them. Margaret watched with interest as the mother gave the baby a dummy to suck. The baby quietened down. It was a smooth landing for a small plane.

The hotel was close to the clinic. Margaret glanced at it as the taxi drove past the modest-looking building. As the taxi drew up at the front of the hotel, she saw two ravens on the small lawn. She crossed her fingers. *Two for a joy,* she thought and then wondered why she had suddenly become superstitious.

Tony and Margaret were on edge. They hardly ate any dinner. They could not sleep properly either. Not even the full English breakfast tempted Margaret in the morning, though Tony had a good plateful. Questions raged through her mind.

The clinic was a short walk from their hotel. The building from outside was not very impressive but once they walked in they felt it was a place that exuded warmth. Margaret pinched herself, *Is this real?* She wondered. She had pictured it in her mind since they got the appointment. They were grateful that the whole clinic was air-conditioned. It was spotless, with photos of healthy smiling babies on the wall.

The receptionist was polite and spoke good English. They had no problem communicating at all. They thought back to the NHS that they had left in Glasgow, the waiting before the appointment, the stuffy waiting room, and the gruff, unhelpful receptionists. The impression here was one of professional competence. The appointment was long. All their details were taken and entered into a computer. They were both given a medical and had an initial meeting with the consultant.

Dr. Patel was a smart-looking man in his forties. He was of medium height, wore glasses, with a small moustache that seemed to be the fashion for all young men in India. He was gentle.

"Mr. and Mrs. Wilson, welcome," he said, "I was looking forward to meeting you. I did my Fellowship in Edinburgh. I have a soft spot for Scotland," he said and smiled, indicating for them to sit down on the cushioned chairs in front of him.

"We're grateful that you agreed to see us at such short notice," said Tony.

"You did say that your return journey had been fixed. I thought meeting and explaining what this entails before you left would be good. You need to undertake this procedure after a lot of thought."

"Yes, we know," said Margaret.

"Let me explain it fully. Please feel free to stop me at any time and ask me questions," he said. He rustled a few papers that gave him some of their details, they presumed, and then began.

"The first thing you need to know is that it would not be simple. You both need a lot of counselling to be sure that you have the inner strength to go through with it. Emotions can run high and such a procedure is not to be undertaken lightly."

They nodded in agreement.

Dr. Patel explained exactly how it would work.

"The embryos that we have are usually frozen. Each embryo is sorted by gender and its viability to produce a healthy baby. Only healthy ones are frozen for use later or for donations. There are more embryos that are possible baby girls than boys."

"Oh I would love a baby girl," said Margaret, and then blushed at her outburst.

"That is very reassuring Mrs. Wilson. Most Indian parents prefer a son, so we have a preponderance of female frozen embryos." He smiled at Margaret and she felt he understood her impatience and excitement.

"The actual procedure is fairly simple but we need you to stay here for at least month." He paused.

"Would that be a problem?" He asked.

"No, luckily we're both teachers. We get six weeks summer holidays," Tony replied.

"Good, that's the first problem solved."

Margaret was still in a state of shock. She was reeling from the suddenness of it all. Some of the time, she wondered if it was real. Her excitement at the possibility of becoming a mother was increasing with each bit of information that Dr. Patel gave them.

"Normally I would say at least a year. We need to be sure that you really want to go ahead with this. We advise the patients to go back to their country, think carefully of all the issues rising from it and only then will we go ahead."

Dr. Patel's words made sense to Tony.

"There is some good news for you. I have some healthy embryos that would be a perfect match in many ways for you, just donated earlier this month."

Tony and Margaret looked at each other.

"You mean we can go ahead now with the procedure?"

Margaret almost jumped out of her chair.

"No I'm sorry. I didn't mean that you do it right away. I would prefer you both to go back to Glasgow, discuss it with your family and think about the implications."

"But," Margaret interrupted, "we've waited years for a baby and have been talking about nothing else for two weeks. We're absolutely positive it's right for us."

"I understand your need for immediate action, and I understand that you've been trying for a baby for some time. Also another trip to India will be expensive but you must understand Mrs Wilson, we do not handle these cases in a hurry. It is important for us to do things by the book."

"You just said that you have the perfect embryo," protested Margaret. Her head was buzzing with excitement.

"No, I'm sorry," said Dr. Patel, in a voice that brooked no further argument. "I do want you to consider all the implications, talk with your doctor in Glasgow before you decide."

"He's right you know," Tony agreed and squeezed her hand.
Dr. Patel showed them all the paper work, the costs, some testimonies from other couples and informed them that the timing of their visit would depend on Margaret's cycle. They were grateful for the thorough and detailed discussion they had with him.

They walked back to the hotel armed with all the information they had been given. Tony accepted it was right to go back to Glasgow and plan it. Margaret was sure she needed no time to think at all. She felt the months were slipping by and she wasn't getting any younger.

"Why can't we do it just now? Tony, can't we talk to him and persuade him?" she pleaded.

"Look Margaret, I'd rather defer to his expertise. He sees couples like us everyday. He knows best."

"I'm sure there aren't many from the UK, surely," Margaret disagreed.

"Okay, he did say apart from Barbara there were no other parents from abroad, well other white European ones, as it's all still fairly new," Tony nodded.

"Well why can't we insist? He did say that he has perfect embryos. What if they are given to someone else? What if they deteriorate after some time," she shuddered. She was clutching at straws.

"No Margaret, I think he's right. Let's do it the right way. I still need to get my head round all that Dr. Patel said today."

Tony got up and paced up and down the room. He looked out of the window and saw a girl in school uniform walking beside a young woman. They looked like each other. That normal everyday scene could turn out to be so different for them. He was confused. He imagined walking an Indian girl to school in Glasgow with him. 'Would it be fair on that child?' he wondered briefly. He looked at Margaret, her eyes bright with hope, looking at him, imploring him to fulfil her deep need.

"We'll be taking an Indian baby back to Glasgow," said Tony quietly. She looked at him, annoyed that he could not understand that every cell in her body ached to be a mum.

"Tony, it will be our baby. She'll be in my womb for nine months." Margaret cried. "We talked about this. Why are you saying such awful things now?" she sobbed.

"I know we've talked about this. I just need time. Surely you can understand that?" said Tony.

"No, no I don't. All I know is that I'm getting older by the day. We can't adopt and this is our only hope. It's almost like fate. It feels right." Margaret ran into the bathroom banging the door shut.

"Margaret, I'm not saying no, just that I need time."

Margaret did not open the door. Tony heard her sobbing.

Margaret stood in front of the sink and washed her face. The mirror showed the wrinkles around her eyes. Time was rushing past. To be a mother was more important than anything in the world. She came out of the bathroom calm and composed and told him he was right.

The following few days were difficult. Their minds could not stop dwelling on the enormity of what they had learned. A baby was within their grasp. Margaret felt her whole being come alive with hope. Hope that had eluded her for so long and had made her life a misery but the doctor was right, they had so much to think about and plan. Bringing a baby into the world, a baby that was genetically different from them was an enormous step. Their mood swung from wild excitement to deep doubts.

"Must take our minds off this if we can," suggested Tony, delving into a new guide book on Bombay. Margaret agreed.

They spent the last few days going around Bombay sightseeing. They processed the photographs of their stay in Goa and did some shopping before they left for Glasgow. The mundane, normal activities calmed them both.

*

The next few months in Glasgow saw them planning the future, nursing hopes that they would have their baby at last. They made a pact that they would not say a word to the family and keep it their secret. If the embryo implantation was successful, and Margaret became pregnant they would wait till it became obvious. Hopes rose and Margaret was thrilled with the possibility of her long-awaited dream being fulfilled. She held on to Tony, filled with excitement that something she had hoped and longed for was becoming a reality.

Margaret pictured herself, waddling around, resigning from her job, raising her baby, dressing the baby, a picture postcard life as a mum. Perfect. The thought of a genetically different child who might cause a stir, not only in her family but in the community at large, was something she brushed aside. Her thoughts were full of the untrammelled joy of holding the infant she would give birth to and nurture all her life.

Chapter 6

It was the week after the exams. Tina had the iPod dock on loudly, and Beyonce's album was belting out the lyrics that she sang along to as she cleaned the room. She picked up all the bits of paper, revision work, past papers that had grown into shabby little mounds and lying in piles around the room. She put them into a black bin bag. She chucked them out, feeling a sense of accomplishment. Margaret and Tony came in and sat on her bed. Margaret had a big bag in her hand.

"So what have I done then, both of you in my room! This must be serious," said Tina as she turned down the music.

"Tina, love, we want to talk to you." Margaret began hesitantly.

"Oh, I'm surely in trouble then," said Tina grimaced, a little confused as she could not remember doing anything untoward.

"I know I came in well after midnight last Friday but we were celebrating the end of the exams and I was with Keisha," she added, still not entirely sure why they were both there.

Her dad got up and put his arm around her.

"Listen, it's not about that night at all. This is more serious. You are eighteen now. There's never a right time to tell you, so."

Tony gave her a squeeze.

"What he means is," Margaret interrupted. "You know that we've never kept anything from you, and now that you have decided to take this gap year to India we thought that you might want to find more about the lady donor..." she hesitated.

Tina swallowed hard. She had put off raising this topic since the last time, wondering how to go about it and here they were giving her a chance to open up.

"Mum, dad, you know I love you more than anything else, but." she hesitated. "You're right. I've been thinking about finding my real… I mean the lady who donated…"

Tina stopped talking, took a deep breath, and her eyes glinted with tears.

"Look love," said Margaret, "we understand. This bag has everything I recorded and all the details of my years of infertility. It also has things from our Indian trips…a few papers of the time at the clinic in Mumbai. Maybe that'll help. I don't know much with the confidentiality that the clinic has. I'm sorry. I don't have much. There is a paper on embryo donation and an adoption certificate but they gave us little detail about the donor."

A patch of red started at Margaret's neck and slowly spread onto her face. Her voice had become a whisper.

They seemed to talk in phrases, whole sentences cut short with emotion, all of them embarrassed, trying to avoid causing any pain to the other. They did not want a repeat of the other night. Tony came to the rescue.

"Sweetheart, listen, mum and I've had a long talk about this. You're old enough now to know what you want. We're totally supportive of this decision. We'll do all we can to help you."

"But I thought… that you didn't want me to find out about her. Mum. I won't go if you don't want me to. I won't do anything to hurt you…" Tina shuffled her feet.

It was Tony who he seemed to know what to do. He had gone over to comfort Margaret but found himself back over to reassure Tina. He sat beside her, held her hands and said, "We need to talk about this properly. We want to help you sweetheart."

He kissed her forehead, and she crumpled into his arms. They talked for ages, all three at times skirting the issue, choosing words carefully, but it was the best thing they had ever done, as

Tina felt a great weight lift from her heart. She understood their concerns and was happy that they had accepted her need for this quest to continue. They pointed out how futile it might be.

"I know, I know but I need to do this. Even if this trip achieves nothing, I must do it. I never want to say later, "If only I'd tried," said Tina.

Her steely resolve impressed Tony.

"You must go then," he said and gave her arm a squeeze. Tina looked deep into Margaret's eyes.

"You have my blessing too," said Margaret. "Heading off to India all alone, at such a young age, your mum can't help but worry." she whispered holding Tina tightly.

"I…I too have something to say to you. I don't know how to…"

They both looked at her; Margaret's eyebrows rose up a fraction.

"I meant to tell you but…"

"What is it Tina?"

"Well I've been seeing Jenny. She's a counsellor…" Tina started hesitating, watching their reaction then explained.

"Of course, and we'd like to meet her Tina. Why don't you make an appointment and we can all see her together?" Tony suggested.

"I'll call her first thing tomorrow."

As soon as they left her room, Tina opened the bag her mum had given her and put all its contents on her bed. She sat still for a moment taking it all in, a big scrapbook of sorts, diaries, brochures, photos, and some letters with Indian postmarks and others with USA postmarks. Yellowed papers, even a piece of ribbon that must have held all those papers together were scattered on the duvet. She inhaled deeply, looking wide-eyed at the things in front of her.

Where to begin?

She touched each of the things. A faint aroma of old dust rose from the collection. A shiver of excitement rushed through her. She searched for the clinic. There was an old brown envelope with "Patel Infertility Clinic" on the cover that was inside a poly pocket.

The contents of that single brown envelope could change her life forever. It was her only chance to find out who she really was. Her gateway to the truth, something she'd yearned for, something she'd craved for. Everything she ever wanted, everything she could ever wish for was in the envelope. It was something beyond her wildest dreams that she could ever come across.

She took the papers out of the envelope carefully. There was a brochure and a few other papers. Photos of babies on the cover made her think of her own baby photos. She felt breathless, as if her heart would stop. No, she could not do it.

She left it lying on the bed and paced the room. She drank some water. Fear and excitement made her palms sweat. Tina stayed up all night, devouring all the contents that were on the bed.

Margaret found her in the morning sprawled asleep in an uncomfortable posture with all the stuff in a mess around her.

"My poor baby" she said under her breath and left her to sleep a bit longer.

*

The Wilsons stood at Jenny's door. Tony rang the bell. They could hear the trill of the doorbell and brisk footsteps coming towards the door. Margaret looked around taking in the old garden that had been tended with care. Neat privet hedges surrounded the house. One huge rowan tree cast its shadow on the stone exterior of the house. The terracotta pot spilled over with evergreen plants and some purple pansy blossoms decorated the edges. The door creaked open. Jenny welcomed them in.

Tina looked nervous as she introduced them.

"My mum, Margaret and dad, Tony."

"Come in, Come in" she ushered them in to the same room that Tina was familiar with.

"It's so good to meet you both."

Jenny got extra two chairs for the parents.

"Do sit down and make yourself comfortable."

"We came to thank you, Tina said you were a great help to her." Tony said.

"Well I was only doing my job. Tina is a lovely young girl and is coping rather well." She gave a bright smile to Tina.

"Tina could have come to us anytime. I know that sometimes it is good to have someone objective to talk to." Tony added.

"Yes." Jenny nodded. "Tina has been so loving and protective of you." She paused looking at Margaret.

Margaret held Tina's hand. "I understand it can't be easy to deal with such a big issue. I mean she's still only a child."

"Well, she's eighteen, a very determined young lady really," said Jenny with a gentle smile.

They all agreed. The clock struck eleven and there was an awkward silence.

"Did you show them your list of clinics that you have downloaded?" Jenny asked Tina.

Tina fidgeted, looked up at her mum.

"Actually, we're going to help her with all the information that we have." Margaret said.

"So you are supportive of her search then? That's wonderful news Tina. Come on, not like you to be so quiet."

Tina gave a faint smile.

"Mum and dad have agreed to me going to India. Things have happened so quickly I can't believe how lucky I am."

"Tina that's great news, but a word of caution, what if you can't find anything about her? It is nearly nineteen years since."

"I know but at least now I have the address of the clinic."

"That's a great start. Wish you all the best in your search Tina." Jenny gave her a hug. "Remember to email me if ever you need me. In fact I quite fancy a trip to Mumbai myself. Why don't you take me along?" she joked.

They all laughed. "We'd be going with her too, if it was not so costly," said Margaret.

"I'll keep in touch, thanks again Jenny, for all your help." Tina returned her hug.

"Jenny is genuinely interested in you. I can see why you were able to talk to her, a very pleasant woman."

Margaret agreed.

"Now we need to start getting all your travel arrangements in place. How long you want to stay there, the visa, injections, changing money to rupees…"

"Tony, really!" Margaret shook her head.

"What? All these need to be done quickly, the gap year will not last all that long you know, and it will fly past if we don't get these things done on time." Tony's mind was busy planning.

"Stop going at hundred miles an hour," Margaret cautioned.

"Eh? Look it shows only twenty eight miles on the speedometer," he joked.

"You know what I mean," Margaret and Tina exchanged a smile.

Margaret felt a sense of relief. Talking things through with Jenny left her feeling that an enormous weight had been lifted from her shoulders. She only wished she could speak to her sister, Brenda about it all. Weren't sisters supposed to be supportive? Brenda was difficult at the best of times, or as Tony put it, a heartless bitch.

*

The meeting on Saturday was as Margaret had expected. Brenda was moody and resented everything in her life. She had to look after her mum. Brenda had been happy to be at her mum's when the going was good and she could rely on her mum to provide delicious, home cooked food. Now it was a chore. It was hard work. She hated driving all the way to spend the day cooking a meal and cleaning the house when she did little in her own house. Margaret was also finding balancing her work, and supporting her mum difficult. Brenda had often complained of her loneliness and Margaret had challenged her to show some care for the mum who adored her. Brenda had accepted reluctantly, making scathing remarks about how she was bearing the brunt of looking after old mum when all Margaret did was take care of her "poxy" job.

It wasn't long before Brenda started her jibes about Margaret getting older and letting herself go.

It was Brenda, her words, her sarcasm; her relentless nagging that made Margaret's life a misery. Her fortieth birthday was approaching. Brenda had bought her a beautiful bracelet. She had commissioned it and the stunning design in silver was unique. Unfortunately, Margaret had hardly finished thanking her when Brenda ruined the moment in her inimitable way.

Brenda had reiterated that "Life begins at forty" was in reality a sham. According to her, life after the big four "O" was on a downward spiral.

"You look older than forty. Why don't you get a good haircut and get some decent clothes," was her cutting remark. "It's harder for you hen, with no kids and just loneliness when you get older. Not much of a future to look forward to. Is it?" she said, relishing the fact that her sister's life would be worse than hers.

"I have my career at least," retorted Margaret.

"Margaret, why don't you take some bloody time off work and look after mum?" Brenda's eyes blazed accusingly.

"For goodness sake, you know the spring term is the busiest, with pupils' SQA exams and reports…"

Before Margaret could finish, Brenda thumped her hand on the coffee table and said loudly "Any bloody excuse. You always wriggle out of your duty to mum."

The people in the café looked around, shaking their heads at Brenda. Margaret was furious.

"I'm not listening to this nonsense anymore," she said rising from her chair.

"Yeah, run away, that's your answer to everything," shouted Brenda.

Margaret hurried out on to the big staircase of the store leading towards the exit. As she walked down the stairs, the whiff of the perfume counter was strong as she headed to the revolving door. She stood outside in the fresh, cold air for a moment, clenching her hands.

Brenda's generosity as always became meaningless with her vicious tongue. Their meetings ended with words said that soured their relationship further.

'*Families*,' thought Margaret, laughing inwardly at how she was desperate to have one of her own, yet her sister had made her life a misery. "*Not just my sister, you are my friend*" were the words on one of the cards Brenda had sent her. 'How could she even write such words,' thought Margaret as she hurried home.

The Saturday crowd in town surged on the pavements. She wished she had stayed home and relaxed but there was so much housework to catch up with and there was all the marking of pupils' work too. She took the train back home.

Chapter 7

Margaret came home to find a letter from India was on the door mat. Her tiredness and worry vanished. She sat down and tore it open. Dr. Patel had replied to their letter. Their second visit to Bombay for the embryo transfer was going ahead. Having received information from her G.P, he indicated the best time for her to arrive in India and advised her to make her travel arrangements. She wished Tony was there to share the news. He was away playing golf. She could not relax. Her housework and school work remained untouched. She sat reading the letter over and over again.

The well-thumbed letters from Barbara, with photos of their baby, were in her bedroom. She went upstairs and took them out of the drawer and touched the photo of the baby.

"One step closer to my dream," she thought to herself.

Tony came back to see her seated with a pile of books on pregnancy, childcare and baby catalogues from Mothercare. The brochures of the clinic with bouncy babies were on the top of the books. He could see the joy in her eyes and he feared for her. *What if the whole thing went wrong? What if the pregnancy was not successful?*

Margaret was like a woman with a mission. She was obsessed with the visit to Bombay. She started buying clothes for the baby. Barbara and she called each other up and spoke over the phone, Margaret tried to find out every little bit information. Margaret persuaded Tony to paint the spare room, but he managed to dissuade her from making it a nursery as other members of the family could find out. He was caught up in her enthusiasm and had only positive thoughts. The nervousness he felt at the beginning slowly changed to one of joy. He too looked forward to their trip.

The changing seasons made work in the garden a continuous pleasure. The autumn colours and stunning sunsets burnished the greens to gold and browns, a season that changed from warmth to cold in a matter of few days. Scotland was tingling with beautiful crisp and cold days. Betty had thankfully recovered from her illness and was on her feet again. Margaret's relationship with Brenda had improved since Betty made fewer demands on her time.

She called Margaret.

"James said that you and Tony are going back to India." Brenda asked Margaret.

"We like the people so much and it is a big country so we thought of going again," said Margaret.

"I hate poor countries. I know James is crazy about India. How can you bear all that dirt and poverty? And the smell!" she said.

Margaret could imagine her sister at the other end of the phone, "I don't think you'd like it," she said genuinely.

"James talks about five star hotels that are out of this world. He showed me the brochure of Lake Palace Hotel. That one with an unpronounceable name, you know the hotel shown in the James Bond film, *Octopussy*. Maybe I should make a trip just to these nice hotels."

"No, no, you'd hate it Brenda. I know you. I mean there's such poverty, the poor kids on the street and the noise, the stench. I know that you wouldn't be able to bear it."

"Well you were all praising it last time, when James was out there."

"The heat, I know Brenda, that the heat would just finish you," Margaret added quickly.

"I suppose you're right, I can't even bear Majorca in the summer," said Brenda.

"Hey, I almost think that you're trying to put me off," laughed Brenda. "I can't stand all the people anyway."

"Brenda, for God's sake!" said Margaret.

"Well I'm only telling the truth. They're just not like us are they?" Brenda chuckled.

"People are just people." Margaret's brow knit in annoyance.

"I've had an experience that I'll never forget. Don't tell me you don't remember, Ashok! They're different from us. Even their food is smelly. There are too many bloody Indian restaurants here. They stink the place," Brenda observed, oblivious to Margaret's mounting anger at the other end of the phone.

"I need to go," said Margaret.

"Listen, James likes his Darjeeling tea. Why don't you get him some when you're in India and I do like the fancy silk scarves? Get me some, right?" said Brenda, without a hint of shame.

Margaret wanted to bang the phone down.

"Okay," she said and rang off.

Tony heard Margaret banging the pots in the kitchen.

"What's up? Not Brenda again? What's it this time?" asked Tony.

"She's doing my head in. God she's so ignorant," Margaret shredded the lettuce for the salad with force almost like ripping its heart out.

Tony put the salad bowl near her and picked some tomatoes from the plant on the window sill.

"These have come out well this year," he said, tasting the home grown ones as he sliced them for the salad.

"She was going on about our trip to India. I wish you'd not mentioned it to James."

"Oh forget Brenda! She always gets your back up. James thinks we're just going on a holiday. He kept talking about Rishikesh and how wonderful it is to go up to the source of the Ganges River."

They ate their dinner of pork chops, mash and a salad with relish. After watching the evening news, they went to the garden to work, a hobby that they both still enjoyed.

Margaret tended to the tiny seedlings with care. Life sprouting after the dark winter and early spring always made her feel better. Working in the fresh air and getting her hands in the soil was a perfect antidote to all the worry about their next trip to India. They spent an hour outside in the garden and then she showered and after, sat down to mark the SQA exam papers. Advanced Higher Papers, was the first step in the pupils' future achievements and their careers. Their entry to a university or work could depend on her assessment. Long into the night the work kept her busy. She went to bed exhausted.

In the morning, her first thoughts were of the dream of her holding a tiny baby. She hugged herself as she and Tony got ready for work. *Would the dream become a reality soon?* She wondered as she drove to work. She played Steve Wonder's "Isn't She Lovely?" on the car stereo, humming the words, as the sun dappled golden on the horizon. A billboard advertising Huggies nappies, with a cute baby caught her eye as she drove on and an inexplicable frisson of joy filled her.

*

The next morning Tina's obsession with finding out all that she could about Indian fertility clinics was back. After a strong cup of tea she sat decided to do more research on the net. She switched on her laptop and googled 'India medical tourism embryo donation.' She was amazed at the information. There was so much to read through.

Medical Tourism – a $2.3 billion U.S Dollar industry

Surrogacy and Infertility Clinics – Testimonials

Embryo donation.

The internet had an enormous amount of websites and articles on the subject. She typed in the name of the clinic, Patel Infertility Clinic Mumbai: A Patient Friendly Infertility Clinic appeared on the home page. She was relieved to find that it had not changed its name or gone out of business. Here it was in black and white, her past, the tenuous link to her origins. A shiver of excitement and fear ran through her. Tina took a deep breath. She stopped for a minute. She wiped the sweat from her hands on her jeans, and continued reading.

The website had a wealth of information. There were pictures of babies, videos and even a comic book explaining infertility and the process that patients had to undergo. It looked so professional and clinical, a world away from the emotional turmoil that she was undergoing. This was her link to her genetic mother, maybe even to both her parents. She read each and every word on the website, not wanting to miss anything. The most important information that she wanted was not there. She had been hoping for a list of embryo donors.

How stupid of me? She chided herself. *They would never make that so public.*

She closed her eyes.

The image of an Indian woman in a sari with the same features as herself appeared in a flash. Tina got off the chair and stretched herself. This was hopeless. The website had only made her imagination soar. Her mum was right. The envelope had contained the clinic's leaflet and letters showing dates of appointments all those years ago, and the name of the woman who had donated the embryo. E.A. Thomas. Her heart missed a beat. This was her mother; the egg had come from her womb. It was a British name, not an Indian one as she had imagined it would be. It was a small clue. At least she had a name. The only way was to go to India and look for this woman, find out if the doctors at the clinic would help her trace the woman who had donated the egg. In her troubled mind she expected there was little chance of getting confidential information from the clinic.

Her mobile's ring tone was insistent. She ignored it for a while. It was Keisha's tenth message. This last one said, 'Pl, pl, mst c u.' Tina looked at the laptop and sighed. She was getting nowhere. She closed her laptop and picked up her phone.

"Keisha, what's up?"

She heard her sob, "The fuckin' bastard," she said. "He's dumped me."

"I'll come straight over," said Tina.

She got her jacket and rushed out the door.

"Mum, off to Keisha's," she shouted as she ran out of the driveway. Margaret stood up from the flowerbed, a clutch of weeds dangling in her hand.

When Tina reached the bed-sit ten minutes later Keisha opened the door. Her eyes were red and swollen with tears. She swept the riot of curls that hung in disarray her from her face, but they sprang back again. Tina gave her a hug.

"I'll kill him, I hate him..." sobbed Keisha as she showed her the text.

"I'm sure he's off with that bitch Sonya," Keisha frowned and walked over to the tiny kitchenette and took out another glass for Tina. The bottles of Smirnoff and tonic sat on the coffee table. She poured a shot and offered it to Tina. They drank and talked, Tina remembered her own first love and the heart-ache that had followed their break up.

They sat in the tiny bed-sit, talking for hours, Keisha's bare feet swinging off the sofa-bed or curled tight under her. The bottle of vodka helped blur the edges. Later, they phoned for a pizza. The mood changed.

"I'll call round to his and trash all his clothes. I'll break his iPod dock and his Wii games." Keisha giggled as they planned more and more bizarre acts of revenge.

"Oh, what's the use, we're wasting our time. Let's forget these men, these losers. Who needs them anyway?" she said winking at Tina, her mood getting better.

"God I'm hungry." Keisha bit into her pepperoni pizza. "How is your trip to India coming along?"

"Mum and dad have been great. We're checking out all the fares and stuff," said Tina brightening up.

"Maybe I'll join you too. Nothing much here now for me, and I can't get a bloody summer job either. I'll come with you. Yeah, that's it. I'll be bored outta my skull here anyway. Let's get two gorgeous Indian men. I'm all for that, Goa here I come," Keisha's voice rose in excitement.

Tina's face darkened.

"I'd prefer to go on my own," she said quietly.

"What? No way man, here I am your best pal and ready to shell out my meagre savings for the experience of a life time. I'm coming. You can't stop me," Keisha went on.

Tina got up abruptly, took the pizza boxes to the bin. She crushed them with her hands and the put them down on the floor and jumped on them.

"Hey, that's my job, I love doing that," said Keisha joining her.

"So tell me how much is the fare? What jabs and medical stuff should I go through for the trip?"

"No Keisha, I don't want you to come. This is something I need to do on my own." Tina turned away from her piercing glance.

"I don't get it! Why ever not? We've done everything together since Primary One. What's the big secret? Have you got some nice guy stashed away out there? Bollywood here I come," Keisha smiled and danced around the room and threw a cushion at Tina.

Tina's eyes narrowed and she glowered. She flung the cushion back at Keisha, with all her might as if to attack her.

"Oh, shut up Keisha. Everything is always about you. Selfish, you only think of yourself." Tina grabbed her jacket and banged the door as she made a quick exit.

Keisha stood at the door shocked.

Chapter 8

For Margaret and Tony the second trip to the clinic in Bombay came all too soon. The formalities were over, the long distance phone calls, the worries, the days and nights of tossing and turning in their minds, the enormity of the undertaking were over.

They met a group of Scottish tourists in the hotel. Fergus McAllen was their chosen guide. He had been to India many times and he took them to areas off the beaten track. Margaret and Tony were drawn to the crowd in the bar when they returned from a walk on the second night in Bombay.

Refreshed after the walk, and nerves still tingling with excitement at their appointment with Dr. Patel, they ordered a drink and sat with the Scottish couples. Fergus was talking of an oracle and his own experience of it. They listened, fascinated with this mysterious aspect of India that they had heard so much about from the other tourists in the bar last evening.

Was Fergus at the bar telling a tall tale? They edged closer to listen to his fantastic meeting with the nadi or the oracle of the leaves, as he called it. They leaned over to catch his words.

"It was so bloody accurate. I was stunned. This has been the most incredible event during my stay here," said Fergus. "Go on have a try, you may not be called. I was a total sceptic like all of you."

He then related some of things that the sage had interpreted from the ancient leaves. They listened. Tony laughed at the gullibility of all the people listening intently, including his wife.

Back in their hotel room, Margaret said that she was going to see the sage. She insisted that they give their thumb impression.

"God men in India! Come on, you're not serious?" he looked at her, surprised at how she had been taken in so easily.

Margaret looked at him with a strange glint in her eye.

"I don't believe in it at all, but I'm going with an open mind. It's like readings of the tarot card or the crystal ball. Why not spend a few hours finding out? Imagine what a tale to tell when we get home, like Fergus holding court in the bar this evening," she giggled.

"Aye, well, okay, for a laugh then," he agreed.

"Let's hurry downstairs and give our thumb impressions. Fergus said that a young man Sekhar is taking them just now," she said.

They stifled their bubbling laughter as they bounded down the stairs and thought of challenging this oracle. Neither of them believed any of the tales that Fergus had told them so charmingly.

The banyan tree filled half the area of the grounds of the ashram. The branches had bent down to the ground and formed their own little saplings as banyans tended to do and joined the huge mother tree to form a complex whole. The brown boughs steeped into the earth like stumps of new growth all mushrooming, linking together to form a huge mass. The dusty green leaves, were healthy and thick. It was an incredible sight for them. They had never seen a tropical tree of such proportions in their lives.

Sekhar took them into a tiny bungalow set in the grounds. A terracotta tiled roof veered down on a faded white-washed brick building. On the veranda, a man bowed and welcomed them in. He was sorting a pile of what looked like old wooden slats. They were the leaves, lying around in bundles. The ancient script was inscribed in vegetable dye, like dark ink on the leaves that were hard and dry and almost like wooden slats.

"It's a form of poetry," said Sekhar, indicating the script on the wooden slats. "It's written in verse form." They saw some strange, looped writing that looked like squiggles and very different from any European scripts that they had seen before.

"Its ancient Tamil, Pali maybe, a script perhaps even older than Sanskrit," he continued. "That's why we need interpreters like the sage, who is trained to make sense of it. It's an ancient skill that has been preserved and passed down from generation to generation."

Their sceptical minds took in the strangeness of their surroundings. They nodded. He guided them and they walked through the veranda to the inner hall to meet the sage. Tony took note, 'plenty to add to the tales that he would weave to friends back in Glasgow,' he thought to himself.

In the tiny hall of the simple house, they sat on the rough mat, both finding it hard to sit on the stony floor that they could feel under the mat. The thin curtain on the door at the side parted and an old man in saffron robes stood before them. Sekhar bowed and formed his hands in a reverential *Namaste* and spoke to him in Tamil. The sage acknowledged them with a slight bow and sat on the small rug in front of them and looked at the papers with the two thumbprints, her left and his right thumbprint that they had given to Sekhar the previous day.

As he spoke Sekhar translated.

"Yes, I will read your leaves. You are the first British couple, though there have been many Christians and Muslims from other parts of the world who have come here before. I could only find yours," he said turning to Margaret. He picked up a leaf. Margaret confirmed that she was the daughter of Betty and Angus and the sage began reading the poems.

Sekhar switched on the cassette tape recorder. The sage read the poems and at the end of each stanza he interpreted it in modern Tamil. He paused and Sekhar translated it into English and asked if they had any questions.

The sage started relating some incidents of her early life. He reported her date of birth, the love of her life, her dad's death, foreign travel, health and wealth so accurately that she sat stunned. Her family, descriptions of her sister and mother, the operation on her knee at the age of eight took her by surprise.

Even Tony did not know about some small details he mentioned like the black and white pet dog that she had as a child. He told her that she was working as a teacher. The facts that hit her the hardest were those of her late marriage and her desperate need to have a baby. It was these details that made the tears rise up at her throat. She swallowed them back and gripped the mat on the floor.

"You were meant to come to this reading of the nadi," the sage paused. "A momentous event is going to take place for you in this country. You'll come back to India. There is a connection," said the sage. "A baby is from here. The past is in the future," he said enigmatically. He ended the reading and put the leaf away carefully on the pile in front of him.

The whole episode left them both stunned. They watched as the sage rose. Sekhar took the cassette out and thanked the sage.
They folded their hands and said namaste. Tony took a wad of notes from his pocket to give to him. The sage left without touching it.

"Well donate it to the ashram. The office is in the next building." Sekhar said,

He handed them the cassette.

They walked out into the bright sunshine. The leaves of the old banyan tree swayed in the light breeze.

"I, we never asked him any questions," said Tony.

She nodded, but seemed in a daze.

A baby, those words stunned her. She could not get past those words.

The hour had passed like the water flowing past in a river. Only the odd sounds of car horns or birds chirping had interrupted the astonishing revelations. A taxi sped them back to the hotel through the dusty streets with scrubby trees and the cow that stood in the middle of the road, the strange but usual sights in India. They had witnessed something stranger, something that they could not explain.

A five thousand year old scripture on a leaf had Margaret's life inscribed on it.

'The past is in the future,' the sage's words rang in her ears. 'What did he mean? Why had she not asked him what it meant?'

As they went to bed that night, Tony remarked that it was just a coincidence and they should put it to the back of their minds. She tossed and turned, unable to focus on anything but that cryptic word 'baby.' She could not get rid the image of the oracle, the nadi or the words telling her that she had a connection with India. She knew in her heart that her dream, her desperate need for a baby would be fulfilled in this country, thousands of miles from Glasgow.

Two days later they arrived at the clinic, determined to give it their all. This was their only chance. Margaret hoped that everything would work out without a hitch. She had important things to worry about, her health, and whether or not the procedure would be a success. Tony was anxious that the legal and financial side would also run smoothly.

The pictures adorning the walls in the clinic showed bouncing babies and happy mothers. She recognised a photo of Barbara holding her infant son, her face wreathed in a broad smile. It stood out as they were the only white couple amongst all the Indian families on the wall. Margaret closed her eyes and said a short prayer. She had never felt more desperate. She wanted this to work more than anything else in the world. She held Tony's hand, and both were sweating slightly as they clung to each other for support.

"The doctor will see you now," said the petite girl in a white sari. She smiled as she led them both to Dr. Patel's room. The air conditioner buzzed silently. The room was familiar. Margaret had relived this visit to the clinic a hundred times or more in her mind. Dr. Patel explained that the embryo was ready and that they had a few more frozen ones if the first attempt did not succeed. He assured them that he would respect their wishes to go by the British guidelines of inserting only two embryos as they did not want multiple births or complications. They had to arrive early the next morning.

They left the room, holding onto each other. In less than twenty four hours, their lives could change forever. Dr. Patel gave very little information about the donor except to say that she was in good health, was an educated person aware of the implications of her donations and that she had signed her consent forms. He showed the documents to them. The only thing that struck Margaret and Tony was that the woman's name was E.A. Thomas. They had expected an Indian name, different, not Christian- sounding. It reassured Margaret. Tony was more puzzled and intrigued but the doctor would not give more information as they had very strict guidelines on confidentiality that they had to follow.

E. A. Thomas. Margaret kept repeating the name in her head for most of the afternoon. What did the initials stand for she wondered? What did the lady look like? Thoughts about the donor kept recurring. Tony stayed silent, going over the risks and hoping that the attempt would be successful. Thoughts of how he would cope with Margaret if this did not work, kept him occupied. The rain came on as they left the building.

It was a short walk to the hotel. They hoped to escape the downpour but it turned out to be an experience that they'd never forget. July and August were the monsoon months in Bombay. They couldn't escape. They ran laughing into the hotel lobby, totally soaked. Margaret watched the sheets of water lashing against the hotel walls and windows. Tony ran up to the room to get the camera to take photographs. He clicked away not wanting to miss any angles that might give the photos an edge. As the rain died away, they walked up to the room, took a warm shower and changed. The TV news ran some information of the high tide and parts of Bombay being flooded.

"Of course these are islands. I keep forgetting that," said Tony

"Yes, Mr. Geography teacher," said Margaret laughing at how the ferocity of Mother Nature's monsoon downpours had made them forget the simple, geographical fact that Bombay had been founded originally on a cluster of seven islands.

"Let's go to the church this evening if the rain lets up," she said.

"Religious are we?" he asked.

"I just feel like praying. I can't explain. I remember being with Barbara in that church in Goa." Margaret examined her nails.

Her face was serious.

"Are you sure? This rain may not stop, you know." Tony looked out of the window at the rain still falling heavily outside.

"I won't go if you don't want to."

Margaret sounded disappointed.

"We'll see how it turns out this evening," he said, picking up the Times of India.

Later as the rain abated they spoke to the hotel reception.

"Are all the churches in Bombay Roman Catholic ones?"

"No, there is St. Thomas Cathedral, an Anglican church. It's beautiful, near Flora Fountain. Not far," said the receptionist.

They took a taxi to the cathedral.

They stopped to have a look at Flora Fountain. Tony checked his tourist guide. The traffic around the fountain was very busy.

They moved on to the cathedral.

The church was simple compared to the gilded rich altars of the Portuguese churches that Margaret had seen in Goa. They sat down on one of the pews and prayed quietly. 'God let the oracle be true, let me please have my baby,' pleaded Margaret silently. The faint sound of the rain outside was just audible.

Later, as they walked around the churchyard, in the light drizzle, they were surprised by the number of Britons whose graves were in the cemetery. The marble tablets were engraved with moving elegies. Margaret was touched. The graves of generals, clerks and young maids were clustered together. Some had died very young, many of malaria. Perhaps in death they had reached equality, thought Tony. He looked at the memorials on the walls of the church for many who had served the Raj. There was one for Henry Robertson Bowers, a lieutenant of the Royal Indian Marines who had lost his life in the Scott Antarctic Expedition on the return journey from the Pole, on or about the 27th March, 1912. Tony and Margaret felt a strong link to the country. They had a coffee after the visit to the church. Tony pulled his tourist guide book out of his jacket.

"What are you looking at now?" asked Margaret.

"Flora Fountain, It's very interesting."

Tony showed her the page with all the details.

"The Roman goddess on the top in Portland white stone. She carries the flowers and fruits." Margaret took in some of the words.

"There is even a poem," said Tony and read it to her. Her mind was on other things. She heard his voice in the background.

"Hmm…not very good," commented Tony "Maybe lost a lot in translation," he added.

"What?" Margaret was distracted.

"Margaret, Flora Fountain's supposed to be like Piccadilly Circus."

"We live in Glasgow. I don't know much about London's Piccadilly Circus," she chortled.

"London, a great city of course," he teased her.

"No I think Glasgow is better," she argued.

They laughed together. The outing had relaxed them a little.

They returned to the hotel and the rain started in earnest again. The ferocity of the monsoon surprised them. They had read and seen the devastation it caused on TV but being in the centre of a downpour was amazing.

Thankfully the next morning was bright and fresh with no rain. It was as if the Gods had washed the city for a new beginning. They left for the clinic, more nervous than ever before.

The actual transplant was so simple that Margaret was surprised. She had known it was not surgery but this was more like a cervical smear. Back in her room, she kept crossing her fingers and sending prayers to the God.

The curtains in the room fluttered. Just a few hours ago she and Tony had walked over to the clinic and now their life had changed. The doctors had allowed her to stay for that day then she was to return to the hotel. Margaret had expected it to be a complicated procedure with a longer stay in the clinic. Now it seemed like an anticlimax. She rubbed her tummy gently. She wanted to feel different.

Tony sat beside her and held her hand but said nothing. They hugged each other, feeling a sense of togetherness like never before? Absorbed in their own worlds they wanted to relate to each other their deepest joy and trepidation but words refused to come as easily as they had before. Conversation evaded them now. Hours of talk seemed superfluous in this moment of sheer joy and fear.

After several minutes, Tony said, "Are you okay, do you want anything?"

"No I'm fine."

"I'll get some coffee," he said.

She nodded.

Margaret looked out of the window. There was still no sign of rain. A clear blue sky with the mid day sun showering its heat was what was visible. She lay back on the bed and closed her eyes.

Tony came in with a flask of coffee.

"How are you feeling, sweetheart?" Tony poured a cup for both of them.

"I wish I knew Tony," she said.

They sipped the coffee.

It was the agonising wait after the transplant that was difficult. Margaret was scared to walk in case she shook the embryo out. She stayed in bed more hours than she should. The doctor advised her to be normal, take her mind off it, even go for some sight seeing as long as she did not strain herself. But both Tony and Margaret stayed within the confines of their hotel. Margaret checked herself often for any signs of bleeding. She lived on tenterhooks, elation and doubt constantly warring on her mind. The first attempt was successful. The doctor confirmed her pregnancy. They both wept with joy. They wanted to thank the woman who had given them a gift that they never thought was possible. Margaret secretly thanked her a million times in her heart and prayed that her life was fulfilled and happy.

*

A few yards away, Tina stopped in her tracks. She turned back to look at Keisha's flat, but the door was shut. She walked on slowly, not sure whether or not to return and apologize. Rain drizzled soft and cool on her face. It was a welcome relief. Tina looked up, baring her face to the rain, wanting it to cool the rage in her heart.

Her footsteps traced the way back to Keisha's bed-sit. She rang the bell.

"I'm sorry..." tears welled up.

Keisha took her hand and pulled her in. "It's OK. Tell me what's up."

The soothing words stirred more tears. Tina's secret, years of heart searching, turmoil and fears came out in a torrent. She related incidents, the scenes from childhood that seemed vague almost dreamlike at times.

"I remember walking over to a stranger at a supermarket because she looked more like me than my mum. I must have been three or four years old. I put my arm beside hers and kept looking at it. It was the same shade. The lady smiled and ruffled my hair. I can remember my mum's puzzled look, but she took me back to the aisle and we carried on shopping. I hated it, constantly being asked who the white lady was at school. That still annoys me, even today. Remember the family album we did in Primary one? All the kids in the class asked why I was a dirty colour in the family photo?"

Tina bit her nails, a childhood habit that comforted her.

"I know...I had my fair share too. The kids called me all sorts of names. What's all that rubbish about "sticks and stones may break my bones but words will never..."

"At least your dad is Nigerian. That made it easier for the kids to understand. I'm still trying to work out who I really am. I need to find that missing piece of my life. That's why I'm going to India. I want to trace my origins. Can you understand Keisha? I'm sorry. I'm so confused. I don't know what to do."

Keisha looked at her friend, a crushed, sad woman, harbouring a deep wound. Tina seemed unable to come to terms with her identity or lack of identity.

"Why didn't you ever talk to me about this? Wish I could help in some way."

Tina explained everything, the trip to India, her plan to visit the clinic that had facilitated the embryo transfer and how she hoped that the doctors would give her the name of the lady who had donated the egg.

Keisha's laptop was on and Tina showed her the link to Patel's clinic. Keisha came up with a daring idea.

"Just try it, you've nothing to lose, go on do it now." Keisha goaded her.

Tina emailed the clinic and requested a placement for her IT experience in their office.

"It's probably after midnight in Mumbai now, said Tina. They'll probably never reply."

Chapter 9

Much to Tina's surprise she got a reply the next afternoon, saying that they would be delighted to offer a student placement for six months as she was the first student from Scotland who had made such a request. Both Dr. Patel and his wife had completed their Fellowship in Edinburgh and they had fond memories of Scotland. They were delighted to return the favour. Tina could not believe her luck, and it gave her a new vigour in her quest.

The next few weeks were a whirl of activity. She applied for the visa. The Indian Consulate in Edinburgh was efficient and she got her six months' visa with little trouble. Tony helped her book the flights and hotel, even Margaret joined in shopping for light clothes and water tablets. She organised Tina's injections with the doctors. Tina was all set for the trip of her lifetime. But before she left for India she needed to get as much information as possible and find out the rest of her story from her mum. Tony brought over his collection of books on India.

"Dad I had ignored all these before, I think I need to read up a bit on it. Keisha said she'd get some DVD's on India."

"That's a good idea. Also call on James," he suggested. "He often goes to India on business trips."

"Sure I'll do that, if that cow is not around," said Tina.

"Hey less of that, young lady," admonished Tony.

Margaret came in from the garden.

"Mum, forget about that garden."

"The garden needs constant care, just like you do," she joked.

"Aye, at least plants don't talk back," laughed Tony.

*

Glasgow was grey and misty as the Wilson's arrived early in the morning. Their flight had been held up in Bombay due to technical problems. They were tired and jet lagged, but the feeling of elation had not subsided.

Brenda was on the phone the next day.

"So how was the second holiday in India? Monsoon rains I was told."

"Yes there was a bit of it but we were okay. The hotel was good."

"Did much sightseeing eh? Must see your photos." Brenda's voice was needling.

"Yes, just a little bit. We wanted to have a relaxing holiday. How is mum?" Margaret changed the subject.

"I coped okay. She's fine now. I've got an agency nurse. It's too much for me to look after her if it happens again."

"I understand Brenda. That's a good idea," said Margaret, happy that she had changed the topic effectively.

Brenda had something else that excited her.

"Remember James's fortieth birthday in November. I've booked a five-star restaurant. It's a surprise for him. I'll talk to you all about the arrangements soon. Bye," she rang off.

Margaret avoided Brenda for the next two months. The start of the new term was a good enough excuse. Brenda phoned her occasionally but seemed busy organising James's birthday and her short breaks to Europe.

"I've brought you and Tony some lovely things from Spain. I must see you." Then her voice rose in excitement. "I'm thinking of buying a villa in Spain. James is reluctant but I'll persuade him. Just give me time," she said.

"Be careful, there are a few scams about buying out there," warned Margaret.

"I'm not that easily taken in. Don't worry."

Brenda loved the sound of her own voice. She boasted about the various villas that she had seen in the brochures.

"Margaret you must take a look at the brochure. You and Tony could stay in ours during your long holidays."

"That would be lovely Brenda, but right now I'm so busy at work. Syllabus changes again. It's The Highers this time. We've just got used to Standard Grade."

"Oh, your school stuff is so boring, Mags. Why don't you relax? Let's go out and get hammered." Brenda giggled.

"No really Brenda no can do,"

"See you at the September weekend then?" Brenda insisted

"Yes, maybe…"said Margaret hesitantly.

"You're such a bore since you came home from your trip. Anyway I've plenty to do. Bye." Brenda rang off. Margaret was grateful that she did not have to explain anything to Brenda. She hoped that the pregnancy would not show. She wanted time to get used to the idea herself before others knew. The first trimester should go safely she prayed and she did not want any one to know till that was over.

Each day was a new beginning for Tony and Margaret. Her skin expanding over the belly was like a map of her future. She touched it every morning, thanking the donor and praying for everything to go safely. Every cell in her body wanted to experience the moments of change. She revelled at the thought of the little life in her womb. Giving birth to a new life! She loved the baby of her dreams already. Every moment that she was not at work, she was imagining the miracle growing inside her.

The garden work was coming to an end and Margaret was grateful for the onset of winter. She would relax, relish the moments when the baby kicked. She scoured the magazines for Indian looking babies and wondered how hers would look. She wanted to dress her, pamper her, hold her so tight and not let her go. She dreamed of the baby's smell that would take her breath away, the skin soft and tender, the little fingers and toes that she would treasure, to hold and kiss. Nothing in the world could match this feeling. No one would understand what her longing had been like, not even Tony.

Tony treated Margaret with touching tenderness. He hoped that the nine months would pass without any complications. This new feeling of being responsible for a tiny baby took him by surprise. He also had worries. What if the baby was so different that they could not feel anything for it? How would the baby be treated by the family?

Brenda had been kept at bay for a few months. Now it was November. James's fortieth birthday party was to be held at the Radisson Hotel. This was a party that they could not avoid. Margaret tried on the dress that would conceal her bump, a long, black dress with a plunging neckline that hopefully would draw attention to her cleavage.

Brenda's first words to Margaret were "You've put the beef on haven't you?"

Margaret gave her a tight smile and moved to wish James a happy birthday and give him his present. Luckily Brenda was too excited explaining the evening's entertainment to Tony and showing off her new dress to all her friends to notice the change in her sister.

It was at the toast to James when Brenda's beady eyes noted that Margaret refused the champagne. She ran over to her and stuck a champagne flute in her hands.

"I'm not letting you do your mad diet thing on my James's big day. Come on, down it in one," she laughed.

Margaret put the glass down and rushed to the toilet.

"She's so sensitive our Mags." Brenda's snigger was heard by all.

Tony ran after Margaret, telling Brenda to carry on and that he would see to her. They had to tell the family. There was no way out. When all the guests had left, Tony and Margaret decided that it was the right moment. James, Brenda and Betty were a bit tipsy and the glow of the good dinner, dance and merrymaking was etched on their faces.

"We've got some good news," said Tony smiling at Margaret and holding her hand.

"Yes, you've won the lottery!" shouted Brenda.

"No Brenda, even better than that," said Margaret her eyes glowing with happiness. "We're going to be...going to have a baby."

They all congratulated them. Hugging her, Betty shed a few tears of joy.

"Oh so lovely, after all these years. God has answered your prayers. This is wonderful news." Her mum wiped her tears.
James congratulated both of them.

"Amy will be so pleased to have a cousin at last," he said shaking Tony's hand. "It'll be a life long responsibility but you'll never ever regret it"

Brenda stumbled towards them and held back a bit. Then she laughed and hugged Margaret.

"When is the baby due?"

"Second week of March," Margaret smiled happily.

"An Easter baby, how wonderful," she cooed. "Let's all drink to that," she said ordering another bottle of champagne.

"I think you've had enough," whispered James in her ear.

The attentive waiter brought the bottle and the champagne cork popped. They raised the glasses.

"To the new parents," said James. They all raised their glasses that sparkled in the chandelier light.

"Fucking brilliant," said Brenda downing a big sip of champagne. "This is a bloody miracle, ten years and then…," she stopped, turned to Margaret, stared at her and said "I thought you had stopped that IVF stuff long ago."

Margaret turned pale, and then turned to Tony. He took her hand and said, "We've something more to tell you." They all looked at him expectantly. Tony explained about the embryo transplant. There was absolute silence for a few moments. The news stunned them all.

"Well we're so lucky. She *is* a miracle." He sipped the champagne and held Margaret's hand tightly.

"Jesus Christ, what are you saying?"

Brenda took another big gulp of her champagne. Her face was bright pink. The blonde curls that had been coiffed so perfectly at the start of the evening lay in straggly tendrils over her shoulders. The light glinted in her bright blue eyes, cold as steel as she exclaimed in a loud voice:

"You're having a black baby! My God!"

*

Brenda's racist reaction shocked Margaret but she was too excited about the changes in her body and the months of preparation for the most important event of her life and she cared little about other people. A warm sensation of love enveloped her being. She wanted the best for the baby. Now she could indulge in all that she had wanted to do. Love for a baby that was not even born was so strong that she thought about her every day, every moment. She bought baby clothes, for every season, making sure that she had enough for each growing stage. She read and re-read the books on bringing up a baby. Some of the instructions clashed with each other so she eventually kept to one book and followed it to the letter. Even Tony had to put up with her strict diet of eating healthily, though sometimes cravings took over and he laughed at her incongruous combination of pizza with pineapple and pickled onion.

However, she did not neglect her school work either. There was a new vigour in everything she did.

Tony watched the transformation in her and adored her happy, loving self. She was more like the Margaret he had fallen in love with. They both had so much to look forward to. The new responsibility made him look at his future plans. He even made a will and took care of all the finances with care. When and if Margaret worried, whether it was about any tiny change in her body or at the ante-natal classes if she failed to follow what she was told, he reassured her.

Brenda saw them occasionally at Betty's and did not say much. She wanted to keep her distance and yet she was curious. She did not want to shut her sister out of her life. Amy was still keen on going to her Aunt Margaret's house and she dropped in at weekends when Margaret offered to baby sit.

The pregnancy progressed without any problems and Margaret was grateful that she could work and that she kept in good health. The glow that she felt in her heart was showing on her face. Even Brenda commented on her radiant looks.

"Mind you, as soon as you have the baby, everything goes; your hair falls out and your body sags; it's not exactly wonderful," she observed grumpily when they were at Betty's having tea one weekend. Margaret just smiled at her sweetly and did not rise to the bait.

The scan picture, a black and white photo that showed a fuzzy shape, was her treasure. Margaret looked at it every day. Each stage of the pregnancy was a voyage of discovery.

The amniocentesis test was nerve-wracking. There were moments when she felt low and she prayed that everything would be okay and then there were the highs, knowing that the miracle was happening.

Looking at the garden, Margaret watched the tiny sapling that she had planted in the spring, blossoming and taking roots. She drank Earl Grey tea looking out at the frost-covered ground and the young plant growing in the harsh weather when everything else in the garden seemed to be resting. She marvelled at Mother Nature battling against all odds, sustaining life in the cold month of February. The faint sunshine brightened the green of the lawn and she could just see the place where she had planted crocuses and narcissi. Every morning she looked for the buds to appear, impatient that the bulbs were still playing hide and seek.

The baby kicked inside her. She placed her hand on her tummy. A tiny tear coursed down her cheek. She was big, waddling in her maternity dress. Brenda's barbs had been relentless, toned down only when her mother gave her a piece of her mind.

"How could you bring such shame on the family Margaret?" she had asked when she had met her at her mum's. There was no remorse or apology for her behaviour.

"What will I say to Amy? Christ did you even think about any of us?" she had harangued her.

"Stop it Brenda," her mother had intervened as Margaret rose to leave the room.

"I'll never let her play with Amy. She'll never be part of my family."

Margaret left, banging the door behind her.

It still hurt. Her only sister was rejecting what was the most important thing in her life. Her mother was caught in the middle trying to mediate between them.

"I don't want you to break up the family Brenda," warned her mum. "A baby is a joyful addition to any family. Stop being so bigoted!"

"Bigoted! Me? Why do you always take her side? Can't you see mum how it's going to cause problems for all of us?" she had retorted.

"No I don't see what the problem is at all. It's a baby and she'll be welcome as my granddaughter any day."

*

Margaret's pregnancy progressed smoothly. She kept thinking of the phrase "A baby made, unmade". '*Why on such a lovely morning did her mind dwell on this,*' she scolded herself. She glanced out of the window at the faint pink in the sky of the early morn. The frosty dew like crystal tips on the grass, shone like diamonds. The garden was surprising in its budding beauty. The grass was a rich emerald now, dotted with amethysts, narcissi and bright golden crocuses. Overnight the colours seemed to have sprung alive, offering a morning gift on waking.

Margaret filled the kettle and switched it on. She felt a shooting pain. She lurched forward. It was happening, everything she'd waited for, everything she'd read about. It was the baby. Finally the baby was coming. She called out to Tony.

Sleepy-eyed and dishevelled, Tony came into the kitchen. His pyjama top unbuttoned, flapping on to his arm, his bare feet white against the cold stone floor, he opened his screwed-up eyes a bit wider. He stood for a few seconds still in sleep mode. Then he realised as her whimpers turned to cries of pain.

"Are you okay?"

His eyes were now wide open and his forehead had creased in concern.

"You need to get the bag I have packed and take me to the hospital," she said between gritted teeth the pain obvious in her eyes.

"The waters have broken?" The sweat beads formed on his forehead and his eyes widened.

"No, I just want to get ready. Calm down," she said as she noticed his body shaking slightly.

They hugged each other. The steam gushed out of the kettle, a tiny roar and then it switched itself off. Margaret took the two mugs, put a couple of tea bags in and poured in the hot water. Tony took the milk out of the fridge, hands shaking, looking at her all the time. He gulped the scalding tea and ran up the stairs to get the case and get ready. She followed him up slowly.

Twenty hours later, little Tina Jasmine Wilson squealed her way into the world.

"Nothing wrong with her lungs," said the nurse as she held the baby girl to Margaret. "Here mum, you can hold her now."

Drowsy and straining, Margaret reached for her. She nestled her close.

Bliss.

Nothing else mattered. It was perfect, the cosy warmth of her skin against hers. Margaret noted that the baby fingers curled in a tight fist. The hours of painful labour, the epidural, the numbness she had felt, faded from her mind. She remembered Tony's pale face as he was brought in after they had prepped her for labour. She remembered the screen placed in front of her and the vague feelings of tugs and pulling below as they tried to bring the baby out.

Hours later she was exhausted but still her baby refused to come. C-section was spoken then there was the flurry of doctors as she was wheeled into the operating theatre. Her nervousness and pain abated as the obstetrician and anaesthetist spoke to her kindly. She held on to Tony as he bit his lips and held her hand, his pale face taking on a red hue. He tried talking to her of their holiday in Goa, the orange sunsets and the tropical night with bright stars, as she waited to go under.

The first sound she heard as she surfaced was a baby's feeble cry. She was impatient for the baby to be brought to her for that first cuddle. Then she fell into a deep sleep, tired and weary after the ordeal. She did not remember them stitching her up or the fact that the baby and Tony were taken away to the nursery.

The family waited outside, James, Betty, and Brenda. Tony came out of the room.

"She's awake and holding the baby. Sorry I called you. The C-section threw me. They're both fine." He looked shattered yet happy. James put his arm round him, and said nothing. Betty sat up straight and said a quiet prayer.

"Thank God," she mumbled.

"That baby nearly killed Margaret, didn't she?" Brenda said. James shot her a look that stopped her saying any more.

"Go home Brenda," he said with clenched teeth.

"I want to see my sister. I do love her, you know that," she said, standing behind her mum as if shielding herself.

Betty shook her head. "We'll come again tomorrow. Give her, and the baby, our love," she said and took Brenda's hand as if to draw her away.

"Go and have a wee look but don't stay long," said Tony, relieved and feeling his whole body unwinding from a tension that he had been unaware of.

They all peeked into the room and a nurse hovered around, making sure that they left soon.

James drove the car, immersed in his own thoughts.

"She's lovely, the baby," said Betty. Brenda drummed her fingers on her bag and said nothing. James smiled at Betty, looking at her in the rear view mirror and nodded.

"Yes, she's bonny," he said.

They dropped Betty off and then picked up Amy from the neighbours.

"Mum how's my wee cousin? Is it a girl or a boy?"

Amy's blonde ringlets swayed and her blue eyes were bright as buttons. Her excited voice annoyed Brenda.

"They're both fine and it's a girl. Come on let's get you home. Thanks for watching her, Fiona," she said and left with Amy still asking her questions about her cousin.

"Mum look, Fiona gave me some paper and I made a card for Aunt Margaret and the baby,"

Amy showed her a brightly-coloured card with a match stick couple and a baby in a crib.

"Very good. You're always good at everything," said Brenda and put it aside. "Come, off to bed now. I'll get you some milk."

Later, Brenda slipped onto the sofa beside James.

"She's that excited, daft wee Amy."

She straightened the cushion and put the magazine in a neat pile on the coffee table.

"Of course she'd be excited, with a new baby in the family."

"For Christ sake, James, why don't you say it? It's a bloody *paki*. I don't want my Amy anywhere near her."

"Brenda, have you gone off your head? It's your niece for crying out loud!"

"My niece? Where did you get that from? Open your eyes James. She's not one of us."

"I'm fed up with this," said James turning to Brenda. "It's time you stopped this nonsense?"

"I suppose you're a perfect gentleman. You're a hypocrite."

"What do you mean?"

"I'm sure you feel the same. I just can't accept her. Why don't you ever support me?"

"I can't talk to you anymore." He shook his head and moved to the kitchen, helped himself to a beer and went to his study.

*

The baby gurgled in the pram. Margaret dug the earth, the rich soil crumbling open for the new plants. An earthworm slithered on the brown soil, its body with its serrated lines undulating as it moved on. She worked hard, her efforts concentrated on getting new colour and life into the garden for summer. She wiped the sweat from her brow then she put the spade down and took a breather. A piece of an old newspaper fluttered in the garden.

"Baby Factories," "Outsourced Wombs," "Babies for Sale," Exploitation of Third World Women."

Margaret shuddered as a flash of the headlines in the newspapers of Tina's birth came back to her. The horror of those early days were etched deep in her mind. The photo of her holding Tina with Tony by her side was splashed all over the papers.

Our exclusive: 'An Indian Baby for a Scots couple' announced the *Daily Recorder*.

The lengths to which women would go to have babies were discussed in the media.

"Not a "Place in the Sun" but "A Baby in the Sun" will be our next programme," claimed a local TV station. The phone did not stop ringing. The more the couple kept their distance, the more the news seemed to get worse.

Comfort came in the form of the massive support from women who had tried everything to get pregnant. Soon Tony and Margaret were flooded with letters from all over the UK. They wrote sharing their heart breaking stories.

It was much later that they found who had leaked the news of the birth of their baby to the media. Chantal, the young auxiliary who had taken the photo soon after Tina's birth had seized the opportunity. They had never thought that she would use it to make money from the tabloids. The news stirred up a debate in Parliament and the language of the right wing press was vitriolic. Their happy event was marred by the house being surrounded by paparazzi waiting to get photos of the baby. It did not help when Tony lost his temper and lashed out at an aggressive photographer who put the camera right in Tina's face. They realised that the only way was to share the news and explain to people and the media their wonderful gift. There was a clamour for this most human of experiences.

As they watched the TV coverage of a few minutes in the local station, Tony and Margaret still felt as if they had been forced to take this action. They had wanted Tina's birth to be a private affair. Instead it had turned into a circus.

James was supportive, often visiting without telling Brenda. He formed a special bond with Tina. She smiled her toothless grin at him and his heart melted

"Another baby born in the Thatcher era," said James and added, "even if there are twelve years between them! Amy and now Tina! What a different world these girls have come into eh?" He tickled the baby's chin.

*

James could see that Tina was really excited about her trip to India. She asked him about his big adventure in the late nineteen sixties when he had foolishly followed the Beatles to the Maharishi ashram in India. He brought out the now-faded photos and reminisced with her. She laughed at photographs of him with long hair, colourful beads around his neck, and the ubiquitous Afghan coat with his travelling companion, Toby.

"Weren't you a hippie, uncle?" Tina giggled.

"He was obsessed with India just like his dad. How foolish to go all the way to India, eh?" Brenda butted in frowning at the photos. "I don't know how anyone can go to such awful, poor third world countries. Can't even drink the water there," she shrugged in disgust but pleased that she had added a deprecating dig at James.

"I think he had a cool time. Tell me all about it, Uncle James." Tina sat beside him, flicking the pages of the photo album.

"Bah! I doubt it. I'm quite sure he was ill there. He never got in touch with his family for ages. He wouldn't have come back if his dad had not snuffed it, you know," Brenda added.

She moved away to the kitchen to make their lunch, muttering to herself that it "must've been a bloody waste of time anyway."

As soon as she was out of earshot Tina asked him again.

"So what is India like? Tell me please."

"You'll love it. That was so many years ago," he said and shut the photo album. He sighed. "The India of today is quite different."

"Come on lunch is ready," Brenda called over. James and Tina stared at the plate of curry that Brenda dished out. James chuckled.

"What, why are you sniggering?" she demanded.

They were both quiet.

"Tina will be eating a lot of that there."

"I do love a chicken tikka masala," she added and dug her fork into the fluffy rice.

After lunch James spent an hour telling Tina all he knew of the new prosperous India that he visited for business.

Chapter 10

Back home, Tina opened the pile of books her dad had given her. She looked at the notes and passages Tony had marked on the pages of some of the books. A piece of paper that fell out looked interesting. He had summarized a story from the Mahabharata. She wondered why he had done that and read it.

Karna - The Divine Birth

  Kunti, placed the baby Karna in a basket and asked her maid to set him afloat on Ashwanadi, a tributary of the holy river Ganges in the hope that he would be taken in by another family. He was a boon given to Kunti for her devout prayers but as she was unmarried and scared that she would be accused of being an unwed mother she let him go. The baby was powerful and radiant as his dad, the sun god Surya. The child was found by a charioteer Adhiratha and his wife Radha and raised as their own.

He became a loyal son and fulfilled his duties to his parents. He was also interested in warfare and mastered the craft of archery, equal only to Arjuna, the greatest archer in the world. At the great battle of Kurkshetra, the epic battle of the Mahabharata, he finds out that he is in fact of royal blood and the first son of Kunti, making him the eldest of the Pandava brothers against whom he is ready to battle. In a touching scene he pleads with his mother Kunti not to reveal the secret of his royal birth until his death, as he wished to remain loyal to his adopted parents lineage. He wanted the entire world to recognise him as a Radheya.

'Loyal to his adopted parents lineage.'

Tina would be leaving in the next few days. She felt a wave of confusion cloud her. How could she leave her parents in search of another? She felt numb. Her visit to see Uncle James had made her feel guilty. Whilst he had been out there having the time of his life, these two people, Tony and Margaret were doing all they could to have a baby. And now this scripture, which seemed to hold in it a wisdom she felt she was too young to understand. Just then she heard Keisha. She'd forgotten that she promised to go and check out that new club. Even though Tina was reluctant to make a big deal of her adventure, Keisha was adamant to give her a good send off.

"Has she got her fab rags on Mrs. W?"

Christ I am not ready yet.

She rushed around her room, grabbed her leggings and top to change. Keisha walked in, dressed to the nine's darkly made-up eyes, dangly earrings, black top matched with bright lime shorts and a pair of ridiculously high heeled pink shoes.

"Not those black leggings again. Hold on let me get you something half–decent, I'm not letting you fade into the background on your last night out with me," she said, rummaging through Tina's wardrobe. She came up with an equally bright top and leggings for Tina.

Tina did not demur she put it on quickly.

"Lets go, I'll do my slap on the bus," she said and hurried Keisha out of the room.

*

James sat looking through his old photo album, grinning to himself. Revisiting the good old days with his favourite niece reminded him of a time when things weren't so difficult. Just looking at the photos of himself in his youth made him realise how much he'd lost. With Brenda life had become about constantly trying to please someone else. So much of his life was wrapped up in duty and doing the right thing that he hardly had time to follow his passions anymore, let alone keep up with the Beatles! And then there was the one person he'd left behind.

*

Jimmy and his friend Toby had trekked to the Maharishi's ashram. They had travelled at night on third-class seats in a train that took them northeast into the foothills of the Himalayas. In the early morning a dawning lavender-pink sky illuminated the forested green slopes that rose on either side of the track. When they entered Dehra Dun they felt they had reached one step closer to their dream. Dehra Dun was well known for housing not one, but two elite British-run schools. The city was not just famous for the Tapkeshwar temple, but it was also linked to the two famous legends of both the Ramayana and the Mahabharata. But more importantly for the two adventure seekers it was one of two places with rail stops close to Rishikesh. They reached the ashram and settled down in the periphery, the Beatles were at the centre with the Mahesh Yogi giving them priority over the other worshippers. After a couple of days they managed to catch a glimpse of the Beatles from a distance. They were in awe to see their idols at last. *Anything's possible if you put your mind to it,* he thought.

Ashram life was simple. They rose early to attend the meditation classes and served as volunteers to help with their stay. The beauty of the ashram where nature blended in with the simple structures was a unique experience. Flowers of every hue grew in abundance here.

He thought about his father and the cruel words they'd exchanged before he'd left. He tried to put the last conversation he had had with his father away from his mind but it kept resurfacing.

"Jimmy, son, go to college, find a job and stop this nonsense about going to India." His dad's anger was evident. A tall, muscular man, he was someone used to making all the decisions. No one had ever crossed him.

"You were the one who told me all the tales about your stay in that country, in the British Army."

"That was different. I had a job to do. I wasn't following some long-haired pop group." His voice bristled with a "how dare you" tone.

"I want to go. Nothing will stop me." Jimmy stood defiant, facing him and looking him straight in the eye.

"Who's paying for this crazy idea?" His dad's voice had now changed to a mocking tone.

"I am. I've saved enough from my last job and I've booked the tickets."

"Not a penny from me mind!" his father had shouted. "You get into a scrape there, boy, and I'll not be there for you."

"I don't care. I'm going." Jimmy shouted back. "You try and stop me!"

"You'll stay here and do as you're told!" The voice was now a threat.

Jimmy saw his mum standing at the doorway, indicating to him to stop the argument.

"No I will not. I'm going."

His dad lunged at him. Jimmy moved out of his way. He thought for a moment that his father was going to hit him. His mum hurried to shield him.

They stood glowering at each other.

"Maybe your dad's right, son. It's time to be serious about studying and find a job. He's only thinking of what's good for you," said June, his mum

"Mum for fuck's sake!"

"What was that? How dare you swear at your mum?" His father raised his hand. His mum stopped him.

"Jimmy, you enrol on that course and finish your college course now. If you go on that trip don't come back!"

His father turned away from him and strode out of the room.

"Maybe I won't! I won't have to see you ever again!" Jimmy shouted.

"Jimmy!" said his mum. He picked a glass off the huge brass coffee table.

"Look at this bloody thing, from bloody India. He's got tons of stuff from there and talked all the time about how great it was. Jesus, why's he so angry? Why can't I go if I want to? I'm not asking for a penny from him."

His mum said quietly. "He knows the country, that's why."

"That was ages ago. Don't take his side mum. I'm fed up. I'm going. I don't care what he thinks." His face red and angry, he walked out of the room. His mum stood holding the glass, shaking her head. Two weeks later Jimmy boarded the plane to India. His father did not come to the airport.

The time spent meditating at the ashram made him regret how he had left things with his dad.

One morning Jimmy rose early and went for a walk. He saw a figure by the bright red hibiscus plants, picking flowers and putting them into a basket. She was a vision in the early morning light. To his eyes she was perfect in every way. Jimmy moved over in her direction, throwing surreptitious glances her way. He came close to her and tried to look nonchalantly at her.

"Hello," he said shyly, "I'm Jimmy,"

"Hi, I'm Rita,"

She smiled and he could feel his heart do a million little somersaults. He caught a flower that had fallen to the ground and handed it to her.

"Thanks," she said.

He was mesmerised by her eyes, the dimple on her chin and her smile. But it was her demeanour rather than her looks that made her unbelievably attractive. She had a confident air. Few Indians whom he had met, both men and women had that look of defiance and elegance mixed together. Her features were not spectacular. Her oval face, her lips thin, her pinched-looking nose that was small, her thick hair that she wore bunched up and her glasses, the black frame hiding her warm brown eyes were not beautiful but it was her figure, slim, with curves that transfixed him. She wore a tight skirt that emphasised her tiny waist.

It was a heady time. Jimmy and Toby watched the Beatles at a distance. They saw them attend evening meetings with the Maharishi. Sometimes they said a few words as they passed them in the ashram. The whole experience was incredible.

Jimmy tried his best to create chances to spend time with Rita. The meditating classes were perfect to clear his mind of all his commitments in Glasgow and help him concentrate on the moment. He was smitten and nothing in the world could have changed that idyllic feeling. He looked forward to each morning when she picked the flowers, when he brushed her arm deliberately or stood close enough to smell her hair, feel her skin breathing almost beside him.

He wanted her.

She could see from his body language that that he was hers. She took her time, teasing him, making him want her more.

When it was time to leave, Toby was ready to head home but Jimmy could not bear to part with Rita. He stayed on. Rita had captured his heart. Away from all that he knew, and his fraught relationship with his father meant he didn't want to go home. He wished to treasure each and every moment he had with his new found love. It was not long before Jimmy pledged his undying love for her.

The tropical sky was burnished in silver, their senses heightened. The young couple sat near the Ganges as it flowed in a silvery torrent, brushing over pebbles. It was perfect, a full moon night. The heady scent of the jasmine flowers that she had weaved into a garland lay beside them as they talked of their future together, two young people caught in the surreal high of an unreal world. He bought a cheap silver ring and put it on her finger making promises that he did not know if he could keep.

Rita did her best to make sure that her parents and community never found out about her dangerous liaison. They would only disapprove. She treasured his ring as if it was a promise for life. She believed him, his promise of taking her to Scotland. She trusted his words, especially when he gave her his address in Glasgow. He made rash promises believing that love would conquer all. In the fervour and moments of passion, he thought it was a possibility. They relished the few moments they could snatch from their busy days at the ashram.

The dawn was unbelievably beautiful. The rose-hued sky as they woke up together was glinting with a hint of the rising sun as they stood looking out of their window. Rita rested her head on Jimmy's shoulder wishing that moment never to end. He turned her around and kissed her all over her face and neck and she breathed his woody smell wanting to hold him in her arms for ever. Her dark eyes were half open as his dark green ones examined every feature of her face as he gently pressed her closer to him. He lifted her face to the golden rays from the window and kissed her passionately.

Later that day, as Rita was showing a couple around the ashram, she saw James hurrying towards her. His face was ashen. He was holding a telegram in his hands. She excused herself from the couple and took him aside.

"Jimmy what's wrong? You look awful."

"My dad," he handed the telegram to her.

The telegram read, "Come at once. Dad passed away. Heart attack. Mum."

"Oh My God!" Rita gave him a hug.

"I need to go home," he said

"Of course you must."

Rita explained to the couple and hurried back to his cottage to help him pack. He was devastated. "My dad's only in his fifties. Oh God, I don't know how my mum will cope."

He kept worrying about his mum, the funeral, the ticket to get back to Glasgow. She watched silently and helped in any way she could, holding him when he needed to.

"You don't need that," she said as he took one of her bangles, one of the pink pebbles that they had collected together and the flower that she had in hair and put it in his case.

"I need you always near me. These will be a poor substitute."

He kissed her and held as if he never wanted to leave.

They hired a taxi and got to the train station.

"Rita, I'm so sorry. I never expected this to happen. I can't bear to leave you."

He held her hand tight.

"Jimmy, you must be there for your mum. I understand."

She held back the sob rising in her throat.

"What was she going to do now?"

Her mind was panicking, but this was not the time to say anything to him.

"I'll be back, I love you so much." Jimmy kept squeezing her hand. They could not hold each other at the station. Open signs of affection were not the done thing in India.

"I'll miss you," she said, "please hurry back."

"I will, I promise, I promise. I'll never let you go. You're my life, you're everything to me," he whispered.

"Phone me, write to me," she said as the announcement for the train's departure came booming and crackly on the loudspeaker.

Jimmy scribbled his address on a piece of paper and handed it to her. She put it safely in her handbag. The train moved away and they watched each until they became nothing but a tiny spot in the distance.

*

James took out another box from behind the drawer. It had been left untouched for so long, it looked as if it had never been opened at all. James took in a long breath and opened it. He looked at the photo of a young woman sitting by a rock beside the river. It was a young Indian woman, not more than twenty, with a big smile and curious pose. Then there was a young man, with big hair, another big smile. He looked through the album quickly, recklessly, in desperate search to find a picture of the couple together. There was just one. They were sitting by the river. Smiles all round they looked so much in love. He reached out and stroked her face. *Rita*, he whispered. He put his fingers in between the plastic, paper and the photos to take out something which was tucked away. It was a letter. He unfolded it and read...

Dear Jimmy,

I hope you are well. How's your mum? I'm sorry about your father's passing. It is over two months now and I've not heard from you at all. Oh Jimmy, the days here are so long without you by my side. I fear you are not returning to me. I pray that you come back to me soon. I miss you.

I am writing down the ashram's address again. I won't be here long. This place is too remote for my needs now. I need to be near a hospital. I've always dreamed of living in the big city, the city of dreams. I'll be leaving for Bombay soon. Write to me soon and I will write with my new address. Sushma's friend has offered to help me get a job and support me. Jimmy I have something important to tell you. I wish I could write it down but I can't. Please write.

Please, please write as soon as you get this. I am missing you so much. I want to be held in your arms again.

I love you and I'm waiting for you,
Rita

"James" Brenda shouted from downstairs.

He said nothing.

He quickly folded the letter and put it away in the box.

"James, come and speak to Amy. She's got news for us." Brenda called out louder.

James went downstairs.

Chapter 11

Tina arrived at Mumbai airport in the mid-morning sun. The temperature hit her as she walked down the stairs to the tarmac and into the cool of the terminal building. The white heat of the sun could be glimpsed even from the air-conditioned cool of the arrivals' hall. She moved along with the huge number of passengers who had disembarked with her and waited patiently at the immigration queue.

She noticed that she had merged with the majority of the people at the airport. A strange sense of belonging went through her, though everything around her was different. She stood in line with the non-Indian passport holders, some of Indian origin like her and others from different countries. A Scottish voice made her turn around, but the middle aged man was discussing a business deal with the person next to him. She assumed that the two men were in Mumbai for an IT software Conference. She waited patiently behind the yellow line as it neared her turn, and watched as the immigration officer asked a long list of questions of an older couple who looked harassed. The man's face got redder. He kept fanning himself with a paper and the woman beside had a worried look on her face.

Then it was her turn. She handed the officer her passport and disembarkation card and for some unknown reason her ticket. He looked at the ticket first.

"Holiday? Six months? Very long time," said the immigration officer. "You have relatives here?"

"No, I'm staying at this hotel, for the first night then moving to a friend's, Mr and Mrs Joshi." she said pointing to the address on the disembarkation card.

He seemed unconvinced and mumbled something that sounded like NRI, but did not press her further. She did not volunteer any more information either. He took his time, then stamped and signed her passport. She gave a sigh of relief.

She went down the stairs to collect her luggage. This was the first time she had travelled without her parents on a long haul trip. She was concerned that she could not cope; everything in India, even the airport seemed different. She was nervous as she watched the carousel in the baggage hall. Suitcases were being grabbed by the passengers as the conveyor belt moved around. She looked for her suitcase, worried in case it had not been transferred from her Glasgow to London flight. There were so many black suitcases trundling past her. Her mum's idea of sticking a bright yellow neon label helped her identify it at last. She loaded it onto the trolley and walked through the "Nothing to Declare" channel.

The crowd outside the terminal was enormous. The heat, smell, the noise and the jet lag made her feel disorientated for a moment. The sunshine was searing, the honking of cars, and the sheer number of people made her reel back. She stood hesitating as people moved in a hurry to join their loved ones.

Then she saw Rashmi, waving a bright scarf and holding a placard with her name on it. Rashmi looked so much like her Facebook photograph that Tina would have recognised her without the placard. Rashmi she observed was taller than other women in the crowd, with a big smile that made her high cheekbones more prominent. She was wearing a red salwar kameez, the dazzling colour perfect for the sunny afternoon and a large bindi on her forehead. Tina walked over and Rashmi hurried her into the taxi which had been waiting for her.

"Sorry, we need to get into the taxi, quickly," she said, as the driver loaded the baggage and they got in. The number of cars moving in all directions terrified Tina. It seemed chaotic. They sat back in their seats as Rashmi gave the driver the name of the hotel and then said something in Hindi that Tina did not understand.

"Welcome. Was your flight okay?" she asked Tina, adjusting her dupatta, over her shoulder.

"Yes, thanks for coming. I don't know if I could have managed on my own," said Tina and rested her head back on the seat.

"You'll get used to my city very soon. Everything is bigger, crazier and noisier but you'll never get tired of it. 'The max city' we call it," said Rashmi showing her pride. "I'll drop you at your hotel today. Take some rest. Tomorrow, I'll take you to the Joshi's family home that is near the clinic. You must be exhausted."

The taxi drive terrified Tina as he honked his way out of the narrowest spaces, and swerved wildly to avoid motorbikes and other vehicles. She was relieved when they got to the hotel.

"Be ready tomorrow at 10 am, sharp," said Rashmi and the taxi sped away.

Tina relaxed slightly in the air-conditioned cool of her room. After a shower, she ordered an omelette, a pot of tea and some toast. She unpacked, her mind racing with doubts. Had she done the right thing by flying over here? Everything in India was so strange. The videos that she had watched in Glasgow had not quite captured the huge differences in the culture of the two countries. They had featured five star hotels. It was so different being actually in the city of Mumbai. She remembered the old cine film of her uncle's trip to India. Tina had laughed at her

Uncle James's outrageous clothes and long hair. She put the photo frame of her family on the bedside table and then reached out for the mobile phone that was in her handbag. She paced up and down, dialled her mum on the mobile. She'd promised to call and tell them she'd arrived safely.

"Be careful with your passport, love. Did you have anything to eat? Drink only bottled water." Her mum's voice at the other end of the phone made her realise how far she'd come. Suddenly she felt all alone. The thought of six months on her own in this huge, sprawling, noisy and chaotic city made her apprehensive. She relaxed by taking a long soaking bath. That calmed her down. As the sun set in Tina took her iPod out and listened to some of her favourite tracks. The fear of being in a strange place by herself receded. She began to enjoy the quiet of the room, flicked on the TV, and watched the Indian news. She switched over to the BBC World Service channel. The familiar voices made her relax. Time passed and she fell into a deep sleep early in the evening, the jet lag overwhelming her.

*

The first days in Mumbai were something that Tina would happily forget. Rashmi had taken her to the Joshi's house in a cab. The journey in the taxi, which seemed to bounce over the slightest bump and throw Tina to all corners of the tiny vehicle, was a nightmare. She gripped the strap at the side of the door, as if her life depended on it. Rashmi chatted away, pointing out the landmarks but Tina absorbed little during that trip.

The clinic was a ten minute walk from her new home with the Joshis. Their house was simple with just the basic necessities but her room was in the shade of a huge banyan tree so it was cool. A ceiling fan gave much needed cool air and the bathroom on the same floor was basic but clean.

110

It was the food that Tina found really difficult to get used to. She longed for home-cooked steak pie, fish and chips and her mum's baking. Getting the inescapable "Delhi belly" did not help either. It was Rashmi's strong personality, the strident way she dealt with any problem that helped her the most. Rashmi was efficient and showed a practical edge to solving any problem that Tina encountered. By the end of the month Tina felt strong enough to cope with her new life in India. The unfamiliar became slowly familiar. People woke up early and the whole city was vibrant by seven in the morning. Seven was early in Glasgow. The sun shone so brightly through her window that she woke up with a start. The sounds of the morning pooja at the Joshis, the cycle bells and car horns that rankled her at the start became a natural background noise in the early morning bustle. The food, the strange smells that wafted through the air was all part of her life now. She no longer felt nervous of venturing forth to the streets and daily walk to the clinic. Day by day her confidence grew.

"Everything okay for you? I'll cook jalebis for tiffin, just for you today yes?" Mrs Joshi asked her as she came down that morning.

"Jalebis... I don't know what that is."

"Sweet, very very tasty." She licked her lips.

"Please don't go to any bother Aunty." Tina pleaded. Mrs Joshi's kindness reflected in her copious amount of cooking. Everyday she cooked something new for Tina.

"Like my beti, yes that's what you are, I look after you like my own," she said giving her an affectionate hug.

"Yes, you treat me so well. I can't thank you enough. I tell my mum about you every time I talk to her." Tina gave her a sweet smile.

"Dr. Patel will be happy. He's such a good friend of ours you know."

"To be honest Aunty I don't know how I would have coped without you and uncle."

"So you are talking about me?" said Mr. Joshi walking in adjusting his spectacles that slid down his nose.

"I was just saying how good you both are. I am so grateful to you."

"Arre, beti, you are no problem at all to look after. When Dr. Patel asked me if you could stay with us, I was worried a bit. You know I read a lot about these teenagers in the West but you are okay."

He switched the radio on.

"Chai ready?" he asked his wife and she hurried back to the kitchen.

Mr. Joshi's interest in everything relating to Scotland and Britain and the efforts that he made to impart this to Tina , made it interesting chatting to him. Tina got a better understanding of the deep connections between the two countries. They got into a habit of talking early in the morning most days. He listened to the radio and she sat in the veranda with him, before the hectic day began.

A cool morning breeze wafted over. Mr. Joshi was humming a tune, relaxing on his wicker rocking chair. He swung his head in tune to the beat and repeated some of the words. His glasses lay on his chest. A bhajan, a hymn was emanating from the radio. Tina sat on her wicker chair reading the newspaper.

The creak of the gate opening disturbed the rhythm of his music. Mr. Joshi looked up, obviously annoyed. A young boy made his way over to him and held a piece of paper.

"Donation sir," said the boy, standing deferentially.

"Donation? Why? What for?" Mr. Joshi quizzed the young lad.

"It's for charity," said the boy.

"Charity! Which one?" Mr. Joshi turned off the radio and looked at the nervous young boy.

"It's for the street children of Mumbai. Look sir, it says on this paper."

"Oh, now everyone is onto the "Slum Dog Millionaire" hype. Give me your details."

The boy handed the paper to him. It looked like a letter from where Tina was sitting.

"Hmm, anyone could have written this letter. See this is the problem with India" He said turning to Tina. "Any Tom, Dick or Harry can get away with setting up a charity." He scowled at the boy. "Here take this." He pulled out a wallet from his pocket and gave the boy a few notes and the letter.

"Thanks sir," said the boy and ran out of the gate.

"Tina, I'm too soft. These rascals know it, and they always come to me for donations." He winked at her. She smiled back at him, knowing that he really was a soft touch.

"Did you know that the city of Mumbai itself was donated?"

"Donated? How fascinating. When?"

Her eyebrows arched up.

"Yes, these islands were given to the English King Charles II in dowry on his marriage to Portuguese Princess Catherine of Braganza in 1662.Then it was acquired by the English East India Company on lease from the crown for just a yearly sum of 10 pounds in gold. So cheap, huh?"

"I know so little about the history of our two countries and how they are interconnected. It's amazing. Do tell me more."

"Oh, they teach nothing in schools nowadays. Don't worry young lady before you leave Mumbai, you'll learn a lot more from me."

"I'd love to know more," said Tina.

He nodded.

He switched the radio on and drummed his fingers on the chair to the beat of the bhajan. They heard the loud voice of Mrs. Joshi haranguing the maid and interrupting the calm of the morning. Tina put the Times of India down and headed for the shower. The morning talk with Mr. Joshi became a regular pattern.

*

At work Tina was met with curiosity combined with a great deal of human kindness. She blended in and people spoke to her in Marathi or Hindi and were bemused when she told them of her incomprehension of these languages. Even the little street kids, who tagged along when she walked to the clinic, and some at the clinic, spoke to her in Hindi. She had to explain that she didn't understand. There was some hilarity at her Glaswegian dialect and accent.

Tina observed the scenes of Mumbai were different from Glasgow. The houses with doors and windows wide open, compared to houses in Glasgow shut and in neat compartments were something she had noticed immediately. Houses in Mumbai were built with little concept of planning and slums grew beside main streets; families lived in the corners of shops or pavements.

Then there was the other Mumbai with skyscrapers, hotels and houses that were more luxurious than any she had seen in her life. It was a city of contrasts; one part seemed to live in the Middle Ages. There were carts, poor hygiene, disgusting betel leaf projectiles splattered on the pavements. Children looked malnourished often in rags and scrabbling around for scraps to eat. The poverty shocked her. Often she saw children begging around little shops and working on the trains instead of attending schools. The other half lived in the present, mobiles abounded, luxury cars glided past, the occupants cocooned in their air-conditioned interior. She was confused and delighted in equal measure with her new life. Sometimes she had a deeply unsettling feeling of homesickness and wanted to board the next plane home. Then she shook herself and thought of her quest, that deep need to find her genetic roots reasserted itself, and she was able to face the next day. Phone calls to Keisha and her parents kept her sane. Keisha's texts about her love life made her laugh out loud. She often sent her photos from the phone and Tina felt close to home when she saw the shopping trips that Keisha had undertaken, the crazy colourful clothes or chunky jewellery that she had bought and her wild stories of her University gigs. Brenda started Skyping her and Amy occasionally called from Canada.

Tina started making friends at work. She could not believe how much she had changed. Her work at the clinic and Rashmi's friendship made the transition from someone who longed for the grey, cool Glasgow to someone who was acclimatising to the heat of Mumbai.

She found the constant pressure of huge numbers of people on the streets and the noise and smells of Mumbai difficult to contend with. The people at the clinic were often knocking on her door and inviting her to attend functions and parties. At first she felt so welcome but after a time she found it a bit oppressive. She was used to being on her own. She valued her time alone, to think. Tina wanted her space and time to chill out with her music or even daydream. When she set out for walks along the beach, her friends from the clinic would be unhappy to let her go on her own. Being surrounded by people all the time was tiring and she wanted to point this out to them without offending them. The Joshis took their job seriously. Always solicitous, they cared about her and wanted her to feel at home. Mr. Joshi, an

Anglophile who read all the classics with interest, sat on his armchair during the day under the ceiling fan, waiting to accost Tina when she returned from work.

"Now young lady, look at this book. What great works from Walter Scott? *Bab, baree*! This short story "Two Drovers" is very good, very good. You must read such fine works, good for the mind."

"No I've not read his works. I only did some Shakespeare and Burns at school. I prefer to read Mills & Boon. I can get lots of copies here."

"*Aree, aree*, why do you waste time on such filth? Read these great works. They have meaning for ever. Like our Tagore. Have you read any of Tagore's works? You want to borrow my books?"

"Oh, thanks. I'll try to find time for them." She smirked knowing well that Mills & Boon would be her preference and these will lie in the bottom of the cupboard, but she did not want to seem rude. He was so enthusiastic about his books.

Mills & Boon, the pages of romance had now a more personal meaning since she had met Andrew Saldana at work. He was the consultant working for the IT Company that leased the computers to the clinic. Tina looked forward to his visits. She sighed as she took the books up to her room.

"Tina, beti come down, tiffin is ready."

Mrs. Joshi plied her with her cooking.

"Try this *sandesh,* very nice sweet, Bengali sweet, full of milk and cream. Good for you. You look so thin." She was a chubby lady with a kind face. The couple were a total contrast in looks. He was dark, thin as rake, with black rimmed glasses with thick lenses, glasses that strayed halfway down his nose like a pince-nez. She had light skin, and wore a big bindi on her forehead. Every morning she followed all the Hindu rituals with poojas accompanied by devotional music. She wore colourful saris and glass bangles that tinkled as she walked by. They were a childless couple and took great pride in looking after Tina as they would their own. Tina was glad in many ways that she was not in a place where no one cared. She could always rely on the Joshis for any help she needed in settling into this new country.

*

Diwali was in a few days' time and everyone was gearing up with new clothes for the festival. Tina made a special effort that morning. Rashmi had persuaded her to try the Indian salwar kameez. Rashmi accompanied her to the mall. Tina was overwhelmed with the choice. Western shops competed with Indian silks and fashions. The season of Diwali was like Christmas in Glasgow. Shops were thronging with people and Tina needed the expert to make her final selection on the Indian dress. Though it was like wearing tights and a dress the material and style was very different and she was glad to get help on the colours and matching accessories.

At her office that morning she felt conscious but happy that she could carry off an Indian dress and not feel awkward.

"Hey, you look kinda nice. That Indian dress suits you. See you soon." Tina blushed.

It was Andrew Saldana, whispering softly to her.

"Thanks, yes. I'll see you," she whispered back as she handed a document to him. She could feel Rashmi's eyes on her and the rest of her colleagues sneaking a look at them. Tina watched as Andrew walked away, his muscular shoulders rippling under his pale blue shirt. He towered above the others in the corridor leading to his room.

They had become close in the last few months. They had a lot in common, settling down in a foreign country. Andrew's parents had returned to India after many years in the United

States. He had been born there and felt India to be a country with which he had only tenuous links. He wanted to work for a year in India, to learn about his roots then go back to America. He was applying to the best Ivy League university for his Masters and wanted some work experience that would set him apart from other candidates.

Dating in India was so different from what it was like in Glasgow. Here it was surreptitious, the society disapproving of open shows of affection. Tina was unsure how things worked here. She felt more at ease, hugging and kissing Andrew in public but he was cautious. He belonged to an Anglo-Indian community that was conservative. Despite having lived all his life in America, he deferred to the local culture. The only time he seemed totally relaxed was the odd night when they went to a nightclub where the music scene was so much like anywhere in the world. A lot of western tourists were there too so it felt more like home. It was expensive so they could not go often.

The Bollywood films in the multiplexes were cheaper and they enjoyed the films. Bollywood films were a totally new experience for Tina. She was aware of Bhangra dance that was popular in Glasgow. Her parents had taken her to the Mela in Kelvingrove Park a couple of times and she had enjoyed the colour, food and choreography. The films however were very long musicals and the heroines were stunning to look at. She and Andrew enjoyed the strange love scenes that spanned over a long time with songs as the background to the emotions. Tina and Andrew could not understand the language but they relished being together. Some tunes were catchy and they hummed along with it. She told Keisha about her new interest in Bollywood films. They Skyped each other and Tina would describe some of the storylines.

'Like your Mills & Boon stuff yeah?' Keisha poked fun at her. Keisha txted: 'I'd luv 2 b in Blywd cinema. Get me a role'

Tina replied 'Not so easy, hun.'

Tina forced her mind back to her work. Rashmi walked over to her desk on the pretext of talking to her about work. Tina rustled some papers on her desk, and hid the post-it note on the document Andrew had given her. She waited till Rashmi left and slid open the note.

"Meet me at McDonald's at 6." It was a handy place to meet after work when the others rushed home.

"What's up? I've been waiting?" asked Andrew, pulling her into the air-conditioned cool of the McDonald's building.

"Sorry, Rashmi kept me back. She was talking about Diwali and wants me to go to the party at the clinic."

"I was going to ask you to go with me," he said, tweaking her chin in an affectionate gesture. Tina felt excited. It would be something to look forward to.

They held hands as they ordered their cheese burger meal, commenting on how only lamb was used in the burgers and not beef.

"I wish I could eat a big steak and kidney pie," sighed Tina.

"Why don't you try cooking it yourself?" asked Andrew.

"No, the Joshis are devout Hindus. I don't want to upset them, cooking beef there."

"I must invite you home then. My mum makes a mean kebab with beef. I'm sure you'd love it."

Andrew winked at her and she felt her cheeks burn. Was he joking she wondered about taking her home and introducing her to his parents when they had only been together for a couple of months?

"You like kebabs don't you?"

"Of course, but meeting your family…is it not too early?" Tina hesitated.

"Maybe I'll invite a couple of friends from work then it would be okay. I'll just say that we work together. At Diwali everyone has a party so don't worry. I do want them to like you."

Andrew caressed her arm and looked deep into her eyes.

What if they don't like me? thought Tina.

"You know I'm crazy about you." he said tracing his finger on her cheek. She blushed and felt a shiver of excitement. She took his hand away from her face and squeezed it gently.

"Yes, I know. I feel the same about you," she said softly.

They shared a chocolate milkshake, sipping it with two straws, taking ages to finish it. He looked deep into her almond eyes and she was lost in his smile. He loved her hands, delicate, long fingers that he kept kissing. Her eyes spoke the language of love, even if she said little.

"I wish we had met in Chicago, honey," said Andrew as they walked towards his car. "Then I needn't drop you back at the Joshis."

"What do you mean Andrew?" They sat close together.

"We could have lived in our own digs. Things are so different here."

She clung to him, holding him closer, smelling his aftershave. She loved his accent. When he called her honey, it was endearing. He dropped her outside the house and they talked for another half hour, unable to part and say goodbye.

Mrs. Joshi peeked from her doorway.

"Good, you're back, Tina." She edged out of the house and stood in front of her, wiping her hands on a yellow tea towel. "I was so worried, getting a bit dark now. And this is?" she asked, her eyebrows arching high and her eyes taking the measure of young Andrew.

"He works with me. This is Andrew." Tina introduced them.

"Come, come, chapattis' are ready," she spoke rapidly in Hindi to him.

He smiled graciously and said, "No thanks we ate already."

Mrs. Joshi stared at him. His accent puzzled her. "So, you also from England?" she asked.

"No I…I am from America. Thank you for inviting me in but I need to go," he said and took his leave, winking at Tina when Mrs. Joshi turned to look at her.

"Okay. Bye," said Tina and waved as his car sped away.

"Nice looking boy, good manners too." Mrs. Joshi shook her head approvingly. "Now only thing is you are too young to stay out so late."

I'm getting nagged even three thousand miles from home, thought Tina.

The mobile text whirred in her pocket. She was glad as she could now get away from Mrs. Joshi.

"My cell," she said and ran up to her room and answered it. It was Keisha. They texted often. More often now that she was with Andrew.

"Going to a Guy Fawkes do with Sam. He's so cool. How r A & U?"

Tina texted back, "Luv A so much, who's Sam?"

"My new guy," replied Keisha, straight away.

At work the next day, Rashmi called a staff meeting.

"A new system is being installed next week. All our records from the start of the clinic have to be transferred to the new system. I'm glad we have you Tina, an extra pair of hands is good."

"I'll do my best," smiled Tina.

Would this be an opportunity to see the records that she had had no access to since coming to the clinic three months ago?

Would she at last find her genetic origins maybe even meet the lady who had donated the embryo to her mum?

Her heart beat faster.

Chapter 12

During Diwali, there were lights everywhere. From little diyas in the lowliest slums to the bright multicoloured lights, some were quite garish in the streets. Rangoli patterns filled with colour were on pavements and in the verandas and drive ways of houses. Patterns handed down over generations perhaps, Tina thought as she watched a young woman deftly tracing a design on the street as she walked to the clinic. The music played in the streets even louder. People bustled about wearing new clothes and the shops blazed with adverts of sales and arrivals of new stock. The colours of silk some that she had never seen in Glasgow were vying for attention as saris and dresses were displayed in the shop windows. The smell of firecrackers hung in the air. The smoke made her think of Guy Fawkes night back home, with the huge bonfire and fireworks that she had seen in Strathclyde Park, the show sparkling on the man-made lake as the fireworks were set off on a raft. She could almost smell the roasted chestnuts, candy floss and sausages. Tina got caught up with the excitement all around. The joyous Festival of Light, Diwali, had made the city feverish with preparations. Even the staid clinic had an air of celebrations. Decorations of tinsel and garlands were around the computers and picture frames in the foyer. The staff discussed the sale of saris and sweets on offer in different stores.

At the Joshi household Mrs. Joshi busied herself making sweets and savouries, several days in advance. Mr. Joshi and Tina sat on the veranda, commenting on the sound of firecrackers that kept them up late at night.

"I used to love all that noise and bustle. I spent a huge amount of time buying and setting the crackers off when I was little. Now I'm getting a bit too old for it."

He looked at the pall of smoke that hung in the air. They heard the sound of the gate opening.

Mr. Saxena, the next door neighbour came over with the newspaper.

"Ah, I wondered if the boy didn't deliver it today, come in, come in," said Mr. Joshi.

"These street children are no use, really. I must complain to the newsagent. They never do their work properly," grumbled Mr. Saxena.

"Wouldn't happen in your country, I'm sure," he said looking at Tina.

"I'm sure we've our skivers too," she said smiling.

"Skivers? What are they?" he asked, puzzled.

Tina explained that they were people who made excuses not to work.

"These huge slums, they are a blight on this city. They must get rid of them." Mr. Saxena shook his head in despair.

"Where would the people go?" said Tina thinking of the appalling poverty that she had witnessed.

"Did you know that Dharavi is the second largest slum in Asia?" Mr. Saxena elucidated.

"That's so shocking. I can't bear to watch the kids…" Tina was interrupted.

"People who see it for the first time are unnerved. A huge percentage of this city's people live in the slums," he continued.

"That can't be right?"

Tina was trying to absorb the terrible statistic. Every day in Mumbai she heard more and more bizarre facts. Sometimes she wondered how such a huge country kept going.

"What is more incredible is that this city also features as the eighth on the Forbes list for billionaires. Disgusting difference between the rich and poor eh? You'd never have such differences in your country. Scotland is very rich, right?"

"Well, if it wasn't for our benefits system, I suppose the gap between the rich and poor would be greater in Scotland. I mean I know there is a lot of poverty in Scotland too, but this is awful. At least most people at home have basic necessities."

The two men had arguments very often on this topic. Tina had heard a few. She smiled at Mr. Joshi.

"Tina is like a daughter to me. There's nothing that would shock her. She's a mature young lady for her age, she can form her own opinions," said Mr. Joshi.

Mr. Saxena got up from his chair.

"I must get back to the Mrs. She's so busy with the Diwali preparations that she'll be annoyed if I am not there to help her. Tina, don't listen to everything he says. I'm always right you know." he grinned at her and walked back to his house.

*

Andrew came to pick Tina up from the Joshis for the party in the evening. Mrs Joshi gave a disapproving look but said nothing. "Don't be home too late, Tina," she called after her.

Keshav, the driver, sped through the crowded streets and they moved on to the suburbs, to a new luxurious development. This was part of Mumbai that Tina had not known existed. The gated community in Mumbai was a new experience for her. The *NRI's* as they were called, the non-resident Indians, had flats built in gated estates with state of the art gyms, pool and other facilities.

The flats were centrally air-conditioned, and well maintained. A bit like New York or Dubai skyscrapers that she had seen in films thought Tina, as she looked at the imposing buildings.

She took a deep breath as she waited for the car to come to a stop. She looked in the mirror in the lift and felt confident in the new silk salwar kameez that showed off her slim figure. The pale pink with silver embroidery set off her skin tone and made her look fresh like a new blossom. Her hair was loose and it cascaded down her shoulder, glossy and smooth. His mum opened the door and welcomed her in. She was a pretty lady with a petite figure. She wore her hair in a short bob that made her look very young. Her skirt and blouse were well fitted, in beautiful raw silk. She exuded an air of efficiency and yet had a kind, soft demeanour as she smiled. Tina liked her as soon as she met her.

"Hey Andrew, come on over," shouted a young guy.

"Hi guys, meet Tina." Andrew introduced her to a group of young people.

Tina said, "So many names! Hope you won't think I'm rude but I'll have to ask your names again."

They laughed and asked about her stay in India and some laughed at her accent. A loquacious young girl, Althea De Sousa, took her under her wing.

"So, tell me all about Glasgow."

Her eyes twinkled. She reminded Tina of Keisha.

"Nothing much to tell, really. It's a great city, I love it. It rains a lot."

"We could do with some rain, not just the huge downpours at monsoon times," Althea laughed. "I love everything about Britain. We Anglo-Indians have a soft spot for it always."

Tina had learnt about this tiny community from Andrew. He had related so many interesting facts about them.

"This must be a coincidence. David has some connection with Glasgow, Althea said.

"David," she called over to a friend.

"Oh, sounds interesting. Apart from Dr Patel and his wife who talked about their time in Edinburgh when they did their Fellowship exams, I've not met anyone with Scottish connections. It would be lovely to meet him, thanks." Tina adjusted her dupatta that kept slipping off her shoulders.

"This is David Fernandez, our Scotophil," said Althea. He shook hands with her. He was of medium height and light skinned with unusual dark green eyes. He had a slight build and had a moustache which seemed to be favoured by many young men in India.

"It's my mum who is crazy about anything Scottish," he said almost apologetically. "She's half Scottish."

"Is she? What's the Scottish connection?"

"Oh, I know very little. I think it was my granddad. Not very sure. I've never asked. I just eat all the good stuff like shortbread and mince and potatoes that she makes."

"Mince and tatties," corrected Tina.

"Tatties?" He laughed and Tina felt a frisson of joy. Here was a kindred spirit. Just hearing those simple familiar words made her feel close to him.

"I love his mum's shortbread. You know it tastes a bit like our Mysore pak," Althea joined in.

"What's Mysore pak?" asked Tina.

"A sweet, a bit like shortbread, crumbly, full of butter and yummy!" giggled Althea.

"Why don't you bring her to my house Althea? My mum could talk to her about Scotland. I'm sure she would be happy to meet you." David gave a disarming smile.

"Well, promise me that you'll get your mum to bake all that lovely Scottish stuff. I'll be there right away," Althea joked.

"Next weekend? How about Saturday? Mum always bakes for the weekend, so Althea you can have your fill."

"You bet," said Althea. "Is that okay with you, Tina?" she asked her.

"I'd love that," said Tina.

They exchanged mobile numbers.

The sound of crackers exploding made them jump from their seats.

"Come, let's go watch the firework display," Althea said.

They all moved to the balcony.

Rose and George Saldana looked at their only child, with pride and approved of his choice. A warm glow on his mum's face as she took Tina around the room and introduced her to the other guests, confirmed her approval to Andrew. Rose drew him aside later and said, "She's lovely Andrew, such sweet manners."

Andrew stood beside Tina on the balcony to watch the firework display. Tina whispered to him.

"Do they like me, your parents?"

"Sure, honey, they love you. Mom told me so." He squeezed her hand gently.

The sky brightened with a white light. They looked at the riot of colour as a rocket firework exploded in the sky.

The dinner that followed was as spectacular as the firework display. There were so many dishes of spicy curries and a huge range of sweets.

"This is amazing. How can I eat it all?" Tina giggled.

"Just try a spoonful of each and you'll feel full," said Andrew and he pointed out his favourites and let her taste them from his spoon.

"Why do you celebrate Diwali? Is it not a Hindu festival?" asked Tina.

"Everyone loves this festival in India. It is so full of colour, bigger than Christmas or Thanksgiving in the States. We just join in the fun."

"True, it's like Christmas at home," agreed Tina. "There's a buzz in the air for weeks. The shopping malls have been so crowded and the sales have been fantastic."

She served herself a second helping of the mango ice cream.

"This is so yummy," she said licking the spoon clean.

"Wait for Christmas! My mom goes overboard. She loves it all and makes a big effort. It's a huge celebration in our family. I'm sure you'll love it." Andrew smiled and her heart beat faster as she saw his tender look. She was touched that he was including her in his Christmas plans.

"Mom I'll take Tina back to her hostel. It's getting late." Andrew took the car keys.

"No, Andrew why don't you take the driver? It's so late and it's raining too..." his mum called out.

"It'll be all right. I'll be back soon."

Andrew rushed Tina out before his mum could insist on the driver.

"We can be alone at last," Andrew said as he slid into the driving seat. He kissed her softly on her cheek, then handed her a small parcel. "Happy Diwali" he said.

"I didn't buy you anything," she protested. He put a finger on her mouth and said "Shush, try it on."

She was thrilled to get a gift from him. She opened the little velvet pouch and found a sparkling bangle in it. She put it on straightaway.

"Thank you so much. It's so beautiful," she said, kissing him.
He kissed her back and then said, "Someone as beautiful as you needs beautiful things."

She felt it was a perfect evening and cuddled him. Andrew switched the ignition on and they sped away.

She put her arm out of the window enjoying the cool rain which was falling softly. She admired the bangle that Andrew

129

had given her. It glinted in the passing street lights. They stopped at a quiet road and exchanged kisses. They talked and planned their future together. It was a blissful time.

"Andrew we must leave now. Mrs. Joshi will be waiting up."
Tina pushed him gently away from her. He switched the engine on and drove fast. She was thrilled. Life was wonderful. She had never expected that she would fall in love with someone in India.

Tina had imagined the six months to be one of confusion, heartache and frustration at not getting any information on her genetic roots. Meeting someone with whom she felt so close, was such a great feeling. She loved Andrew and his family had welcomed her too. She was happy and felt that she needed nothing more.

The oncoming car's lights were blinding. She screamed. The car veered and hit a tree. Lights and then a strange darkness as she heard Andrew's voice faintly. The car veered and hit a tree. Lights flashed in her eyes. She hit the dashboard or something hard, and then a strange darkness as she heard Andrew's voice faintly.

*

Tina opened her eyes to blurred images. Was it a dream she wondered? She felt the unfamiliar bed. Tina struggled to get up, feeling as if she was hung over after an all-nighter. It made no sense at all. She crinkled her eyes open. It was white everywhere. White, white walls, bright, everything was unnaturally bright. The sun streamed through the window and made it hard to open her eyes fully. Her head felt heavy. She lay back down then tried to sit up again. The dull aches all over her body made her take a deep breath. She lay back again. She looked round the strange room, at the tiled floor shining in the sunlight and the pale periwinkle blue curtain with tiny red flowers. The disinfectant smell was strong. *Hospital*, she thought. Then she panicked.

Why am I here? she wondered.

The clink as a new bangle on her left arm hit the metal bed frame brought it all back. The bangle was Andrew's Diwali gift to her. She touched it, and felt the intricate filigree work on the smooth band of silver. The beauty of it stunned her again. The scene played back in her mind.

It was the ride back with Andrew. He was dropping her home after the party at his parents house. She recalled the light drizzle on the windscreen as the speeding car approached them with blinding headlights and forced them off the road. She remembered the car going out of control as she grabbed Andrew tightly and they hit something. It was dark. Was it a tree that they had hit she wondered now? Another dull pain in her head made her whimper.

"Mum," she groaned, then "Andrew, oh my God!"

How was he? Was he hurt?

Her heart raced as she looked around the room. She pressed the button beside her.

An auxiliary nurse walked into the room and spoke rapidly in Hindi to her.

"I... I don't understand." Tina whispered. She gestured a phone and said "My mobile, my cell phone" to her.

"Phone, ok" smiled the young lady and opened the drawer in the bedside table and handed her the phone.

"Thanks," she said as she punched Andrew's number immediately.

"Are you okay? Where are you! I want you here," she sobbed.

"I'm fine, just getting a coffee at the kiosk here. Gee am I glad you're okay?" She could hear his footsteps running to her room. A moment later he was with her. She hugged him tight, as he balanced the hot coffee carton in one hand. He put the carton on the table and stroked her hair, as she nuzzled into his shoulder.

"Don't leave me please," she implored.

"No I won't leave you, babe," he said, cuddling her.

"You're okay. It's the shock. The doctors have checked you over. They kept you in overnight just in case." He gave her a kiss on her cheek and cuddled her again.

She saw his bruised arm and the tiny cut above his eye.

"Are you okay?" She touched his arm.

"I'm fine. Thank God we're both not injured. That crazy driver! I could swing for him," Andrew's face darkened in anger.

Just having him around made Tina feel better and the panic subsided.

"Rest. The doctors have said that you can leave after lunch today. I'll stay here and take you home. My mom and I can look after you," he said.

"Oh no Andrew, thank you so much. I'd rather go back to my own bed. Mrs. Joshi will take care of me. She's wonderful."

Tina's tears started to fall onto the pale blue sheets. She sobbed as she thought of her parents so far away in Glasgow and wished they were with her.

"No way! You're coming with me. I want to take care of you," he said wiping her tears. "I've called Mrs. Joshi. She was concerned but she knows that my mom and I'll take care of you, at least for the next few days."

Andrew was insistent. Tina had no strength to refuse his kind offer.

The doctor came at midmorning. Young, dapper looking, with the stethoscope hanging round his neck, he glanced at the notes that the nurse handed him.

"Tina, yes, young lady, you've had a shock but nothing serious. You have a special blood group; you'll know that I'm sure. We kept you in for observation overnight," he added dryly, his lips set in a thin line.

"Thanks Doctor." Andrew's voice was curt. He hoped the doctor would leave.

"You are okay now, young lady," said the doctor. "You may leave after lunch. Make sure you take some rest and recover from the shock. A couple of days off work would be good." He turned on his heel and left, followed by the nurse shuffling her set of notes for the next patient.

"Gee, no bedside manners at all! Christ, where do they train?" said Andrew seething with rage.

"He was only doing his job," said Tina. "Blood group, what did he mean? I wish my mum was here."

She looked ready to sob again. The strain of the accident and the trauma showed as lines formed on her forehead.

"Hey, look I'm here. I'll be always there for you. I'll make sure that everything is fine," Andrew tried to reassure her.

"Oh, I'm scared Andrew, being away from home. Maybe I should go back to Glasgow."

"Stop thinking like that. Listen, nothing will happen to you. The nasty accident has shaken you. Please don't go back to Glasgow. I can't live without you," he said and gave her a cuddle. Tina rested her face on his shoulder. Her mind whirled with doubt and fear.

They left after lunch. The taxi took them to his house. Rose opened the door to the flat. She looked tired and her eyes were red with crying. She said little and showed Tina to her room. Tina looked around the spare room with a bed that his mum had prepared for her. Photos of Andrew from his babyhood to his graduation adorned the walls. His computer table and books were in a corner. American pennants of his team, the Chicago Bulls and their posters were on the wall. She chuckled at his baby photos, a chubby baby swaddled against the cold Chicago winters in padded coats, he looked cute and vulnerable. Her heart flipped as she saw him as a school boy, a backpack heavy on his shoulder, singing in the school choir or playing on the soccer field. The graduation photos held pride of place. He wore his black gown with its bright orange border and a flat cap. He looked happy standing between his parents. She touched his photo and felt guilty as if she had somehow intruded on that very special day. The door was ajar and she heard some voices. Tina edged to the door and heard his mum saying:

"I might have lost you. Why didn't you listen to me?"

She was scolding Andrew.

"The car is a write-off. It's shocking. God, I don't know what I'd do if anything happened to you. Go and take some rest, you look done."

She heard footsteps walking towards the door. Tina moved towards the window quickly. His mum came in with a tray of tea.

"Tina. Have your tea first then you must take some rest. You must be badly shaken after that awful accident. Thank God you're both okay."

Mrs. Saldana brushed back the fringe from her forehead and sat down on the bed and patted it for Tina to sit beside her. They chatted as they drank the tea.

"Thank you so much for letting me stay here, Mrs. Saldana," said Tina.

"Don't worry. It can't be easy, being away from your family in a strange place, especially when you've had a nasty shock like this. I know what that's like. We've been through it all in the States." Her words were sweet. Tina felt better.

"Shall I call you Aunty Rose?" asked Tina, aware that youngsters never addressed older members by name in India.

"That'll be nice, yes, I'd like that Tina" Mrs. Saldana said and continued, "I've asked Andrew to take some rest too. The poor boy has been run off his feet, giving statements to the police, and waiting for you at the hospital. He had not realised how tired he was. He'll join us for dinner later."

She left with the tray and shut the door firmly.

Tina lay on the bed thinking of the events of the last few hours.

The accident had shaken her. She missed her mum but was touched by Andrew and his family's kindness. *I need them both now, my Andrew and my mum*, she thought, smiling to herself.

Chapter 13

Brenda tried to call James at his hotel in Singapore. There was no answer. She was fed up and lonely. James called her after a few hours and as always was in a rush.

"Sorry darling, I've had so much to do. Anything the matter?"

"Why should I call you only if there is something wrong?" Brenda's voice cut him like a piece of ice.

"No of course not, but just too busy now. I'll call you tomorrow. Okay, need to rush," and he was away.

Brenda was livid. His workaholic life style left her bored and fed up with her lonely life but she did not want to leave him. She had everything that she had always wanted, a loving, undemanding man, a beautiful daughter who was married and living in Canada. She had a wealthy comfortable life with nothing to complain about but she felt empty. She was bored. The church work, the games of bridge, helped a few days of the week but seeing her friends with their busy, fulfilled lives with their children milling about at weekends, with parties to celebrate their birthdays and husbands with whom they shared a bridge night or the occasional golf match made her jealous.

James was always at work. When he was at home, he was too tired to do much at all with her. He wanted rest and to see as few people as possible. He needed time on his own. He preferred to go fishing or hiking than meet with a crowd of people. At first Brenda had demanded that she accompany Jimmy on company trips. It was not successful at all. She felt left out, wandering around cities in strange countries with no knowledge of the language and no company. She ended up staying at the hotel room. Alone. James worked long hours and his job was as such that the evening was filled with socialising. Brenda felt abandoned and stopped trying so hard.

The huge house that they had bought was out in the country and few friends made the trip to visit them. Brenda had to make trips to see them and few reciprocated because of the distance to her vast but empty mansion. Her dreams of a house filled with people and huge parties never materialised. Every part of the house was redone to her taste. She still loved it and refused to move out.

Brenda's big worry now was her loneliness. She had no idea how to keep herself occupied. She tried getting involved with the local church, but her heart was not in it. She donated huge sums towards the church funds and her heart swelled with pride when she was given a place of honour at functions. She arranged the flowers, visited the elderly but never wanted to commit herself. Brenda would only help out when she was free. She longed for fulfilment but found it a real bore. The older members were set in their ways, often commenting on the changing society, the topic often about the reckless, feckless young or the cost of living, punctuated by talk of their ailments. Brenda found none of them fitted into her luxurious lifestyle. The local church was losing younger members and the old regulars had been in it all their lives with parochial ideas, not ready to accept any suggestions that Brenda came up with. She stayed with them only to fill some of the winter mornings when a drive into Glasgow was too much of an effort.

Brenda tried the gym. It was a ten mile drive to get there. Two months after the initial enthusiasm, getting all her new gym clothes, the right trainers, the designer tracksuits, the novelty wore off. She lost interest and only went to occasionally when guilt made her attend an odd class or when James pointed out that her membership was up for renewal and that she had hardly used the gym.

One day, Brenda switched the TV on, a background noise to fill the void as she flicked the pages of the weekly magazine. A familiar voice caught her interest. She looked up from the Hello magazine on her knee. It was Alistair McGowan, the impressionist tracing his ancestry. She laughed out loud when Alistair's closing words were, "I was always so proudly Scottish: now to find that I am more a Seamus Singh is humbling."
Intrigued by the programme that showed his roots were Irish and Anglo-Indian, she mulled over its contents as she made herself a cup of tea. She worked late into the night online to read up on the programme.

Here was something to keep her occupied. She drove to the local library the very next morning. They were offering courses on "Tracing Your Family History." The course on finding her ancestry turned out to be fascinating.

Within a few weeks, she was into this new pastime with great swathes of enthusiasm. She constantly talked of it to James on the phone. She started her family tree and filled up all the spaces of the immediate family that she was aware of. This gave her a new sense of purpose. The quest to find out her forbears was like reading and guessing 'whodunit' in a detective novel, but she found it even more exciting.

She revelled in the fact that she had progressed to the next stage where she needed to do research to find out more about her parents lives and those of her grandparents. Brenda realised how little she knew of, or had any idea of, her parents early lives. Betty spent a few afternoons recounting all that she could remember. The dates were a problem. Betty could not give the exact year of some of the events of their lives and that frustrated Brenda. She spent lots of time online and made enquiries at churches to get access to her family records.

"Amy, listen, do you know anything about this family tree thing?"

"What family tree thing?"

Amy put her toddler Charlie down. He ran to the dog straightaway.

"Listen, I'm into finding out about all our past. I've already drawn a family tree and uploaded some photos of us all."

"Mum!" Amy was taken aback, "Not another of your new-found interests? How long will this one last?" she giggled.

"Amy, how could you? I've not even started yet and you're putting a damper on it."

"Sorry. There's a lot of interest here. Quite a few Canadians are into tracing their Scottish ancestors. So, is that what you are trying to do now, discover skeletons in our family cupboard?" she laughed.

"Amy, I'm so into it. It's like a detective story. I just thought you could start one too. Maybe get some details of Bobby's family?"

"Maybe, but right now looking after Charlie, the house and the dog is more than enough for me. Found anything interesting yet?" Amy tried to stop little Charlie pulling the dog's tail.

"Not yet but I'll get it all laid out for you when you come over at Christmas time."

"I've been meaning to talk to you about that mum. We may not be able to come over at Christmas."

Brenda's heart sank. She loved Christmas and the family time together. "Why ever not?"

"Bobby is so busy at work and I don't think we can manage."

This was a terrible blow to Brenda. She put the phone down, her enthusiasm ebbing. The grey in her heart was reflected in the grey clouds outside. She absentmindedly wiped an imaginary speck of dust from the marble mantel piece. She called James, but got the answer phone instead.

"No, I'm not going to feel down-hearted," she told herself and moved back to her study. The table groaned with all her notes, scraps of paper, photocopies of old newspapers and the packaged new software on the "Family Tree". She sat down and was soon engrossed in the work.

Brenda felt sure that she would find some interesting detail about the family that would rock their complacent lives. She wanted something that she could claim that she had done and achieved with her new hobby. She felt maybe James's side of his family would throw up something outrageous, maybe an entrepreneur who had made a fortune in the early part of the century and lost it all, she thought.

*

James sat in his hotel room. He'd hoped that getting away from Brenda would make him have a change of heart but it was useless. Whoever said absence makes the heart grow fonder wasn't married to Brenda, he chuckled to himself. He poured himself another drink and thought of his first love. Rita. For so long he'd folded up his memories of her and stored them away in the back of his mind. The recent discussion with Tina and now this trip to India brought his memories to the surface. He thought back to how he lost the love of his life.

*

The British Airways jumbo jet touched down on the tarmac. Jimmy looked at London's grey sky and wished he was back in the warmth of India.

He had called his mum from the public phone as soon as he had booked his ticket to Glasgow.

"Mum, how are you?"

His voice cracked with grief and hearing her speak made him feel worse.

"Jimmy, oh thank God you're coming home…" she sobbed.

"Mum, I'll be home in a couple of hours."

Jimmy consoled her with a few more words of support. She handed the phone to someone else. It was his Uncle Ronnie.

His uncle picked up the phone, breathing heavily.

"India? What the hell were you doing there for God's sake?" he shouted.

Jimmy said, "I'll talk to you soon. Look after mum."

"Yes, you're Mum, the poor soul. Did you think of her at all?"

Ronnie's hyperventilating voice was loud over the phone.

He could hear voices in the background of people who must have come to convey their condolences.

Neighbours or Uncle Ron's family? Jimmy wondered and then wished he that could see his mum on her own first.

"I'll see you all soon," he said and put the phone down.

Jimmy sat down heavily in the seat. The departure gate sign showed that they had another hour till they boarded the plane. With his head in his hands he looked at the dark blue carpet, his mind in turmoil. Rita, he missed her. He wanted her by his side. His mum's sob had affected him too. He felt guilty that he had been in India when she had needed him most.

Jimmy walked to the window. His plane had arrived and was refuelling. He watched the people unloading the luggage and passengers getting off the flight. There were other planes leaving the runway and soaring into the sky. In less than a couple of hours he'd be back home.

Once the funeral was over and the relatives had left Jimmy realised there was nothing left to say. He sat with his mum in a darkened room. They sat in silence immersed in their own thoughts. Jimmy looked at his mum properly for the first time since he got back from India. She was thinner and gaunt looking. *How could it be?* he thought, *she had looked so full of life only six months ago.*

"I'll warm some of that soup that Lynn brought us," she said getting up from her chair.

"Mum, sit down, I'll do it. Are you keeping well?" Jimmy asked her.

"I'm….it was so sudden…"

"Of course, I know that. But you look a bit pale."

"Just a bit of blood pressure recently," she said.

"Have you been taking your medication? I haven't seen you taking anything."

"I'm okay. I'll get by. I'm just tired that's all." She gave a ghost of a smile. Jimmy was not convinced.

"I'm home now. You're not to worry about anything. I'll get the soup."

They ate the soup and rolls in silence. The house felt strange. His father had been such a huge presence. It was eerie to see all his things and not hear him or see his towering figure in the room. His mum got up to wash the plates whilst he dried them.

Jimmy switched on the TV and they sat down to watch the news. The news channel flickered in the background. Their eyes were on the screen but taking very little in.

"We need to sort all his stuff."

Jimmy shuffled his feet and drummed his fingers on the arm of the sofa.

"Yes, we'll do it in the morning," she said calmly.

After a restless night, they sorted his clothes first. They got bags for charity neatly packed and set them aside in the lounge. Jimmy watched his mum, concerned in case she broke down. She kept his dad's watch and a favourite pen of his but placed everything else in the charity bags.

Lunch was simple, beans on toast. Jimmy sat down at his father's desk cluttered with papers. June, his mum bustled about clearing all the papers and books elsewhere in the tiny study. Old books from his boyhood days were piled high in one corner. Magazines on horse racing were added to the pile. He tried to sort the papers on the desk and after half an hour realised that there was something very wrong.

"These bank statements, have you seen them mum?"

"No son, I just left all the money stuff and everything to your dad."

"Mum did he say anything to you?"

"About what son?"

She looked at him, her eyebrows arched in surprise then returned to sorting out some old yellowed books and papers that were at least twenty years old.

"Have you settled the funeral bills yet?" Jimmy asked her.

"Why do you ask all these questions? Is there something not right?"

"Mum, we're in big trouble." Jimmy's brows furrowed in bemusement.

"Eh? What do you mean?"

"Dad owes ten thousand pounds."

"Ten thousand pounds!"

Her body shook slightly. She put the old books down, dusted her hands and wiped them on the apron that she was still wearing and came to him. She peered at the bank statement that he was holding.

"That can't be right. It must be a mistake."

Her face grew pale, the blood draining from it. Jimmy wondered if he should have kept quiet about it.

"He was getting mean and grumpy every time I spent money. Oh God!"

She rubbed her forehead and shook her head.

"Ten thousand pounds!"

Jimmy said it again, as if saying it aloud would make it go away. Incredulous and stunned at the amount, they sat in silence. Jimmy moved the chair and pulled the drawer out further. At the back there was a pile of betting slips.

"This explains it," he said, turning towards his mum.

"Oh God, not that many!" she said.

"What do you mean?"

"I knew he had the odd flutter at the bookies son, but…"

"Christ, what a mess!"

Jimmy threw the pile of betting slips on the floor.

"Jimmy I'm frightened,"

June started crying and Jimmy held her and smoothed her hair.

"Don't cry Mum, please. I'll do what I can."

The month that followed the funeral was one that Jimmy found hard to cope with. The creditors started arriving. From the undertaker to companies whose bills had not been paid, there was a stream of debt collectors at their door. The only way was to sell the house and wait for the council to re-house them.

A bundle of letters and junk mail was redirected to him by the Building Society that had repossessed their home. They informed him that they would not be redirecting any more of the mail and that he should inform the Post Office of his dad's change of address. There was a letter from Rita, begging for his return. He read it and it wrenched his heart. He ran to make an international phone call to the ashram. It cost over a pound a minute. He had little money and by the time he got the person in the office to understand that he was calling from Glasgow and that he wanted to talk with Rita, the money had run out. He could glean little from that phone call.

"No, no, there's no Rita here. Wrong number..." and the phone went dead.

Surely she hasn't left within three months? he thought. He knew nothing of her family or any other person to contact. *I'll write a letter. There must be someone at the ashram who would know where she is*, he decided but he never got round to writing that letter.

He thought of Rita when he retired to bed, exhausted after trying to find ways of staving off the people at the door and keeping their heads above water.

What can I offer her? he mused. *She's better off without me.*

He thought he should write to her and explain the awful situation when he had some money and a job. He kept her letter in a box with the other things that he had carried all the way from India. They remained apart of him that never died but receded into the background.

When the house was repossessed by the building society, they had to move in with Uncle Ronnie in Fife. Jimmy left his mum with them and stayed in Glasgow doing two jobs, at a factory and as a night porter in a hotel. He was determined to get his mother back to some semblance of their lives before. The Silicon Glen as it was nicknamed was his first step in getting out of the dreadful situation they were in. National Semiconductors took him in and paid for a college course as a day release student. His bright talents were recognised. Jimmy had found his niche.

A year later he rang the ashram. Rita was long gone. No one knew of her. He realised that he had lost her forever. He was devastated. He vowed never to love again.

Chapter 14

Mr. Joshi was cleaning his glasses while he listened to a bhajan on the radio. The morning paper was lying in front of him.

"EXAM RESULTS- University of Mumbai," announced an advertisement on the top of the paper.

"Next year I will be in university. How I will manage to do all that reading I don't know," Tina said to him, catching sight of the headlines.

"You're a fine young lady, living and working in a different country and doing so well. I think you've very goods skills to make a success of life, Tina," he reassured her.

"You're so kind to praise me, Uncle Joshi."
She sat on the chair beside him looking worried.

"No, I don't say things for the sake of it. You must know me better by now. As for the university, I must tell you something interesting."

Tina listened.

"Now, you do know that the University of Mumbai is the largest university in the world for the number of graduates it produces every year?"

Tina listened but didn't say anything. She knew by now not to interrupt Mr Joshi.

"Yes, and it was started by a Scot, Mountstuart Elphinstone, a Scot from Dumbarton. He was an aristocrat, you know, very rich family. I read up on it just the other day. You've given me something very good to do. I'm often at the library looking up Scottish things you know." His eyes twinkled. He stopped and looked briefly at his newspaper.

"I thought it would be a university in the USA or even maybe China. I'm surprised," said Tina interested now in Mr. Joshi's little facts or the trivia on Mumbai or India that he often mentioned.

"Dumbarton! That's close to where I live. It's a town on the Clyde."

Tina was fascinated.

"Well, he started the Native Education in Bombay Presidency in the early 1800's though the others did not agree with him." He said putting the newspaper down. Finally, he thought to himself, a subject this foreign child is interested in! He thought of it as a personal triumph.

"Who objected?" Tina asked.

Mr Joshi smiled and continued.

"I suppose the colonials did not want to spend money on educating the Indians at that time."

"Even Britain had its fair share of poor people who had no access to education so I suppose that must be true." She thought again about what she was saying. "Yes, especially if it was as early as that."

"There was even a William Henderson with an MA from Aberdeen University who suffered poor health and taught at the English school but he left to become a missionary for the Free Church of Scotland and died soon after he arrived back in Scotland. He was the Editor of the Bombay Times in 1839."

"So there were lot of Scots in India all those years ago? Does the 'Bombay Times' still exist?" asked Tina thinking that her other mum, EA Thomas might turn out to be a Scottish woman after all.

"No, that folded years ago."

A loud car horn made them almost jump from their seats.

"The morning roar of traffic has started. I better get ready for work."

Tina rose from her chair to get ready to start the day.

"I'll find out more about Scotland and India for you Tina. It's obviously something you're interested in."

Mr Joshi put his glasses on and picked up the paper, his spectacles sliding down his nose and settling on the tip as usual.

*

"Back at work already? I hope you've recovered fully," said Rashmi, with a solicitous look at Tina who had arrived early.

"I'm fine. Thanks. It was good to be pampered at Mrs. Saldana's. Needless to say that Mrs. Joshi plied me with her dishes when I got back to the house. I'm so lucky to have such good friends so far away from home."

"Excellent, I'm very glad to see you. The new systems are ready to be tested today. I'm pleased that you are back and punctual. Let's get started. Remember if at any time you feel a bit under the weather just tell me and I'll send you home straight away,"

Rashmi said gently.

"Thanks. I'm all set for work. I don't think I could spend another day indoors in this heat."

Tina put her bag down and switched her computer on.

"Will you please start on the records from 1980 and input the data in the new format for me?"

Rashmi showed her the new software and the morning passed in a whirl of activity.

Dr. Patel arrived after his morning clinic to check that the systems were working

"Any glitches? He said. "I hope not. I've paid enough for the new software." He shone a wide smile at all. "How are you feeling today, Tina?" he asked her as he passed her desk.

"Good, thank you," she said, pleased that he still paid some attention to his newest trainee.

"Good, let's hope everything is ready in a week's time," he said. "The transition time could be a bit difficult but I'm relying on my super efficient, Rashmi," he said.

He left soon afterwards.

Tina was grateful she had been granted a long lunch break. Lunch was usually a brief affair but the gossip was good. She got to know the women more as they sat apart from the men and talked of family problems and the latest soaps or TV serials as they were known in India.

"Soaps, yes, my mum watched a few in Glasgow. Coronation Street and Eastenders."

"Serials can be quite addictive! You know yesterday I forgot all about Nitin's homework I was so into that Swayamvara." said Gita

"What's that about?" asked Tina

"They get to match one famous actress with possible suitors, its fun," said Gita.

There was a discussion on the guy who was eliminated. Tina sat half listening. Her mind was on Andrew, as she sipped the tea and ate her sandwich.

"Try some of my bhel puri," said Gita, "Aren't you bored of the sandwich?"

"Thanks I'll just try a bit. Mrs Joshi makes huge meals at night so a sandwich is all I can eat," said Tina crunching the delicious bhel.

She rested her head on her desk as the others got back to work. The office was warm and she was momentarily distracted by her buzzing mobile. Andrew called a few times to see how she was coping all right. He was meeting her after work. She felt a thrill, thinking of being with him again. Love flooded her being. She looked at his photo on her mobile phone and blew a kiss. She looked around to see if anyone had seen her doing it and then hugged herself with the warmth of her feelings. She worked steadily through the lists of patients' records in alphabetical order.

Just as she was leaving work, her mobile rang again. Her heart leapt a beat thinking that it was Andrew again and she picked the phone up without checking who it was.

"Hi gorgeous." She said.

"Aww hello my gorgeous. So happy to hear from me, huh? Missed me much? I had to call and tell you! Sam is moving in with me! I'm so excited."

It was Keisha.

She was talking very quickly in a high pitched voice.

"Brilliant, Keisha, such good news. I hope it all goes well this time."

Tina thought of the last guy who had let Keisha down. She was also glad Keisha hadn't realised why she had said 'hi gorgeous.' Keisha was wrapped up in her own happiness.

"Yeah, of course it will, dummy. You worry too much. He's so cute, I love him," she gushed. "I'll send you pics of him soon. Can't talk for long my credits running low. Skype you later. Bye." Keisha rang off.

Andrew was waiting for Tina when she got outside. Seeing him her heart went aflutter. He stood beside his car, brushing back his hair and talking to the driver. The car park at the clinic was jam-packed. She weaved her way between the cars to him.

"Hey good-looking, how was your first day back?" he said giving her a quick hug.

"It was fine. I managed to tackle the new software systems. I'm a bit tired now though." she said and nodded a hello to the driver, Keshav. He acknowledged it with a slight bow.

They sat in the back of the car and the driver headed towards Worli Sea Face. It was the just place Tina needed that day. Andrew gave Keshav a few rupees for his tea as he parked the car. A cool breeze rustled Tina's dress as they walked on the path and saw other couples with hands entwined, in a world of their own. The Arabian Sea was a dark blue, not the muddy grey that it appeared sometimes. The waves crashed on the sand near the parapet walls, there was the buzz of the traffic in the background and yet a sense of calm came over them both.

They watched the scene that seemed to never change. It was as if that moment was frozen in time. The sea breeze cooled and revived them. They watched the vivid sunset burnishing the beach with an orange glow. The tropical change over from day to night. It seemed sudden and magical. The sky changed from a bright orange to a dark night as if a painter had covered it in quick brushstrokes to get the right shade. The myriad of stars twinkled and a crescent moon rose up high. They sat on the parapet wall, swinging their legs and watching the waves rise and fall. It was mesmerizing and deeply calming. There were a few children hawking nuts, fruits and ice-cream. She watched a young boy roasting peanuts on a big wok and groups of people milled around him for the snack. He placed a small neatly wrapped newspaper cone of nuts into each hand so efficiently and collected the money and gave change quickly, she marvelled at his enterprise. Another young girl had a basket with coconuts cut into little white ribbons for a snack. There was even a man selling candy floss, this is like a fair thought Tina as she watched the beach scene in Mumbai.

They moved to a quieter side, some older couples and some families were taking an evening stroll.

"I love Mumbai," said Tina closing her eyes and breathing the sea air.

"Hey just Mumbai! What about me?" Andrew tickled her. She winced, a big smile spread on her face. She put her head on his shoulder. "I love you more."

Andrew leaned in for a kiss. An old man walking near them, stared at them and then tutted. Tina chose to ignore him but Andrew moved away to respect him.

They stayed out longer than they had intended. Mrs. Joshi fussed when Andrew dropped her home, making a few comments in Marathi. Her disapproval was evident.

"Too late beti, tomorrow you are back at work, you must get good rest no?" she said as Tina tried to squeeze past her to her room.

"Yes, Aunty Joshi, the traffic was very bad," she lied, and managed to sidle her way into her room avoiding any further discussion on the matter.

The weekend stretched before her, she fell asleep dreaming of Andrew.

*

Tina looked forward to meeting David again and wondered what she'd learn from his mother. The Scottish connection made her excited. Would he be able to tell her something that would make Mr. Joshi run to his research? Andrew came over to pick her up. The car dashed and swerved along the road and made the heart stopping ride drive to the house. Tina was glad to get out! Althea was in the veranda with David.

"Come in," he said.

A gorgeous smell of home baking wafted out as David opened the door to his house. Tina's thoughts shifted back home and she relished the delicious aroma as she walked in. A tall gentleman rose from a sofa and held out his hand as David introduced his father to her.

"Tina, I've heard all about you from David. My wife, Beth is waiting to meet you."

"Thank you Mr. Fernandez," Tina said shaking his hand briefly and turned as she heard Beth walking over from the kitchen.

Beth untied her apron, put it over her arm and came over to Tina. David's green eyes and light skin was inherited from his mum obviously, she looked like him, and Tina liked her.

"Thanks for inviting me, Mrs. Fernandez," said Tina

"You are most welcome, Tina," she said and gave her a peck on the cheek. There was something comforting that made Tina want to hold her longer. Maybe it was the smell of the baking that clung to her, thought Tina.

"So how long have you been in India? Are you quite settled in Mumbai?" Mrs. Fernandez asked her kindly as they both sat down.

Both of them smiled as the small talk continued.

After a few minutes Althea broke the exchange of pleasantries with a cutting remark.

"David! Look at Tina and your mum, they're chatting away. Your mum loves anything Scottish doesn't she?"

"I suppose so," said David, busy filling the glasses with soft drinks for everyone. Andrew glanced at the women and then turned his attention back to Mr. Fernandez who was discussing the cricket IPL tests and the ridiculous amount that the players were given. It was a common topic these days.

"The game is being ruined, no longer a game of the gentlemen, such greed," the older man commented.

"Yes the film stars are getting involved and the big businesses too but it's more exciting reducing it from five day test matches," defended David.

"Yes but I prefer the old style game. There was a gentle rhythm to it and it was so enjoyable. You could relax watching it with a cold beer in your hand," Mr. Fernandez reminisced, his eyes glazed over in a fit of nostalgia.

A young Pomeranian puppy bounded in from the garden and jumped on Althea.

"Oh get away, you little rascal," she said and pushed it off her lap.

"It's so cute! Come here, puppy," said Tina. The puppy came over, wagging her tail and excitedly jumped on her lap.

"David, we must train her more. She jumps on all the visitors," complained Mrs. Fernandez.

"She's still young. Come here, Sheba!" David called and tried to get her off Tina.

"Oh, let her stay. Please. She's so playful and lovely," said Tina, holding onto her and ruffling her collar. The puppy licked her arm and squirmed on her lap.

Mrs. Fernandez got up from the sofa.

"I'll go make the tea. Why don't you all come to the table?" she said.

It was a proper high tea, thought Tina. The table was laid beautifully with a linen table cloth embroidered with Indian scenes. The china was sparkling and the three-tiered cake stands were lined with doilies and filled with scrumptious food. There were tiny cucumber sandwiches, delicate salmon and tuna sandwiches and a selection of scones and fairy cakes. There was a plate of shortbread and oatcakes too.

Althea could not resist.

"I'm helping myself to one," she said and helped herself to a piece of shortbread straightaway.

The puppy followed them as they sat at the table and kept at Tina's feet jumping up for attention.

"Sheba seems to have taken to you," said David.

He took the pup out of the room and left her out in the back yard. They could hear her scratching the back door for a while.

"I'm amazed at the Scottish food. How did you learn all this? Was your mum in Scotland?" Tina asked Mrs Fernandez.

"No but she loved baking like most of us Anglos do. There is also a fine cookbook by a Bridget Kumar which has recipes of mince and tatties, and stovies. It's a collection of old recipes handed down over the generations by Scots who had been in India."

"By the way do you know it was Francis Cogan and Andrew Day, the two Scots who landed in Madras in 1639, who started the East India Company? So you could say, but for the Scots sailing here, we might not have had an East India Company, or the Empire or perhaps any of us Anglos," said Mr. Fernandez and gave a dry laugh.

"I'll tell Mr. Joshi, he'll get more research done and give me a long spiel about it," said Tina and explained about Mr. Joshi and his hobby.

"I must ask you about this address in Glasgow," said Mrs. Fernandez and she hurried out of the room and came back with a wooden box. She prised out a paper, yellowed with age and smoothed it out for Tina to have a look.

Chapter 15

Tina stared at the piece of paper for several minutes. She didn't know what to say or do. It certainly looked like a familiar address in Glasgow. Bellview Terrace, yes, she remembered passing it on her many bus journeys into town.

I think it's a regeneration area. I can't be sure. But I think its undergoing some development of new flats there," she commented.

"Right, its okay." Beth said, obviously disappointed. "All I know is that my father lived there in the 1960's or early 70's, I can't be sure, my mother didn't speak of him too much. Its likely he must have moved."

Tina felt her pain. Here she was, a woman without ever knowing her father. It made her realise her resolve more than anything before.

"I'll email my friend Keisha, if you want. Do you have a surname by any chance? It might be easier to trace him."

"No dear, this is all I have. His name was Jimmy, that's all my mother knew."

Mrs Fernandez looked broken.

"I suppose I'm on a wild goose chase. I just had to ask. Not knowing my father is like a big void in my life." She gave a fragile smile.

Tina understood exactly what she meant. She felt a sudden urge to reveal herself. Some days her life in Mumbai felt so false, a plot from one of her much loved romantic novels that she'd read. She felt like a complete fraud. Today she felt, for once she could bear all. She could finally reveal what she was doing miles away from home. In the company of a stranger in whom she saw the pain and sadness she had felt for so long, she felt she didn't need to pretend any longer. She was about to say something about her search for her genetic mother, when David came back in the room and the moment passed.

Mrs. Fernandez took the paper from her hand and placed it in the wooden box and hurried back to put it away.

"Well I could ask Keisha to go round and ask, you never know," offered Tina when she came back to the room.

"That's kind of you dear, thanks." Mrs. Fernandez busied herself stacking the plates on the table.

The whimpering at the door was getting louder. David let Sheba in as Mrs. Fernandez cleared the table and the girls helped take the dishes to the kitchen. The puppy followed Tina again. Althea went with David to choose some music. The pup playfully tugged at Tina's bag which was hanging on the dining chair. It slipped and fell open on the floor. Andrew picked it up for her. The photograph of her parents holding her as a baby fell out of it. He picked the photo and stared at it.

Tina stayed silent.

"Your parents are..." he whispered

"Yes they're white, Scottish..." she whispered back.

"Why, how?"

Andrew's eyebrows knitted in confusion.

"I had assumed..." he seemed stuck for words.

"Andrew, I...meant to tell you. I just never found the right moment." She hesitated.

"So, you're adopted, that's no big deal," he said.

"No, I need to explain."

She swallowed hard. Beads of sweat appeared on her forehead.

She realised that the moment was here. She would have to reveal herself.

"I came to India because I am looking for my…"

"So you are adopted then?" Andrew interrupted still whispering.

"No, oh, this is so difficult. My mum had an embryo transfer."

They heard some footsteps close to the door.

"I'll explain later," Tina said quickly. Andrew stuffed the photo in his pocket out of sight.

Mrs. Fernandez came in and removed the tablecloth.

*

In the lounge, Althea flicked through the CD collection and chose a classical piece by Beethoven.

"We Anglos are into Western music you know," she said with pride, as Tina and Andrew walked in. "Did you learn any music? Western or Indian, Tina?" she asked.

Andrew shifted in his seat. He played with the puppy that had followed them.

"Oh I learnt a few notes on the recorder at primary school but no, nothing like proper music." Tina replied. She glanced at Andrew.

"You've both gone a bit quiet," said Althea.

"That's because you don't let anyone else have a word." said David, laughing and teasing her.

Mrs. Fernandez came in from the kitchen. She had a recipe book with Scottish dishes in it. The well-thumbed book was obviously something she had used and treasured. There were pages of Anglo-Indian dishes with titles such as Captain Chicken, Mutton Chops, Lamb Curry, Mulligatawny Soup and many other ones that Tina had never seen before.

"You choose from this Tina and I'll make it for your next visit," she said, her smile lighting up her face.

Tina squirmed in her seat with embarrassment.

"That's so kind of you but I wouldn't dream of asking you to cook again for me."

"No problem at all dear. I love cooking and it will be a great pleasure for me to try them out again. You can tell me if they are as good as you get in Scotland," she added.

Andrew drew his mobile from his pocket and went out of the room, apologizing, saying that he needed to take a call. He came back in and said that they had to leave straight away as his dad needed the car. They took their leave.

As soon as they were seated in the car, Andrew turned to Tina and said, "I had to pretend that it was a call. We need to talk. Tell me everything," he squeezed her hand gently.

Tina indicated that Keshav was waiting for instructions from him.

"Home, sir?" he asked, in a quiet voice.

"No Keshav, please drive to Worli," Andrew said.

There was a stony silence in the car.

They reached the sea front. Andrew and Tina got out of the car and walked along the beach. The waves were rough. They swelled to a great height and crashed down onto the shore, the white foam receding in new patterns each time. Tina took her sandals off and felt the sand between her toes. They found a quiet place away from the noise of the sea and sat down.

"Well?" Andrew looked at her quizzically

"Andrew, I don't know where to begin."

Tina looked down. Her fingers touched the gritty sand.

"I didn't mean to keep it a secret from you."

"So, why never mention it at all?"

"It's not something that's easy to talk about…" she hesitated.

"Try me. I need to know everything, Tina. So is it like a surrogacy or something?"

"No, my mum had an embryo from another couple inserted… oh this is so awful. I can't explain…" Tears welled up in her eyes and rolled down her cheeks.

Andrew was silent. He looked at the waves and saw the white froth flowing and receding on the shore. The sounds of the traffic and people faded in the background as the silence between them grew. Tina glanced at the sea. It had grown dark already. She watched the moon and stars reflected in the water, the silvery designs undulating on the flowing water. Her heart beat fast. Would Andrew be annoyed that she had kept a secret from him? Would he her hate for it? Would his mum think less of her? The thoughts tossed around her mind like the waves in the sea.

"I'm sorry," he said breaking the silence, "It's not something that one hears everyday. I mean, I can't understand. Does that mean that you're not adopted? But you're not genetically their child?"

"Yes, that's right. Andrew I came to Mumbai, hoping that I could find something about the lady who donated the embryo."

Tina looked deep into Andrew's eyes. He cuddled her. She buried her face in his chest and held him tight.

Chapter 16

Andrew stood looking out of the window that morning. Tina's revelation last night was a lot to take in. Tina, a product of embryo donation, it was such a difficult concept to understand. Yet he loved her for what she was, it surely didn't change his feelings for her, he told himself. He could sense her anxiety and lack of self confidence at times. He had attributed that to her age and being in a different country. But this was such a huge issue. He felt sorry for her, a childhood that must have been perplexing and the difficulties to cope with when she grew up and understood more. His life in Chicago as South Asian American was nothing compared to what she must have gone through, he told himself. Her confusion being a brown child to white parents must have affected her. He felt more tender and loving towards her. He rang her early, talking brightly about their plans for the evening, not touching on what was on his mind. His love for her and need to help her in her search for her biological parent took strong roots.

At the clinic, the week flew past as Tina got to grips with the new system. The data input was not difficult and often texts from Keisha, Althea and Andrew helped reduce the tedium of the work. On Friday, Rashmi showed her the new records to be entered into the system.

"Now these are very sensitive material Tina, do handle them with care. Make sure you don't leave them lying around. We are so short of staff that I'm giving you some of these to do. Do be careful," she said again.

Tina looked at the material and her heart beat faster.

E. A. Thomas, the name stood out like a bolt from the blue. It was same name that was in the brown envelope her mum had given her. Her accident, staying with Andrew and being away from work had taken her focus away from her quest and now, here it was, the lady who had donated the embryo! She felt faint. She tried but could not focus on the paper as the words blurred into a shadowy pool. She drank some water and looked at the papers again. Details of the dates of the embryo donation, the procedure, the name of the doctor, the time and the number of embryos inserted were recorded.

The second section had the names of Margaret and Tony Wilson. Tina looked at the names and felt it was strange to see her parents names staring back at her. A frisson of excitement ran through her. This was the reason she had come all the way to India. She wanted to shout from the rooftops, ring her mum and text Keisha to tell them both all about it. She paused and took a deep breath. Her hands gripped the desk, the knuckles standing up proud. Counting to ten helped calm her.

The feelings of elation were replaced by doubts. How would she find E.A. Thomas in this city of millions of people? The address was nineteen years old. Tina made a quick copy of the papers and put them in her handbag. Her heart thumped with a mixture of guilt and worry tinged with the possibility that she might not be able to find the woman. Would she end up like Beth, she thought, and never find that missing piece?

Rashmi came bustling into the office. She made some hurried remarks to the young man on the next desk then turned to her.

"Tina, where are you with the records? Are you nearly done with the first lot I gave you T – W, was it?"

"I'm just at V. I should be finished with the first section today," she said her voice rising up.

"Good, I'll get you the next section this afternoon. You can get started on them first thing tomorrow."

Rashmi strode away in a hurry.

Tina worked at a pace that kept her mind from straying again. Who could she talk to about her feelings? Andrew had talked to her briefly about her search and promised to help her. She could rely on him. But that inner fear that all this information might lead to nothing enveloped her.

She spent the evening looking at the piece of paper and a map of Mumbai. She googled the address on her laptop and looked for the area. Thane seemed miles away from where she was. How would she get there? She looked up a telephone directory for the name. She drew a blank. She paced up and down her room, wondering how she could access any of the information. Lying on her bed she remembered something that Andrew had said to her.

"Anglo-Indians are a small community. All the families know each other or at least can always find someone who knows the family." This is such a huge city, teeming with millions, how could all the families know each other or of each other she wondered. Doubts crept in again. She shook them off and steeled herself to think about the whole thing in logical steps. What is the next constructive step she asked herself?

The bedside clock showed that it was well past midnight.

Tina decided that Andrew would be the one to ask for help. His family had connections across the city. She decided to call him in the morning and seek his help. She slept a dreamless sleep and woke up feeling slightly more confident to face the day.

Work was busy. Rashmi was under pressure to get the records done and the new system showed up glitches with other features.

"How about all of us doing some overtime today? We could really crack this new system before the weekend is on us." Rashmi suggested.

Most were happy to get the extra hours and the pay. Tina wondered if she could excuse herself but before she could summon up the courage, Rashmi had assumed that all except the two who had asked to be excused immediately were willing.

Tina worked the extra hours. It gave her little chance to meet with Andrew.

"Hey," he called her early next morning as she was getting ready for work. "We're going to have some fun. Guess what? David is having a surprise party for his pal at the Taj Lands End. It's the in place. You must see it! Get your glad rags on."

"Andrew I've been working so hard. I'm tired. I don't feel like partying."

"I'm not taking 'no' for an answer. You'll see why when we get there. I'll be at your door at 7 sharp." He rang off.

Her mind was churning over the name again and again. E.A. Thomas. What would she be like in person? Would she be aware that she had a daughter on the other side of the world? Would she resemble her in any way? Would her father be there?

Questions that she had gone over her mind a thousand times kept recurring. She thought of little else all day and worried about if and when she could get this journey of seeking started at all.

The party at the Taj Sands was a surprise birthday party for one of David's friends. One of their gang had arrived from USA. All had been to the prestigious Bombay Scottish School, so it was a kind of reunion. David felt that Andrew and Tina would have a lot in common with them and they would fit in perfectly and promised a great time.

Tina arrived a bit bleary-eyed and feeling out of sorts but she was stunned by the luxurious hotel. She had never seen such opulence in Glasgow. The hotel lobby was fantastic. Marble floors led them into the restaurant that the friends had booked. They had chosen the 'Vista', a younger, less formal restaurant, with pizzas on the menu.

David and his friends had ordered drinks and they were reminiscing about their school days as Andrew and Tina walked in. One of the boys was singing their school song, and the others were filling in the words every time he struggled to remember them. They were enjoying their reunion, singing loudly.

> There stands our School by Mahim Bay,
> Built on a wondrous site,
> By Scotsmen true in days gone by,
> All honour is their right.
> So proud are we of this great School,
> We sing with right good will -
> Its praise and follow every rule
> To make it greater still.
> Then we would up and cheer and laud
> Our teachers ev'ry one:
> They spare no pains - (nor yet the rod!)
> To see our tasks well done.
> Sing Bombay Scottish School, my lad,
> Our School we thus address.
> Sing Bombay Scottish School, my lass
> Sing Bombay Scottish School

Tina chuckled as she heard the words. They sounded oldie-worldie, something from the past, words that were from a different era to her ears. They joked about their teachers and the house system. Andrew and Tina were amused by the names of the houses. The boys were named after missionaries, MacGregor, Kennedy, MacPherson and Haddow, and the girls after the Queens - Beth, Victoria, Catherine and Anne. They talked about the ancient banyan tree that was in the quadrangle of the school and their exploits on the cricket field. Tina was staggered to find that the school flag was the Scottish saltire and wondered how such strong connections existed in a corner of Mumbai that she had never heard of before in Glasgow.

The pizzas they had ordered arrived piping hot and served with a fresh salad. Tina avoided the salad. The pizzas were eaten with gusto and the cake cut for the birthday girl, Malini. After a bit if banter and argument over what to do next they decided to go to a disco in nearby Bandra.

"I need to go, sorry." Tina turned to Andrew, hoping that he would not mind leaving early.

"The evening has just begun, yaar," said Arvind, "come on let's have some fun."

Andrew drew Tina aside and asked her why she was so on edge. "I don't feel well, my head hurts. Would you mind if we leave?"

Tina looked frail and her red-rimmed eyes were dull with pain. Andrew relented and they left early.

Tina was aware of Andrew's disappointment. She apologised and then rested her head on his shoulder. "Maybe all those extra hours at the computer have done your head in."

He stopped the car at the nearest pharmacy and got her some paracetamol. She was touched by his gentleness and his concern. When they reached the Joshi's house, she pleaded with him to come inside.

"He needs to get some papers for work, Uncle," she said to Mr. Joshi who stared at them from his wicker chair in the veranda, his spectacles falling further down the tip of his nose. He shrugged but his eyes followed them up the stairs and Tina glanced back at the top of the stair to see that he had got off the chair and stood at the bottom of the stairs waiting for their return.

Andrew sat on the bed and she showed him the papers.

Andrew read the papers quietly. He shook his head at the facts in front of him. Lives created with technological wizardry. He marvelled at the meticulous record-keeping of the clinic.

After what seemed like ages, he looked up at her and darted her a quizzical look. "This may be a wild goose chase; I mean there is very little to go on."

Her face fell. She looked as though she was going to burst into tears. He held her hand, calming her.

"Hush, I just don't want you to get your hopes up too high. Thane, it is quite a distance away," he said at last.

Tina looked deep into his eyes. Was he trying to avoid giving her help? Was he embarrassed or reluctant to get involved with her search?

He looked at the collection of papers that she had acquired: maps of Mumbai, telephone numbers jotted down in bits of paper, the railway timetable and finally she had printed out some newspapers of the 1990's with any news that covered the clinic.

"It's nearly twenty years ago Tina. The addresses may have changed and there are so many new buildings too."

"Andrew, you mentioned that the Anglo-Indian community is small. E. A. Thomas has stated in her records that she belonged to that community. Surely there must be some way of finding out if anyone knows of them?"

Tina looked anxious. She rubbed her forehead.

"Okay, if you feel well enough tomorrow, why don't we make a trip to Thane? I'll take the day off. Are you feeling any better?"

It was as if a veil of uncertainty had lifted.

"I'm sure I'll feel better tomorrow." She said.

"Oh dear," exclaimed Andrew, "we forgot completely that the picnic at the Elelphanta Caves is on tomorrow. We'll go on Sunday."

"Yeah can't take another day off. Rashmi is stressed already. Just as well I had applied for leave this Thursday. Okay it'll have to be Sunday then," she said, relieved that they would start the search soon.

Mr. Joshi had climbed up the stairs and was about to knock on the door as they came out of Tina's room.

"Good, good," he said, "don't spend too much time in the room. You can read those papers downstairs you know," he said to Andrew looking quite cross.

"Sorry, uncle we were trying to solve a complicated computer error," Tina explained.

"Next time bring that lap top down Tina, okay?" said Mr. Joshi.

"Message loud and clear, you old fart," mumbled Andrew as he walked out to the car.

"Be ready for the picnic," he said to Tina as she waved him goodbye.

Mr. Joshi waited till his car was out of sight, then looked at Tina and said gently.

"We are responsible for you, you know, just be careful."

Chapter 17

It was a perfect day for the picnic. In November the days were getting cooler and the skies did not turn white hot with heat. Tina had mixed feelings. On the one hand she wanted to get started on the search for the donor lady; on the other meeting with friends for a picnic was an experience that she looked forward to. She liked Althea who made her transition to life in Mumbai so painless. Althea was full of energy and made sure that Tina did not miss having fun during her placement in Mumbai. She was proud of her city and loved to take her around.

The group of friends met at Andrew's and chattered happily about their time off from work. David took charge of the occasion. He seemed to have deep knowledge of the place as he had done the trip many times. Tina instinctively felt close to David. She could not explain why.

They left early to travel during the cool of the morning and reach the caves for lunch time. The two cars were full of young people as they set out for the journey. The caves were not far, only ten kilometres away from central Mumbai. They got off at the Gateway of India to take the short ferry ride to the caves. The Taj hotel, resplendent in its iconic position near the Gateway of India caught her eye immediately. Andrew saw her looking at the Taj and said that he'd treat them all to *Tiffin* there on their return.

They boarded the ferry. As it was Tina's first time on a ferry in India, she was nervous and clung on to Andrew. However, the hour long ride was smooth. They went onto the upper deck and watched the ships plying the Arabian Sea and as David had

169

promised, the sea was not choppy. There were two hundred steps to the caves, and instead of climbing them, they got into the little toy train that took them up to the foot of the hills. Tina was glad that it was still cool.

"The caves were designated a UNESCO Heritage site in 1987," said David.

"Why is it called 'Elephanta caves?'" asked Tina.

"The Portuguese saw an elephant carving at the entrance to the caves and called it that, though the village was originally called 'Gharapuri'. It goes back to the 5th or 6th century and the whole sixty thousand square feet of the temple is carved out of solid rock." David added this extra information that helped them understand.

"Wow, these are such great sculptures, but so many are in such an awful condition. I suppose the Government didn't bother about preserving them," complained Althea.

"No, for once we can't blame the Government. The Portuguese used the statues as target practice and took pot-shots with their rifles at the Indian Gods. They vandalised a lot of the statues," said David.

"How dreadful," they said in unison and continued walking on, remarking at the various sculptures at the wonderful site.

They looked on at awe at the twenty foot magnificent sculpture of Lord Shiva that dominated the site. It was carved in relief, showing the three-headed Shiva. The right half of the face showed him as a young man with sensuous lips, holding a flower embodying life and creativity, the creator of life perhaps and closest to Uma, the feminine side of the creator too. The left half of the face displayed anger, the Destroyer. The face in the middle was contemplative, the preserver, Vishnu, in deep meditation for preserving of humanity. In one sculpture, the cycle of life, death and universe was shown.

"Anyone want to go up Cannon Hill? The Portuguese built a fort with cannons to fend off any invaders. It's a good walk uphill."

David was enthusiastic but the others were slowly wilting in the heat. Tina was relieved when the others declined. They stopped for a cold drink and got back on the boat.

Andrew held Tina close as they stood on the deck of the boat. As the sun got stronger they went down to the lower deck.

"India rocks! It's awesome," he added, "Its ancient heritage makes me so proud."

"Yeah, I agree," said Tina, glad that she had seen at least a bit of Mumbai. They got off the boat and looked forward to the air-conditioned coolness of the Taj hotel.

They entered the rich marble foyer which was welcoming after the heat of the trip. They relaxed into the luxurious cushioned chairs in the "Shamiana" restaurant.

"We can't go to the "Sea Lounge". We need more formal clothes, no jeans, we'd not be allowed in," said Andrew. He winked at Tina as he slid into the chair beside her and whispered to her, "We'll make a special date and I'll take you there."

"I agree, the Sea Lounge has the best views and none of the noise of the fishermen or tourists," said Althea.

All of them seemed to be familiar with the menu and ordered their favourite dishes.

"I'll choose for you if you're not sure," said Andrew.

"I can manage. I'll have the crab cakes please with the coriander dip," said Tina, happy to see one of her favourite dishes there.

"So what are you doing for Christmas?" Althea asked Tina, as she drew out a tiny compact to check her make –up. She reapplied her lipstick with grace and confidence.

"Tina will be with us," said Andrew. "Mum is making her usual elaborate meal and inviting the whole family as always."

The waiters fussed around, placing the cold cokes and setting the plates for the different dishes that they had ordered. The conversation stayed on Christmas, the preparations and the presents. Tina recalled Christmases at home and thought of the cold, dark days filled with shopping in the bright lights of Glasgow. The sounds of the jingles and the same old songs like "Tiger Feet" and "White Christmas" played loudly in the shops had always annoyed her. The jostling in the crowds was always fraught, but now she thought fondly of it.

How different it was going to be here in India!

The *Tiffin* over they left the Taj, and moved onto a multiplex to watch a Bollywood movie. It was pure escapist, with a plot full of action and songs. They relaxed and enjoyed it. As they were leaving, Althea stopped in her tracks and said,

"Oh Gosh, I've lost my gold ring. It must have slipped off." She was anxious. They searched the seats at the cinema, the car and then she said,

"I remember I took it off at the restroom at the Taj. Oh, no, I hope it's not vanished."

Andrew called the Taj, and was told that one of the staff had handed it in. It had been left at the front desk for them to collect. The relief was palpable. The foursome David, Althea, Andrew and Tina left for the Taj while the others called it a day.

"Thank God they have it," said, Althea. "It was my grandma's and I always wear it."

"Lucky it was the Taj. It might have disappeared if it had been any other place," said David.

They came out of the Taj, relieved to have got the ring back. Mumbai was alive when they left the Taj Hotel. The late evening sky darkened with tropical suddenness and stars twinkled above, reflected as tiny shards of light on the waves of the Arabian Sea. It was a normal evening in the busy metropolitan city. Tina was getting used to the noise of street hawkers, mingled with the ubiquitous car horns.

It's the sound of life and living in a subtropical city, she thought as she linked with Andrew and they walked on. Their friends David and Althea were striding up ahead. She moved even closer to Andrew and she felt at home even though so far away from Glasgow. Being with him she was happy.

"How about a drink?" asked David.

"I've read about the Leopold Café in that book, *Shantaram*. Can we go there?" asked Tina.

"It's just across the road, crowded always, yeah, why not? The bar upstairs is okay. Let's go," said David.

The café was exactly as Tina pictured it, a kind of scruffy, busy place full of travellers. The tables had checked tablecloths, a completely different atmosphere to that of the Taj across the road. She noticed that nearly three quarters of the crowd in there were foreign.

"Aye, one Reshma Kebab and a burger please," Tina heard a young guy ordering. She knew that voice. She rushed over to him.

"Hey, Alan, what're doing here?" she said, thrilled to hear the familiar voice of her old schoolmate.

"Christ? Tina, I can't believe it. When did you land here?" Alan turned round and smiled. "Cath, look, here's someone else from Glasgow," he called out to a girl who was busy chatting to a group of backpackers.

Cath came over. "That's cool," she said, "Come on over and join the Scottish gang."

Tina recognised two other girls she knew from Glasgow. She introduced Althea, David and Andrew. The conversation was all about the backpackers plans of travelling around India and their experiences. David and Andrew kept quiet, Althea looked at her watch.

"Bored?" Tina whispered to Andrew.

He nodded.

"Why don't you go up and I'll have a wee chat with my pals and join you soon?" Tina looked at all three.

"No problem, we'll go and order the drinks upstairs," said Andrew. He and David bounded up the stairs, but Althea stayed with Tina.

Andrew and David were sipping their drinks, watching the cricket match, India versus England, on TV. Most of the crowd was engrossed in the game. The owner of the café was with them, commenting on the score and chatting to the customers.

They heard a sound like a light bulb bursting. Their first reaction was that the sound had come from the TV.

"Crackers, fireworks? Strange, is it…" David's voice trailed off.

Then they heard the sound of a machine gun followed by screams. The owner jumped off his seat and ran halfway down the stairs. He took one look at the scene below and raced back up again.

"Shooting! Guns!" The owner came running up, "Duck down! Hide!" he screamed and hid himself under a table. Their survival instinct kicked in and they dived under the tables too.

"Tina, Althea… Oh my God, they're downstairs…"
Andrew's words died on his lips. Fear enveloped the room like a blanket. A few seconds later they heard glass shattering downstairs and more screams.

Downstairs was pandemonium. Tina shivered as she watched the horror unfold. Two young men with backpacks had walked into the café armed with machine guns. They opened fire and shot at random. Althea held Tina as she fell with her leg spouting blood. A piece of glass from one of the huge mirrors had ricocheted off a wall opposite her and had hit her leg. A waiter pushed all of them under a table as he took cover too.

They lay there terrified. It seemed to last forever, the gunmen continued their shooting, again aiming at anything or anyone whom they caught sight of. Tina whimpered. Althea took a silky dupatta which was lying on the floor and wrapped it around the wound on Tina's leg. Fear made Tina quieten down.

Bombed, shot at and terrorised.

The change had happened in seconds. From a lively café with people laughing, drinking and chatting to an eerie silence. People had ducked, pushed, crouched under tables and taken refuge. The sound from the semi-automatic gunfire gun was loud and Tina shivered. Adrenaline coursed through each of their bodies and sweat poured out. Moans were stifled. Some stuffed their mouths with handkerchiefs, scarves or *pupates*. It felt like an ordeal that lasted hours but the twenty minutes that the two young men had spent blasting their guns was suddenly over. Tina watched in shock as one of the young men nonchalantly threw a hand grenade into the centre of the room as they walked out of the café. The sound of the blast was incredible. It shook the floor and left a crater that smouldered.

They felt their end had come.

There was a deathly silence, followed by some of the injured moaning. The silence was broken as the waiters crawled out from under the tables and sprang into action, going to other tables to help the injured while some others in the café ran out.

The mist of smoke cleared slowly.

Tina inhaled the strong smell of cordite that hung in the air. Shattered glass tinkled in the silence then whimpers and muffled screams broke out as if the drawn breaths were released. Slowly the screams became louder. Blood oozed out of wounds that were visible. Tina saw the wound on her leg and almost fainted. Althea held her arm and tried to keep the bandage in place but it was a vain attempt. Broken glass bangles and pieces of mirrors crunched underneath as some people started to take steps out of their hiding places. Some emerged warily, from under the tables as the crowd from the upper floor dashed down the stairs.

Andrew and David rushed downstairs to see seven bodies covered in gunshot wounds, lying grotesquely on the floor. They stumbled over them, ashamed at their own callousness as they ran towards the girls. Althea had eased herself from under the table and was struggling onto her feet. David thanked God as he saw that the two girls were alive. He glanced at a calendar that stood askew on the wall, flecks of blood sprinkled over it.

Tina stayed frozen on the spot, under the table, moaning. She felt Althea tugging at her as she tried to prise her out. Andrew crouched down towards Tina. Her bandaged leg was visible, the wound exposed as the silky dupatta had eased off and fallen on the floor. He instinctively tore his shirt and bandaged her wound properly. Tina looked pale and about to faint. Andrew held her close to him, smoothing her hair and kissing her lightly. He kept talking to her softly, willing her to live. He had no idea how deep the wound was or if her bleeding had stopped.

As soon as he heard the ambulance siren he ran out, carrying Tina. He pushed past the surging people to get her in the ambulance first.

"She's injured; get her to a hospital," he croaked.

Other injured were also hoisted in. The ambulance raced to the nearest hospital carrying as many of the wounded as possible. It screeched to a halt at JJ hospital which was already heaving with patients. The critically injured were wheeled in first. Tina lay on a trolley and Andrew did not rest until he found a doctor to attend to her.

The next few hours were filled with anxiety as the doctors worked on the critically ill. The police arrived and tried to help people and control the crowd of relatives in the hospital looking for their loved one but the chaos continued in the hospital which was stretched to its limit in manpower and facilities.

"Her parents! Oh my God, Althea, do you know their number?" asked Andrew, his face pale and lined with worry. Althea searched for the mobile in Tina's bag and gave it to Andrew. He tried the number but the phone lines were all dead.

"Jesus, how do we get in touch with them?"

Andrew slapped his forehead in despair.

"Should we try the British Embassy?" suggested David.

"None of the phones are working. Shit!"

Andrew kept pressing all the numbers he could think of. Then he remembered and took out his Blackberry and texted a message quickly to the British Embassy website.

'Tina Brown, UK citizen injured, JJ hospital, HELP.'

Terrorists had struck Mumbai.

Chapter 18

In Glasgow Margaret and Tony were at their wits end. They had spent hours trying to reach Tina. The British Embassy in India could not be contacted, while the foreign office had only a vague idea of the sheer scale of what was happening. They dashed over to Brenda when they remembered that James was in Pune for an IT Conference.

"Call James, Brenda, please. Tina is in hospital." Margaret rushed into the house as soon as Brenda opened the door.

"Hospital, why, what's happened?" Brenda seemed blissfully unaware of the bombing in Mumbai.

"Brenda, have you not watched the news? It's all over the TV."

"I was busy with my research; I'm doing the family tree." She switched the TV remote beside her to find the shocking scenes of the flames shooting out of the Taj Palace hotel.

"I didn't realise, oh god how awful? Are you sure Tina's injured?"

"Brenda, there's not a moment to lose. Please call James. He is in India, right?"

Brenda picked up the phone slowly.

"I'll see if he's at the hotel. He's often away at meetings," she said.

Brenda dialled the number and gave the receptionist James's room number. She handed the phone to Margaret who mumbled thanks as she put the receiver to her ear.

"James, Margaret here. It's Tina. Can you get to Mumbai? Tina is in…" Margaret's voice trailed away into a sob.

Tony took the phone from her and explained what had

happened.

"She's in hospital. We need your help James. Pune is not far from Mumbai. Can you drive there?" Tony implored, his voice shaking. "The foreign Office is advising us not to travel and there are no airlines going to Mumbai. You're our only hope."

"No problem, I'll leave straight away. Look as soon as I arrive in Mumbai I'll get news to you. Don't worry; I'm sure she's in safe hands." James sounded calm and decisive.

Brenda was standing fuming in the background. Her eyes were venting fear and loathing, as she paced up and down watching the awful scenes on the TV from the corner of her eye and then, turning back, she saw Tony about to put down the phone.

"I can't thank you enough."

Before Tony could finish the sentence Brenda grabbed the phone from him.

"You're not going anywhere near that terrorist city, James. You've your own family to think of," Brenda screeched into the phone.

They heard the decisive click of the phone being slammed down. Brenda turned on Tony and Margaret. She vented her anger and confusion at Tony.

"How could you do this to my James? How could you ask him to go to a place where there are bombs and terrorists? If it is so dangerous for you to go there how can you expect James to be there?"

Brenda was crying.

"I don't want him anywhere near that place. You hear me!"

"Brenda we'd do the same if it was Amy. Please try to understand," Brenda's sobs grew louder. She was getting hysterical.

"If anything, anything happens to him. God help you!" she screamed, covering her face and sobbing loudly.

179

"Brenda, please we need to be together now, please."
Margaret tried to hug her but Brenda shrugged her off.

"I'll make some tea," said Tony.

"Tea! I don't want a bloody cup of tea." Brenda shouted.

"We just have to wait now. It would be better if we could all calm down a bit."

Tony went in to the kitchen to make the tea.

Margaret sat beside Brenda and stroked her hair. Brenda jerked free of her and moved away from her as though just her proximity was unbearable.

"Brenda we're desperate. We've no idea when the airport will open there. We're trying to get a flight to anywhere in India, to get to Tina as soon as we can."

"Oh shut up, stop it, just shut up," Brenda screamed. "That child has brought nothing but sorrow to our family."

*

Tina lay on the stretcher, her eyes closed. The wound had already coloured the new bandage red. Andrew kept trying the phone. He sent a message to the British Embassy.

'Tina Brown, UK citizen injured, JJ hospital, HELP.'

David and Althea sat huddled together in deep prayer, preferring a space where they could meditate in quiet. The sight of others crying, howling with grief, heightened the tension and shook them. Althea kept touching the cross on her silver chain and kept repeating prayers that came to her. The human suffering was hard to bear. Althea zoned into her own mind and kept thinking of the events that had changed such a wonderful day to one of horror.

A doctor in a white coat hurried towards them. They crowded round him.

"Are any of you her family?" he asked.

"I'm her boyfriend," Andrew said.

"Its good that you brought her in quickly and the bandage helped. She has lost blood and needs a transfusion, otherwise she's okay, no other injuries. The problem is she has a very unusual blood group, the Bombay Blood Group. I checked the Blood Bank store. They have none. I've just contacted our list of donors," he said and rushed away.

"Bombay Blood Group? After the Diwali accident I remember that doc saying something about her blood group!" he said.

"Calm down Andrew, you've saved her," said Althea. "God is on our side, I'm sure they'll find a donor," she hugged him, tears stinging her eyes.

Andrew lowered his head. He was distraught.

He felt helpless. Bombay Blood Group! Andrew tried desperately again on the phone to call her parents number. The phone lines were still down. A pint of Bombay Blood Group was crucial to save her life.

Beth and Brian Fernandez rushed into the foyer. Althea turned and ran towards them.

"David is he...? My son, my baby is he hurt? Althea, tell me please?"

"Aunty, he's fine, he's with us. Come with me." She took them both over to see David.

"David, thank goodness you're okay!" She hugged him tightly.

"Mum I'm fine but it is Tina..." Then they spoke all at once about Tina's wound, the bleeding and the need for something called 'Bombay Blood Group.'

"Jesus, I've got that blood group! Maybe I can help," Beth explained. "Let's go find a doctor," she said calmly.

Althea crossed herself and thanked God for this amazing coincidence, as Beth was taken in for further blood matching. Andrew's relief turned to anger and worry.

Brian explained to Andrew. "The Bombay Blood group does not belong to A or B and it's not group O either because of the absence of Antigen 'H'. Beth knew she had the rare blood group because she had to have an IVF treatment to have David. Only 0.001% of the population has this group."

Andrew looked at him baffled. *Blood*, he thought to himself, *ties families together*. The fluid that connects, claimed to be thicker than water, was vital for survival.

It had been everywhere today; seeping the ground outside the cafe, splattered across people's clothes and face. How it transformed from a bright red to a darkened maroon, stained white sheets in ghostly patterns. Blood, easily transported in plastic bags to save the lives of patients, the fluid that ran deep in person to person, that ties one to their family.

"It's okay. I know it can be quite a technical matter, you weren't to know," said Brian gently.

"I hope her parents get here quickly," said Andrew. "I wonder if the British Embassy got my email." He started checking his messages on the Blackberry.

The next few hours were filled with anxiety as the doctors gave Tina the transfusion. Police arrived to try and help control the crowd of relatives. Large numbers of people scrambled the place searching for their loved ones. Others stood anxiously waiting for good news, Tina's friends spent a restless night in the corridor worrying about her recovery, Andrew worried if the blood transfusion would be performed on time.

They were all oblivious to the fact that the terror attacks were continuing in other parts of Mumbai.

The hazy sun of dawn broke through the windows and the streaks of light lifted the darkness. Althea opened her eyes and hoped that God had answered her prayers. She whispered a prayer as the faint light of the new day dawned. The full scale of last night's horror was beginning to reveal itself in the soft light. The hospital's corridors remained crowded with people who were waiting patiently. The orange hues brightened and dispelled the darkness. Andrew's sleepless eyes were red-rimmed.

Althea and Andrew stood up as they saw the doctor striding towards them. A quick crowd of people surrounded him, asking about their relatives. He tried to ignore them but was getting increasingly annoyed. Finally he turned to Andrew.

"The procedure went very well. A hundred per cent success. It is very good Mrs. Fernandez arrived when she did."

He rushed off. A crowd followed him, accosting him with further questions.

Andrew's shoulders heaved and sobs broke out. Althea hugged him tightly. They clung to each other with tears in their eyes. David and his dad were outside the theatre, waiting for Beth. Andrew hurried over to give them the news.

"Tina's stable and doing well. Thank God. How's Mrs Fernandez? Is she okay?"

"Thank goodness Tina is okay. My mum is fine," David replied.

"Your mom's an angel. I can't thank her enough."

Andrew grabbed David and gave him a hug.

"By the way, there was a young man from the British Consulate. He was saying he was organising something. A transfer to Jaslok hospital, I think," said David.

"That's great news. Does that mean her parents have been informed?" asked Andrew.

"I have no idea," David's tired voice was barely audible.

Andrew and Althea rushed to Tina's room and asked the nurse for information. She was busy and said she would talk to them when she was free. They waited again, hopes rising that she would be transferred to Jaslok Hospital as the state of the art facilities would mean she would get the best after care. The

183

British consulate had insisted that their citizens should be transferred and made all the necessary arrangements for the transfer as Jaslok hospital. There was a great sense of relief that Tina had that extra help from the embassy officials.

*

Meanwhile Beth lay in the hospital bed, flashes of her life unravelled slowly.

'David' her heart cried out. The thought that she might have lost him in a senseless terrorist attack made her whole body shudder with fear. Her mind cast back to the pain she went through to have him. She and George were desperate for a son.

The months of gruelling infertility tests and then the IVF procedure she had endured to have him made her cherish him more. She spent countless hours marvelling at his perfection. She looked at his dark, virgin olive green eyes and in his light skin saw a likeness to her mother. It is true, *time is a great healer,* she told herself. The thought of nearly losing David was something she could not bear to think about. Her whole body shook again, the pain of her thoughts of losing him only another mother could understand.

The sirens of ambulances outside were still audible. The hospital was still thronging with people; she said a prayer for all the mothers who may lose their children on this awful night. And for George and her mother, may God rest their souls.

This poor girl, Tina lying in a hospital so far away from her parents, she thought, I'm glad I could help her.

All she wanted to do now was to go back home, and be with David and Brian.

*

For Tina's friends, it was important that they stayed by her bedside. Andrew would not leave her side for a moment. The scale and horror of the attacks was apparent to all of them only days after their ordeal. They learnt much later that the horror at Leopold café was only the start. The news reports described each scene in great detail. In the next few days Andrew, Althea and David watched scenes on the TV with anguish, as ten young men went rampaging through the city and killed innocent people across eight locations.

After they had left the café, the waiters and the owner had helped the injured, getting wounds bandaged and calmed everyone. The smell of gunfire had hung heavy in the air. A sulphurous smell had wafted around. The carnage was awful. There was blood and glass shrapnel everywhere. The papers showed pictures of the chaos. Some tables were upturned; the checked tablecloths were soaked in blood. There were people in clothes that were torn, some had scrambled into small places and caught their sleeves or hems. Some of those near the bomb had their faces blackened, with tears of fear running down their cheeks forming unsightly lines. Many witnesses had given statements to the press. They described how they had seen grotesque bodies lying close by and how they had watched helpless as the callous shooting had carried on. The shockwaves were palpable. They also criticised the police who had arrived twenty minutes later at the cafe.

The iconic Taj Hotel was held by the men for another three days. The world held its breath at the audacity of these young men, who were willing to go to any lengths for their cause. They simply weren't suicidal but a destructive force that did nothing but harm to innocent human life. Terrorism had wrecked many parts of the world and Mumbai many times before but this carnage was incredible with a huge loss of life.

Mumbai was a city left paralysed.

In Pune, James left as soon as he got the phone call from Glasgow.

"Driver, jaldi," said James, "I want to get to Mumbai as soon as possible."

"Yes, sir," said the driver, pressing the accelerator and the car jumped to a higher rev and raced across the road.

The hundred and twenty kilometres should not take more than an hour and half, James told himself. He rested his head on the car seat worried about Tina. He momentarily remembered slamming the phone down on Brenda and regretted it. He hoped she needn't be so dramatic.

The small case with his change of clothes and toiletries lay beside him on the seat. Traffic on the main roads was busy; the honking and noise of the scooters, auto rickshaws a blur in the background of the air-conditioned car. The images flashing across the window screen took several moments to process. An entire family were riding a tiny motor scooter, a child stood in the front, and a mother was hanging onto her partner, her red sari sat tight around her body, her curly hair obscuring her vision. The scooter weaved its way between the cow standing right in the middle of a busy road and the rest of the swirling traffic. Mumbai was chaotic at the best of times.

He arrived at the hospital glad to find that Tina was recovering after the operation. James emailed Margaret and Tony right away to say that she was alive and being looked after well.

"Thank God, Thank God," cried Margaret to Tony when she saw the email.

"The Embassy said she was fine, had reassured me, but I'm so glad James has seen her. I feel so much better. Email back and give her my love; tell her we'll be there as soon as possible."

Tony replied immediately. "James, we're trying to get the first flight possible. Please stay by her side, till we arrive."

"I will, I promise," James replied. "Don't worry she's fine. The staff here and her friends are amazing and she's being really well looked after. The whole city is rallying around."

James did his best to reassure them both.

The hospital orderly walked down the corridor, with a food trolley. The smell of food made Andrew realise that they had not eaten properly for hours.

"I'll stay," said Althea, "I'm full of coffee and don't feel like eating anything now. Why don't you and James go and have something to eat, Andrew?"

"I need to book a hotel to stay in anyway. Is there anything nearby?" asked James.

They drove to the Regency, a decent four-star hotel nearby and ordered a drink after James had checked in.

"It was touch and go you know," said Andrew. "We could have lost Tina."

"I want to know everything, tell me," said James, nursing his lager, cool and refreshing in his hand.

"Tina lost a lot of blood and she has a very rare blood group." Andrew shook his head thinking of the tense hours that they had spent at JJ hospital.

"Did the hospital not have a blood bank?"

"They do but, Bombay Blood group is so rare," said Andrew. "I've never heard such a preposterous thing. You mean a, b, or o."

"No it's a very rare group that is peculiar to only a few people in the Indian population." Andrew shivered. The toll it had taken on him was visible.

James found the news incredible. They sipped their beer, while Andrew explained the bombing that had involved them all.

"We've been very fortunate. Beth, my friend David's mom has

the same blood group and donated it without any hesitation."

"How lucky for Tina? I must meet this lady and thank her."

"I'll ask David and let you know. I'm sure she would like to meet with Tina's family too," said Andrew.

He got out his Blackberry and emailed David who replied immediately. They arranged to meet the following day in the afternoon.

"Let's get back and give Althea a break," said Andrew.

They went back to the hospital. The skyscraper building of the hospital looked foreboding in the grey evening light. Each of the men sat in the car thinking about all that was still happening in Mumbai. The images of the terrorist attacks were all over the city. The pictures of the Taj hotel burning were thrust in front of everyone. There was world coverage of the incident, shown in the local TV stations. The city reeled with horror story after horror story, while each survivor or the relatives of those who were killed, picked up their lives and tried to move on.

The next, grim few days for James and Tina's friends were ones of unstinting support for the lucky young girl who had survived. When the siege was finally brought to an end, a huge sigh of relief went up around the world and in Mumbai. The ease with which they had carried out the atrocity was shocking. Tales of bravery of the policemen and ordinary people who helped the wounded were relayed everyday in the media. A semblance of normality inched its way into the lives of the people.

Tina lay in her hospital bed only vaguely aware of what was happening around her.

Chapter 19

The florist shop at the hospital was as good as any for their selection of flowers, thought James as he bought the biggest and prettiest bouquet that they had. There was a mixture of white and red roses with a lovely pale green fern arranged in an exquisite way. The perfume from the roses was pungent, unlike roses that he had bought in Scotland. He wrote a simple message,

"Thanks for saving Tina" and signed it. He hurried towards Andrew's car and the driver opened the door for him.

"Is it far, their house?" asked James.

"No, not really but with traffic restrictions everywhere it may take us longer than normal," said Andrew.

In twenty minutes they drew up in front of a house in Bandra. David opened the door and welcomed them both in.

"You must be James," he said and held out his hand. "Please have a seat."

Beth walked in. James stood up and dropped the flowers on the floor. David and Andrew bent down to retrieve the flowers.

James and Beth stared at each other.

He hesitated.

"Mrs. Fernandez, pleased to meet you" he said after what seemed ages. He spoke very quietly, his eyes widening in surprise. The dimple on her chin and her tiny nose were so much like Rita. *How could it be*? His heart beat faster.

She smiled and his heart melted. Her hands tugged at her skirt and smoothed it, nervously doing it again. The boys looked up. Andrew gave the bouquet to James. He took it wordlessly from him. James moved up closer to her, and handed her the flowers.

There was a pause then he cleared his throat and said,
"Mrs. Fernandez, I don't know how to thank you. I'm lost for words. Thank you so much for saving Tina."

His voice was still soft and trembling.

"Please call me Beth. She's such a lovely girl. I did nothing special," she said and smiled again. "It's so good to meet you." They looked at each other. The olive green eyes that she could see in David stared back at her. She smoothed her skirt and smiled at him. Tightness caught at her throat and she felt a strange sensation throughout her body that perplexed her. She looked at the flowers and the strong perfume of the roses made her nose crinkle.

"Oh these are so lovely. Thank you. I'll put them in a vase."

"Let me make some tea," she added, walking back to the kitchen.

"Mum do we have some of the shortbread you made yesterday?" David called after her.

James sat down heavily on the sofa and wiped his forehead with a handkerchief. Over forty years ago and she looked as if she had just walked back into his life again. It was the same Rita whom he had loved as an eighteen year old and to whom he had professed his undying love. He had promised her the world.
James looked around. The photograph on the wall that he had not noticed as he came in was right in front of him.

"My grandparents," said David, not aware that James was sweating profusely and shaking slightly. The photograph showed Rita with John. A sepia image, a cameo of a life together was framed and hung on the wall.

James felt ill.

"Are you feeling hot? Our weather must be really hard for you to adjust to."

David checked that the ceiling fan was at its highest setting.

Before he could answer, Beth walked in with the tea and shortbread. James kept looking at her, conscious that he was staring at her and unable to stop it. She seemed nervous too but kept herself busy pouring the tea and serving it around.

Brian was explaining about the dreadful events of the terrorist attack in Mumbai and the fact that Tina was lucky to have escaped the horror at Leopold Café.

"Enough about the bomb! Let's stop being morbid."

David turned to James.

"Mr. Campbell, is this your first time in India?"

James had to turn his attention to David. He noticed his green eyes as he answered the questions posed to him. His mind was whirling and trying to get back to what people around him were saying was an effort. He felt his face was getting redder and tried to calm himself down by taking a deep breath.

"Please call me James," he replied. Before anyone could answer, Andrew interrupted.

"He's an IT businessman. He must have come here many times before."

James nodded. He sipped the tea, wishing he could have a cold drink instead. He was confused with this sudden revelation that he was connected so closely to the family. Beth offered him a few more pieces of shortbread. She smiled at him and his heart was flapping like a trapped bird.

"No… thanks, I've had enough but it was delicious," said James with a semblance of normality.

"I better get some more hot tea," she said and whisked away the tray. She took her time and came back with the teapot and a small wooden box. James's eyes widened when he saw the wooden box. He knew straightaway that it was Rita's.

She laid the teapot and the box on the coffee table carefully.

"More tea anyone?" she asked as she poured a cup for Andrew

and herself. Then she opened the box and took out a yellowed piece of paper and handed it to James.

"This was my mum's. She passed away and I found it when I was sorting her things." she said. "I've wondered why she kept this scrap of paper for all these years. Do you know where this place is in Glasgow, James?"

The familiar scrawl of his teenage years was in front of him.

22, Bellview Terrace,
Glasgow 12

He was grateful that he had not put his name on it and breathed a huge sigh of relief. He felt as if he was in a play on stage. He was there and yet it felt remote and strange. His mind was not registering everything as his thoughts were hammering around his head. Should he tell this woman the truth?
Beth fumbled through the rest of the box and recounted what was in it.

"This cheap ring, a dried flower, a small hanky, a half burnt candle, a pebble, even a small twig, oh, what a sad little collection. It must have meant a lot to her."

Beth looked at James as though she was reading his mind. He looked at his watch and the whites of his knuckles showed as he clenched and unclenched his fists. His face was bright red. He mumbled something that she could not hear clearly.

"David, please get a glass of cold water. I think it is the heat."
She closed the box and promptly forgot about its existence. She was more concerned about her visitor.

"James, take it easy. Our bedroom is air-conditioned if you want me to switch it on and you can lie down for a while. You look unwell."

"No," he croaked, "I...I think I should leave now, if you don't mind. You've been so kind."

Andrew agreed.

"It must be all the strain of seeing Tina and this bombing in Mumbai has rattled everyone," said Andrew and they said their goodbyes and headed for the car.

"Are you okay James? You do look awful," said Andrew. "Should I take you back to the hospital and get a doctor to see you?"

"No thanks, it must be the heat. I'll be okay with some rest."

James got into the car and sat back, resting his head on the seat. He was relieved that Andrew did not ask him any questions. He struggled with the enormity of what he had found out. Strange as it might seem, he was glad of the noisy road and the chaos that was a drive in Mumbai. Cars hooted and swerved, ancient jalopies vied with brand new BMWs and Mercs. The huge four by fours were a menace, occupying the middle of the road and forcing other vehicles to the edge.

James sighed with relief when they reached the hotel.

"Thanks so much Andrew. If you don't mind I'll head to my room and take some rest."

"Fine, James. I'll see you at the hospital later on or tomorrow maybe. You take care."

"Make it tomorrow. I'm not feeling too great," he said.

The car sped away. James collected his room key and walked up to his room, his mind reeling with confusion.   *Beth, my daughter?* The question flashed like a red hot poker.

On the hotel bed he tossed and turned. He remembered the letter that Rita had written to him all those years ago. There had been a desperate plea for James to send for her and the tone was one of despair that he had not contacted her at all for months on end. She had mentioned her plight, her pregnancy and he had ignored her. In his helplessness he had thought it was something she had concocted to get him back. He had felt trapped.

As a young eighteen year old with no visible financial support he could do little. In all these years he had never once thought of such a consequence of his six month stay in India. He never imagined that he would come face to face with his own flesh and blood all these years later. Old memories chewed and bitten then forgotten with the passage of time resurged in vivid colours, stunning him.

There was no easy answer. Glasgow and his life with Brenda and Amy was his reality. How could they accept such a shocking new fact? He was struggling with it himself. *Christ! What would Brenda do if she found out?* He imagined her face iridescent with anger. He drank the mini bar dry.

James decided that he would leave India without saying anything to anyone but as he tried to sleep, Beth's smile haunted him. He thought of Rita and wandered what her life was like after he left.

*

Meanwhile Beth wondered about James's strange behaviour.

"Must be the Delhi belly, though he has been here often enough according to Andrew," mused Brian.

She was quiet. She thought of her mum and her elusive dad. Could it be James? If only she had his surname. Jimmy and James and a person from Glasgow, was that not too much of a coincidence, she kept asking herself. She kept turning over all that her mum Rita had said to her about her life and Jimmy.

Chapter 20

Rita sat down on the rock which had been the couple's favourite spot. The pebbles were clean and white. Their special place where their love had been all-consuming was beside the River Ganges. Its waters flowed in a torrent, fresh from the source up high in the mountains. The clear water had cleansed them that day. The blue sky and white fluffy clouds were reflected in the waters at the side where it was still, held back by rocks as the rest of it gushed down. This was where she felt at one with Jimmy.

She rubbed her stomach imagining the new life that would bring them closer. She had been shocked at first, blamed herself and worried about how Jimmy would react. After a lot of thought she had decided it was a sign from the Almighty that they were going to be together forever. A bond, a link was forged that was growing inside her, their blood, bones, skin and cells all joined as one. Their love was strong. She never doubted for a moment that he would be anything but supportive.

She put her hand in the water. A cold shiver ran up her spine. It was chilly, stone cold like her heart as she searched for an answer to her dilemma. How was she going to cope with a child with no one to support her? Her parents would be devastated. An unmarried mother, an illegitimate child, she squirmed as she thought about her predicament. She had no choice; she could never ask them for help. It would break their hearts. Despair rent her soul. She sat for a long time wandering what she should do. She prayed for Jimmy's return.

When she returned to the cottage and switched the light on, its rays fell on a wooden box on the table. She opened it. The scribbled note with Jimmy's address was in there but there was no name. The box became one of the things that she clung to, along with the twigs, a leaf, the pebbles and the ring that he had given her. She made up her mind to write to him.

The blue of the airmail letter was crisp and fresh to her touch. She opened it and wrote her address clearly in capital letters. She decided she needed to leave the ashram and find somewhere safe. She would travel to Bombay.

The reply to her letter never came. She wrote several more, pleading for a word from him. Nothing. The silence rent her heart.

*

The train pulled in at Victoria Station, Bombay. The Victorian Gothic structure overwhelmed her. Rita had known only Bangalore, the quieter city where she was born. Her parents still lived there. The only other city she knew was Rishikesh, where she had lived for her work. This gigantic sprawling city frightened her. The noise of the station and the sheer volume of traffic outside made her head spin. She stood outside Victoria station with all her worldly possessions in a suitcase and a bag. Her eyes darted about looking for Alicia. She found her standing beside the stone sculptures of a lion and tiger, the symbol of Britain and India, at the entrance. She was relieved when she saw Alicia in a bright blue dress waving at her.

"Hi, great to see you," said Alicia, giving her a big hug.

"Nice to see you, Alicia. Thank God you're here," she replied. "It's so busy here!"

"Yeah nearly two million every day travel to and from here I believe. It's always busy," Alicia said "Let's get you straight home and then you can tell me all about life in the ashram," she giggled.

They got into a taxi, and the black and yellow cab veered out of the parking bay. The driver pressed the horn loudly as he overtook a motorbike with a family on board adjusting their bags. The smell of petrol fumes mingled with the heat and made their journey uncomfortable. Both put handkerchiefs to their mouths to stop inhaling the noxious fumes. The vehicle made a dreadful sound as the driver drove it through the manic traffic. It was a bumpy ride through Bombay. Rita's first impression of Bombay was negative. She could hardly hear what Alicia said to her, watching the people driving in and out of the tiniest of spaces. She was relieved when she felt the sea breeze on her face.

Jimmy what have I done bringing our baby to this huge city. How will I survive? Confused thoughts raced through her mind. *Why didn't you keep your promise? Why have you abandoned me?* She tried to hide her despair from her new friend and looked out at the passing scenes of the city.

Hers was an uncertain future.

Jimmy had left her with only a promise and a note of his address back in Glasgow. Rita feared bearing an illegitimate child alone in a city that she hardly knew but she had no choice but to move away to Bombay. It was the city of dreams. The poor from the villages and others who embraced anonymity found their home in this cosmopolitan, bustling city. It was the city not only of the film world of fantasy but the thriving metropolis where jobs were plenty and where a single woman working and bringing up a family was not unusual. The most important factor was that Rita could get away from her church-going parents and prevent the scandal that would have devastated her family. They accepted her lie, that the ashram had given her a job in Mumbai. She would live a lie all her life now. She would have to sever relationships with her parents when they insisted on visiting her.

Bombay in all its garish vibrancy, the city which she had seen on TV and in films was to be her haven. Nerves jangling with fear and worry, she got out of the taxi as it pulled up at Alicia's building.

The weather-worn board had Vikas Sherwood Park emblazoned on the front.

They walked up a dark staircase. A young man helped carry her suitcase to the first floor flat.

"Welcome to Bombay and your new home," said Alicia, with a bright smile.

Rita felt the baby kick. She put her hand protectively on her tummy and smiled back at Alicia. Rita put her bag and suitcase down in the room. The ceiling fan swirled above giving some respite from the heat. She sat down on the bed.

"Hope the room is okay? I've made some cold nimbu pani, come have some," said Alicia, standing at the door.

"Oh the room is lovely, thanks. Yes, a cold drink would be nice," said Rita.

They sat on the wicker chairs on the balcony of Alicia's flat.

Alicia explained her routine and her rules which were reasonable. The room had to be kept tidy. They had to share the kitchen and cook for each other, taking turns. When she got a job, she could pay her rent for the room.

"I can't thank you enough." Rita's voice faltered.

"Look, don't feel too worried. My life's story is similar to yours. But when we have no choice we rise to the occasion and do the best we can."

Alicia sipped her juice. Rita nodded.

Alicia recounted her story. It was equally harrowing. Left by her lover, she had struggled to bring up her son up on her own.

"God's always there. He shows the way. The church helped me a lot," she said and touched the cross hanging around her neck.

Rita nodded again.

"I can give you some of my savings now…," started Rita.

"Listen, you need to keep all that you can for the little one. You can help me though. I'm looking for a tutor for the destitute women's project at my church," she said with a smile.

"I'd love to do that," Rita replied, glad that she could repay her in some way.

"That's settled then. First thing tomorrow I'll take you to my doctor and get you checked over."

Life with Alicia went ahead smoothly. She was easy to get along with. Rita settled into the work and the routine.

She wrote another letter to Jimmy, giving him her new address in Bombay. She waited anxiously for a reply.

Her pregnancy was showing now. She could feel the baby moving. She so very much wanted him to be with her. Every night she prayed that a letter from him would arrive. Rita dreamed of him coming to take her away to set up their home together. She wondered how the baby would look. Would the baby be like him? She wanted that so she could think of their love always.

Whenever Alicia reminded her not to keep hoping, she cast her words aside.

"Jimmy is different. He would not desert me, not now, and not when he knows our baby is due."

She waited in vain for his reply. She never gave up on him and hoped he would be there when the baby arrived.

The women she helped were young, vulnerable and abandoned by their families. Some had even been sold off to prostitution by their parents and had no way of supporting themselves. The pimps discovered that they were pregnant and chased them away. They had nowhere to go.

Fundraising and campaigning for them with government agencies was a thankless task. When Alicia was out doing the hard grind of meeting with officials, Rita held fort, helping with the day-to-day problems of the refuge. Life in Bombay became the norm for her within a short time.

Rita devised a day that would have some meaning for the women. An hour of literacy was the start of the day after daily prayers. Most of the women had a very short concentration span. Sewing was a skill that could be taught with minimum outlay. She managed to get donations of soft material for babies from local shops and a couple of old sewing machines. They loved music and dance, so she got a cheap radio and encouraged them to sing along while they worked. They took turns at cooking and nutrition was added to their knowledge. When babies were born, hygiene on how and why to sterilise bottles was taught. Most took to the regime, but one or two were slow to learn anything at all.

Her work with the ten young destitute women was challenging but rewarding. Any time she felt despair at her position, she looked at the abject poverty of the women in the refuge and thanked God that she was not one of them. She had to turn away at least three or four young women every week. There was no space or provision for them.

One Saturday morning began with a flurry of activity. Rita was woken early before the normal six a.m. trill of the alarm clock. One of the girls had to be taken to hospital. The girl had a still born baby, something that Rita had not thought of. She was terrified. The image of the young girl as she came back the next day, bereft, with a glazed look in her eyes, scared her. Rita kept feeling for her baby's movements, thankful at each kick or ripple of her tummy. She did not want to lose the only thing that mattered to her in the whole world.

The monsoon downpours were something she had not experienced before. They tore at the flimsy tarpaulin that they had put on top of the thatched roof of the refuge. Pools of stagnant water were all over the church grounds.

Alicia and Rita sat after their dinner, resting and listening to music on the radio. Rita looked out of the window at the never-ending rain.

"Don't worry. We're used to it. We need it for water supply for the rest of the year," Alicia claimed laughing.

"It looks so fierce at times," said Rita. She did not feel cold, but the thought of the cascading water all over the flats and on the women's refuge made her body give an involuntary shudder.

"Not long to go now," reminded Alicia, as she dried their clothes on the long poles on the top of the room operating a pulley. "Feeling okay?"

"Fine, I hope the baby comes when the rain has subsided a bit," she said.

"We'll manage just like others," said Alicia. "Have you thought of names?"

"Not yet," she said. Definitely something that Jimmy would recognise, she thought to herself.

The rain made music on the window pane, a kind of drumming that annoyed to begin with then became a backdrop to her thoughts as she lay in bed. It was in Jimmy's passport that she had noticed his second name, James Ashley but could not remember his surname. Ashley, she could use that for a boy or a girl. Her mother's name Beth if it was a girl or her Dad's Vincent if it was a boy, she thought to herself. She smiled and rubbed her stomach and whispered, Vincent Ashley or Elizabeth Ashley, then hauled herself to the side. She was heavy. Sleep was difficult as she was not comfortable in any position. The rain music faded to a soft rhythm. She dozed off.

*

Alicia held her hand as she screamed in pain. Childbirth without Jimmy by her side was a scene Rita had never envisaged. It was harsh, the pain doubled not shared with him to hold her or comfort her. The baby, Elizabeth Ashley, arrived as dawn broke over a clear sky. The monsoon had stopped in the middle of the night. The six pound healthy baby squealed till she held her to her breast. The haze of pain vanished as she held her tenderly. Every bit of her body marvelled at this tiny life that filled her with a joy that she had never felt before. She kissed her as the baby struggled to find her nipple. Alicia blessed them, saying a short prayer and kissing them both on the forehead.

Jimmy, Jimmy wish you were here, she's so beautiful, our baby daughter, Rita's heart and mind went out to him in that bitter-sweet moment.

"She's beautiful. God Bless you both," Alicia said.

Rita's eyes glowed with a hint of tears of joy. She nodded and held the baby tight.

"She's so fair and in good health. You're a very lucky lady," said the doctor and she left the room.

The nurse bustled about. The maternity room had a lot of things to be tidied away before the next lady could be wheeled in. The nurse on duty was a withered old woman who looked as if she held all the world's woes on her shoulders. She had seen enough births to make her blasé about the whole thing. A normal delivery was good as she had no extra duties to perform.

"A girl child. Only trouble. They cost a lot and are only a burden," she tutted.

Nothing, not even the words of the nurse, bothered either of them. Alicia was glad that it had been a normal birth and Rita was overwhelmed just holding Elizabeth.

She prayed that one day Jimmy could see their beautiful baby daughter.

The birth of her daughter made Rita realise that staying with Alicia was not practical. Working as a volunteer was okay for a few months but with a young child to bring up, she needed a career. The schooling, health care, clothes for the child would cost money and she could not rely on Alicia's generosity forever. She had to carve out a future for herself and her daughter.

"Alicia, I'm planning to move to another place soon, what with Elizabeth and…" Rita said to her one evening as Alicia started to discuss her plans for the women's refuge.

Alicia looked at her.

"I'm not surprised Rita." There was not a hint of sarcasm or hurt in her voice.

"I must get Beth into a good school and think of her future. You do understand…" Rita paused.

"I totally understand. In fact I was going to suggest the same to you. A career with prospects for you and a good education for the little one is very important."

"I'll never forget what you've done for me and I'll help out with the refuge when I can." Rita added, breathing a sigh of relief that Alicia had taken it so well.

"Would you believe I have another request for your room? The girl is in the same situation as you, educated and abandoned by her lover."

"As soon as I get a flat I'll move," Rita smiled at her. "I have a job lined up already."

"Is it with John Kerr's company by any chance?" Alicia winked at her.

"What do you mean?"

A deep blush crept up on her cheeks.

"I have eyes, my dear." She laughed.

"I thought you saw him only once when he came in with that big donation for the refuge?" asked Rita was perplexed that Alicia had noticed her friendship with John.

"I knew him well before that. His wife was also involved with the women's refuge."

Rita's face fell. The disappointment in her eyes was obvious.

"His... wife?"

"I know he's quite taken with you. Don't worry. He's a recent widower and a very decent man with a good heart."

"He's been very kind. I didn't apply to his company!" said Rita, a slow smile spreading on her face.

"Why not?" Alicia looked surprised.

"I...he's asked me out. He spoke to me several times on the phone." Rita blushed. Her new found feeling of being wanted and loved cast a glow on her face.

"Yes, I did notice. I really hope you two get together dear. It would be so good for little Beth."

"I've got a job at the Bank of Baroda. I start on the first next month," Rita added.

Alicia came over to her and gave her a hug.

"You're a hardworking, loving mother and a good friend. It's time you found some happiness in your life. I hope God is kind to you. Remember I'm always here for you if you need me."

Rita had tears in her eyes at Alicia's kind words. She was indebted to her for ever. Kindness from strangers when one is at the end of one's tether is unexpected. Rita wondered how she would have coped if Alicia had not stepped in when she needed help so badly.

Chapter 21

Margaret and Tony arrived in Mumbai three days later. They were traumatised. Not having been able to help their daughter was evident on their faces, pale, wan and eyes with bags underneath showing sleepless nights. The waiting period in Glasgow with no idea when they could reach Tina's bedside had taken its toll.

Seeing James at the airport and hearing his calm words made them feel a bit better. Andrew had booked the same Regency hotel for them that James was staying in.

"You can freshen up at the hotel, check in, then go to the hospital," said James.

"No, I want to go straight to the hospital, please," said Margaret.

In the nineteen years since they had last visited Mumbai, the city had changed completely. The drive from the airport was agony for Margaret and Tony. So close to Tina and yet it took them well over an hour and a half to get to the hospital. The congested, snarled roads made them irritable and more anxious.

They arrived at the hospital their nerves jangling.

"Tina, my baby."

Margaret hugged and kissed her over and over again. Tony joined in and they sobbed, hugging each other and their tears flowed.

"Mum, mum I missed you so much, mum, Oh My God, it was awful," Tina cried, holding her mum tight. Slowly the sobs grew quieter.

"Let me look at you. Does it hurt, my baby?"

Margaret wanted to take her pain away and her tears did not stop. Tony stroked Tina's hair and cuddled her.

They saw that the wound on her leg was heavily bandaged.

After all those hours on edge waiting to see Tina, her parents could not believe they were with her, holding her at last. They all talked at the same time, or paused, just touched each other to feel each other's skin, thanking God inwardly. Then Tony remembered that James and Andrew were outside waiting.

He asked them to come in. As they walked in they heard Margaret say, "As soon as you're better we're taking you back home."

Andrew and Tina exchanged glances.

"Tony, why don't you both go to the hotel? Check in, freshen up and have a rest. The jet lag will floor you soon." James insisted.

Margaret agreed, reluctantly, to leave Tina's bedside.

The minute she was in the car, waves of tiredness lashed over her. She felt disorientated. Too many things had happened in the last few days. In their hotel room, the TV blared with news of the chaos that had been present during the three days of the siege. The news coverage was pointing out the Government's ineptness in handling the attack. Those ten young men could hold a huge city to ransom was a condemnation of the people who ruled. There was deep anger at the lack of help for the survivors and the delay in tackling the terrorists.

Tony and Margaret realised that they had been lucky as at least Tina was alive and recovering from the trauma. The TV pictures had shown death and destruction on a scale unimaginable. They switched the TV off and showered and took a rest.

James met them again at lunch. He was sitting in the dining room with his bag at his feet.

"Look I have to get back to Pune. Now that you're here…"

"Of course I understand, James," said Tony. "You need to get back to your work. You look so stressed. Looking after Tina must have been an added worry. I can't thank you enough."

"I don't know what we'd have done without you James," said Margaret, giving him a big hug.

"Tina has made good friends in such a short time, especially Andrew, so you will be well looked after."

Margaret had already sensed an intimacy between Tina and Andrew. Tina's eyes lit up every time Andrew was in the room. The way they looked at each other relayed a closeness that Margaret had recognised right away.

"I'll see you all back at Glasgow."

James added "I think I'll be leaving on the first available flight as soon as I get back to Pune. The conference is over anyway."

James left after lunch. The sooner he could get away from Mumbai the better, he thought to himself. The scenes of meeting Beth kept obsessing his mind. The long drive back to Pune was when he had to make his mind up. Should he confront his past or ignore it and hope that it would go away? The longer he thought about it, the more confused he became. Finally, he decided to go back home. Maybe he could think clearly when he was in his familiar territory, not in India where everything was still chaotic. He suppressed his deep feelings of guilt.

*

The house was in darkness when the taxi dropped him off. Glasgow with its grey skies seemed to reflect his mood. He opened the door and found her sitting in the dark. He switched the lamps on. The huge mirror reflected his haggard face, lined with worry.

"Hey, why are the lights not on? I'm tired. It was a bloody long flight."

He dropped the suitcase and bent down to kiss her.

Brenda turned her face away.

He moved on to the decanter on the table and half filled a glass with malt whisky.

"Am I glad to be home!" he said and slumped on the sofa beside Brenda and took a big sip of his whisky. Home comforts, the glass in his hand gave him a momentary feeling of contentment.

She was strangely quiet.

"I missed this."

The amber liquid warmed him. She said nothing.

He turned and looked at her.

"Is everything okay? You're awfully quiet. You do look a bit pale, not coming down with anything are you?"

Brenda glared back at him.

He noticed that her nagging, loquacious normalcy was absent.

He had called her from the airport and she had not answered the mobile or the landline. James felt the atmosphere was icy with resentment.

"Are you not well, darling?" his voice showed concern.

"How dare you call me darling?"

Her voice chilled him to the core. It was deep, not the high pitched, whiny voice that he was used to when she was annoyed.

"What! What do you mean?" James was taken aback.

"Why didn't you stay in that god forsaken place?"

She spat out the words and ran up the stairs.

He was stunned. He had never expected such a reception. He was exhausted and it was the last thing he needed right then, a row with Brenda over something trivial. Was she annoyed that he had not brought the usual duty free perfume or a designer watch? Surely not this time, what with Tina in hospital and the mad scramble to get a flight back? How could she want anything at all?

"Brenda!" he called out.

"Go back to your Indian floozy, your bloody home," she screamed.

He heard her slam the door of their bedroom. He stood stock still, rooted to the spot. Had he heard her right? What did she know? How did she know?

He trudged up the stairs slowly, deep in thought. The sight at the top of the stairs stopped him dead in his tracks. All over the corridor were boxes from the spare room. They were spread out, an awful mess filling every bit of the landing. His father's memorabilia from his stay in India was scattered all over. Then he recognised some of the boxes from the attic. He held his breath. Years of marriage broken by a few items in an old brown box? How could it unravel at this time? What had she seen? What did she know? His mind could not focus.

His collection of vinyl records, 45's, 78's, Beatles Albums, his souvenirs from the ashram and photographs lay strewn on the floor. He searched for the letter from Rita. There was no sign of it anywhere.

He sat on the top stair, an abject figure with his head in his hands. The jetlag and the whisky made his head feel as if it was splitting down the middle. He closed his eyes and rested his head on the balustrade, hoping this nightmare would end.

All these years a part of his life had been squirreled away in a corner, in an old box, a box of memories that he had never thought would amount to anything. It was scrolling back, spawning tentacles, reaching out to reassert its rightful place in his consciousness. Even more it was slithering dangerously into his relationship with Brenda.

The door of their bedroom opened. Brenda flung his pyjamas out and shut the door again. He got up and knocked on the door.

There was no answer. He could hear her sobs. He grabbed the bottle of whisky and walked slowly up the stairs and into the spare room. He drank till he had finished the bottle, and then lay on the bed, wide-eyed for a while. Later he fell asleep, curled into a foetal position, his tie still hanging askew from his undone collar. Jet lagged and hung over, he heard the noise of movement downstairs.

The smell of freshly-brewed coffee and the sound of the shower woke him up. James took a moment to find his bearings. He slid off the bed, his right shoulder and neck aching slightly. He gingerly stepped down the stairs. The need for a caffeine input was urgent. The bubbling hot coffee in the machine made a hiss as he helped himself; the welcoming aroma filled the room. The hot ceramic on his fingers, the searing hot liquid down his throat was soothing in a strange way. He felt he could face the day now.

Brenda came down in a dark blue velvet track suit. Her hair was wet from the shower, the flowery perfume of her shampoo that was all too familiar to him, made him edge towards her. She took slices of home-made bread, made in the bread machine and put them in the toaster. The delicious aroma filled the room.

"Brenda, we need to talk. Give me a chance to explain..." James beseeched.

Her subterranean hostility lay like a thick blanket around them.

"Our whole life has been a lie." Her voice shook.

Then she turned around and looked directly at him. She looked at him as though he was a stranger to her. Her aloof eyes threw incriminating glances at him.

"Let's hear it then," she challenged.

The slices popped up in the toaster. She put them on a plate, spread some butter on them. The golden blobs melted slowly, filling in the tiny spaces on the toast. She took a new jar of blackberry jam and tried to unscrew the top.

James took the jar from her hand and opened it in a trice. Brenda spread the jam.

"Brenda, it was such a long time ago. Why bring it up now? Listen to me, please."

"I'm waiting," she said, the tone like a whiplash.

They walked over to the conservatory. The pale sun was streaking the sky, a dawn luminescence that spread slowly. James sat down with his coffee. Brenda carried her toast and orange juice, both of them unconsciously following a ritual, a habit of all these years together. She looked at the toast with loathing. She put the plate down as if it did not belong to her.

"Why James, why did you never mention her at all?"

James sipped the coffee, his hands shaking now. He placed the mug on the glass topped wicker table.

"I was nineteen, just a crazy teen in an exotic country," he started.

"So that bank account with all the money going to an Indian address, what was that?"

"Remember how I talked about helping other people? I've been sending that money since our dot.com profits soared. That was when we moved to this house fifteen, or was it seventeen years ago."

"To her, that's why it was a bloody secret?"

Brenda's steely voice with a deprecating smile stung him.

"No of course not, it was to a charity." James squirmed in his seat. Her accusations were annoying him. "Look I had no contact with her at all. I…"

"So why did you keep the bloody things, a stupid wooden box and other measly things from the ashram? What in God's name do they mean to you? I hauled them over to this house when we moved. Christ! What a fool I was. I thought they were your dad's stuff."

"Some of the things are my dad's stuff…,"

"No James, you're lying! I saw the silly things from her, the dumb stuff like a pebble and sheets of silly poems describing her. How could you even think of a *that woman* as a lover?"

She shook her head in despair.

"Brenda! For fuck's sake!"

"Yeah, swear at me all you want but it was your doing."

"Jesus! I've had it with you! You'll never ever understand."

He got up to leave.

Then facing her said in a loud voice, "You'll be glad to know that I had a daughter with her."

"What! A daughter! Amy is your daughter, not some *paki*?" Brenda screamed.

"Fuck off," he screamed back. "I'm going back to India," and he walked out of the room.

She sat transfixed for a few moments, stunned. Then she ran after him, striding up the stairs following him. He went to the bathroom and shut the door in her face.

The two of them sat on either side of the door. Confused, angry, still tired, he stripped and stood under the hot shower. The stinging hot water cascaded down his shoulders, prickling, a sensation that he welcomed. Brenda banged on the door. Primal sounds emanated from her. Expletives that he had never heard her use before now skewered his heart. She threw a heavy object at the door and shouted out: "You won't get away with it. Never!"

He heard her footsteps fading away as she ran down the stairs. He stood under the shower for ages, till his skin was red raw, the toes and fingers almost white at the tips, hating himself, not sure why he had said what he had. Words that could never be taken back again, wounding the person he had loved so much and the mother of his Amy.

He felt sick.

He was torn between doing the right thing by both of the people he felt responsible for, Beth in India and Brenda and Amy who had been with him all his adult life. He came out of the shower. He picked up all the boxes that were still lying around. He put all his father's things back into their boxes and then sat with his things from the ashram.

His life with Rita re-emerged even more strongly. The smell of the camphor incense from the ashram was still in the box when he opened it. Transported back to those heady days, he sat down on the stairs, realising that he could not walk away from that part of his life anymore. He had to at least let Beth know and form some sort of connection with her. That was something he had to do. He owed that to Rita. He owed it to his daughter, Beth.

Brenda ran back to their bedroom and locked the door. She had ignored his pleas to her as she ran up the stairs. He packed a small bag, and then knocked on Brenda's door. She did not open it. He said loudly:

"I'm away for a few days. I'll call you."

The break would hopefully allow Brenda to calm down and maybe understand his feelings too. He drove to an airport hotel and booked the next flight to London as it was easier to get a flight back to India from there. He called her from the hotel but Brenda refused to talk to him.

The next day James was on the flight back to Bombay. The two Indian passengers beside him were talking about the airport bookshops.

"A vending machine for books, a good idea, so much easier and available if you're stuck overnight, as often happens nowadays," said one of them.

"Yeah, just got this Booker winner, Adiga."

The man was showing the book, "The White Tiger" to his

friend.

"India seems to produce a lot of Booker winners."

"Yes, they have some excellent writers of course. Salman Rushdie's Booker of Bookers is set in Bombay."

James's mind strayed from their words. He was grateful when dinner was served and then the lights were switched off. The two co-passengers stopped their conversation and settled into the film that was showing. He put his eye mask on, hoping that he would fall asleep. He was restless, trying to find the right words to tell Beth what he knew. Should he ring her and talk to her first or go and see her and tell her personally? These scenes which kept floating in his mind were interrupted with the words that Brenda had screamed at him.

It was the worst long haul flight that he had ever endured. He arrived in Mumbai looking the worse for wear and exhausted.

Chapter 22

Tina stood at the window of her parents hotel suite. The management had upgraded them free so that Tina could stay with them. A gentle breeze, with a faint perfume of "night queen" the night blooming jasmine or "cestrum nocturnum" wafted in. Mr. Joshi had told her this name when she had asked him about the gorgeous perfume when she had seen the flowers in his house.

The bright stars of a tropical night sky twinkled, silver dots on a velvet background. A meteor streaked through the sky. She breathed in the night air, as if she wanted to fill her whole self with the country, become part of it. Tina loved the warm air at night, the noise, the feeling of life around all the time. She felt at home in India though she missed so many aspects of Glasgow. The changing seasons, when autumn tinged the whole of Scotland in its golden hues, came to her mind. The scrunch of leaves under her winter boots, the crisp and cold air that refreshed her spirits as she walked to school, winding her scarf around tightly to keep out the chill, made her shudder even now on reflection.

The horrific ordeal of 26/11, as it was referred to in the country, left a deep scar. She needed her parents. The crisis had proved how much she loved and missed them, how much she was part of their life, how she was cherished in love of an unquestioning kind. She had recovered physically from the terrifying siege at the Leopold Café in November but there were things worrying her, pulling her in different directions. She had only a month left of her visa and she wanted to stay and be with

Andrew but her parents were desperate to get her back home, concerned about her safety. Also, having got some information about her genetic mother, Tina wanted to try to find her. She spent another restless night.

Morning chores over, she sat reading an article in the India Today, that gave an insight into the terrorist attack, an analysis that was well-researched and asked searching questions of people in authority. Margaret was sitting across from her, doing a Sudoku. It was a peaceful time.

The phone rang. Margaret picked it up. She listened and put the phone down.

"That was Dad. He's managed to get our tickets. We'll be leaving early next week. I'm so relieved." Margaret's tired face brightened a bit.

Tina looked up from the magazine. She was torn again. She wanted to go back home with her parents. Glasgow, after the nightmarish event in Mumbai would be familiar and safe but, she wanted to be with Andrew. The terrorist attack had happened in such a dramatic, unexpected way that she had not even talked to him about what they were going to do when her visa was up in a month's time. She said nothing to her mum. Andrew would be there this evening after work. Tina decided to have a long chat with him.

"I'll start making a list of all that we should do before we leave. There are so many people to thank! You're so lucky to have such good friends, Tina."

Margaret went into the next room and came back with a notepad to make her list.

Andrew called Tina and invited her for a drive in the evening. Her mum gave her permission, rather reluctantly. Tina was going out with Andrew for the first time after her hospitalisation.

Her parents had wanted her within their sight always since they had arrived.

"Don't drive out too far. Text me. Andrew, please don't stay out too long," her mother begged.

Margaret's concern made the young ones giggle once they got into the car. They went to their favourite walkway in Worli seafront. They walked close to the shore line then sat on the sand and relished their time together.

"Andrew, I'm leaving next week. Dad's got the tickets."

Tina's eyes glistened with tears.

"Hey, I thought you had a whole month to go. Was your visa not valid till mid-January?"

"Yeah, but they want to take me back as soon as possible."

"I can understand that. But, gee, what about us?"

Andrew ran his hand through his hair.

"I don't want to leave you. I…I love you Andrew."

Tina held him tightly and tears coursed down her cheeks. He wiped them gently.

"I love you too. I can't live without you."

Andrew kissed her wet eyelids. "Next week! That doesn't give us much time for anything." He looked despondent. "Look I'll do anything to be with you. I don't want you to leave. Shall I have a word with your mum and dad?"

Andrew tried to shake her from her passivity.

"No, Andrew I don't think they'll accept any reason for my staying on here. It's been too traumatic for all of us."

"So you want to leave too?"

"No, Andrew! God, more than anything, I want to stay with you, I do. Oh, I'm so confused."

Tina shook her head.

"Listen, what about your job. It's a kind of contract isn't it? Tell them you need to finish the six months placement," Andrew suggested.

"My parents have already spoken to Dr. Patel. He has been very understanding and fully accepts that I must go back with my parents."

"I'm not letting you go," said Andrew. "I love you too much. We'll work something out." he tried to reassure her.

They watched the waves rising higher and crashing on to the shore. The white foam flowed over the shells and crabs that scuttled in the sand. The awful bombing had brought them even closer. Losing each other again was not something that either of them could bear to think of but they arrived back at the hotel still not sure of how to prevent Tina going back to Glasgow.

"I'll be with you every day. I'll ask for a few days off before you leave," said Andrew as she bade him goodbye.

Margaret was at the door, fussing, making sure that Tina was not too tired after the drive.

"You go straight to bed and take some rest. I'll call you when dinner is ready," she said giving her a cuddle.

Tina washed the sand off her feet and lay on the bed. Only a week left in Mumbai! She closed her eyes. Her mind went blank, the paucity of thought broken by her mum knocking on the door.

"Your favourite, darling, steak and kidney pie. The hotel has been so good to make it for us but I don't know how tasty it will be," she said, as she dished a hot piece of pie onto each plate.

"Looks and smells delicious mum."

Tina pulled up the chair and smiled at Tony who had a napkin tucked under his neck ready for the meal.

"Indian wine that tastes this good! Whatever next?" said Tony sipping his glass of wine then read the label on the bottle, holding it with his other hand.

As soon as they finished the meal, the phone rang. It was Mrs. Fernandez.

"I just heard from Andrew that you're leaving next week, Tina?"

"Yes, auntie."

"You must bring your parents here for dinner."

"I don't think we'll have much time."

Tina tried to excuse herself.

"No, no dear. I insist. David wants to say goodbye to you properly and I must meet your parents and tell them what a charming young girl you are. I'll expect you all on Sunday night. 7pm okay?"

"They too wanted to meet you and thank you but felt that maybe we would be imposing on you auntie."

"Not at all, Tina! I would love to see you all before you leave for Glasgow. Maybe your parents will be able to tell me more about your lovely country Scotland."

*

Tony and Margaret enjoyed their early morning daily stroll. It was pristine, before the day's humidity broke through. On their return, they kept busy, wrapping some of the last minute gifts that they had bought for all who had helped Tina.

The drive to Beth's house was raucous. The roads were jam packed. The cacophony of horns made Margaret wince and hold onto the straps in the car. Keshav, the driver gave fleeting grimaces and nodded when Andrew pointed out the reckless drivers on the road. The brazenness of some drivers who cut in expecting their right of way made the journey scary. By the time they reached the house all four of them wanted a quiet few minutes to compose themselves.

Beth was happy to see them and plied them with a refreshing nimbu pani, fresh lime juice chilled to perfection in a large jug. David and Brian kept the conversation going on the Bollywood stars making a commitment to work for Mumbai and help elect more educated young councillors.

"They didn't care when the terrorists were ripping Mumbai and bombs were affecting the poor markets," said Brian.

"The Taj, their favourite playground, the haunt of the rich gets bombed and they're all making a huge fuss about how they love Mumbai," David agreed.

Andrew moved the chat to cricket and sport to alleviate Tina's feelings of horror at them revisiting the topic of the bombings. Beth checked on the food and reeled off the culinary choices for the evening. She had made a special effort and offered a range of dishes. Sheba, the puppy came rushing in and jumped on Tina. She cuddled the pup and kept her on her lap. Andrew and she exchanged glances, remembering the last time with Sheba.

"David, put Sheba away in the back garden. Let's all go to the dining room," said Beth.

They followed her to the room and sat down.

The dinner was sumptuous. Tony and Margaret marvelled at the Scottish recipes surviving after such a long period in India. They joked about the lack of malt whisky in India and the fact that a company was exporting whisky to Scotland. Brian offered to make the coffee. Beth relaxed. She brought in her yellowed recipe book and they discussed some of the things that could not be made in India, such as "Clooty dumplings" which needed lard, a fat that was not easily available in Mumbai. The smell of fresh brewed coffee was in the air.

The door bell rang. Tina, Margaret and Tony jerked their head up as they heard a familiar voice.

"David, hope I'm not interrupting your evening."

It was James's deep voice, unmistakeable to their ears.

"James, do come in, what a surprise! I thought you were in Glasgow," said David welcoming him in.

"I need to talk to your mum. It's urgent. I know that Tony and Margaret are here."

David looked surprised.

"Keshav the driver told me," James added. "I must see your mum. It's urgent."

All of them crowded into the lounge. Brian was still in the kitchen.

"James, what are you doing here?" Tony asked. The others waited for an answer. James looked tired, unkempt and on edge.

"Beth," he said ignoring the others, "I must talk to you. Privately," he added.

Shaken by his presence and his request, Beth took him to the dining room and the others stayed in the lounge. Brian came out of the kitchen and she ushered him to the lounge. Perplexed he did as she wanted him.

In the lounge, David played a classical DVD on the CD player.

The room was suffused with the strains of Beethoven. They sat down on the sofa, each wondering why James had turned up and wondering about his strange behaviour.

"Beth, let me explain," he began. The candour with which he spoke took her breath away. The tale of the ashram that she had heard so many times from her mother was now being retold by him.

"You're...Jimmy?" she said at last.

"Yes, I'm Jimmy. I'm James Campbell, the same Jimmy that your mum often referred to. That piece of paper with the address

221

on it was in my writing. It was my address in Glasgow. You're my daughter."

She looked at him open-mouthed, not understanding a word of what he was saying. Then, slowly, it sank in. Her father! She had often wanted to meet him but never in her wildest dreams had she thought that she ever would.

"I'm so sorry. I didn't even know about you," James rambled on. "I mean I had lost touch with Rita and…"

He looked at her, alarmed at her blank face.

She just looked at him and smoothed her skirt as if that was all that mattered, the crease of her skirt being flattened out perfectly. James took out a sepia tinted photo of Rita and himself on the banks of the Ganges. Beth took it from him and squinted at. The colours in the photo had almost faded.

"Mum," she said in a whisper. She smoothed her skirt, mumbled something that sounded like, "Oh sweet Lord."

She sat there motionless, as if she had not heard a word that he had said. Then she looked up at him.

"The dimple on the chin! Oh God!"

She rubbed her chin, over the indent. Then she shook her head in disbelief.

"I had to tell you the truth. I can't live with a lie." He said.

James's words came rushing out.

Beth sat staring at him. James and her mum! The shock ran through her whole body. All her life she had wanted to meet this man who had abandoned her mum and her. She had imagined it so many times, how she would hate him and demand answers to all the questions that had preyed on her mind since infancy. Why had he abandoned them? Why had he not replied to her mother's letters? Why had he not looked for her, his daughter? Instead she felt numb. Words were like a discordant noise to her. She tried to get up, felt faint and sat back down. James ran to the kitchen to get water. He was putting the glass to her lips when Brian looked in from the lounge.

"What's happening?"

He leaned over Beth's chair, glowered at James and said sternly, "Leave her alone."

The rest of the guests arrived, looking concerned at Beth and her pale shaking figure. They crowded in at the doorway.

"Mum, mum, are you okay?"

David was beside her.

A sepulchral quiet descended on the house. Sheba barked to be let in. David brought her in. She jumped on Beth's lap and licked her face. Beth held her tightly.

"I'm so sorry. I'll leave now," James said and walked out of the room.

Sensing that there was something serious, Tony, Margaret, Tina and Andrew took their leave and caught up with James.

James looked flushed and shaken. A red patch on his neck had risen way over to his face. He hurried away from them.

"Go with him, Tony, don't leave James alone. He looks awful," said Margaret.

She joined Tina and Andrew and they got into their car.

Tony hailed a taxi.

"Are you staying at the Regency?" he asked James.

"Yes," nodded James.

The driver played some plaintive Bollywood ballad. It seemed the right soulful tune for the drive. He tapped to the beat on his steering wheel and shook his head to the tune. The music played as background as James tried to find words to explain what had happened, to Tony.

"I had to see Beth, tell her the truth," James said after a short pause.

"The truth?"

Tony arched his eyebrows in question, not sure what James was referring to.

"Beth...is my daughter," James stated.

It was Tony's turn to be stunned. He tried to grapple with words to say something.

"Did I hear you right? Oh my God! How can that be?"

James took nearly all of the drive to describe the whole saga to him.

"Tony, I had to tell Beth, right?" He was looking for some support.

"Of course but Jesus, this is so incredible! I mean you having a daughter all those years ago!"

Tony was still coming to terms with this incredible news.

"Brenda can't understand at all."

James looked angry thinking of his short stay in Glasgow.

"It's too much to take in, even for me. It can't be easy for her. Give her time."

"No, I don't think Brenda will accept this at all."

James rubbed his hands together. Tony tapped him on the shoulder.

"James, I'm sure it will get better with time."

James told him of the scene at Glasgow and the futility of him trying to explain to Brenda. "For God's sake, even I didn't know Beth existed till I came here." He said.

He recounted all that had happened between Brenda and him. Tony listened to him, still reeling from the incredible story. The taxi arrived at the hotel.

"Christ we both a need a drink!" said Tony, as they made their way in.

The bar at the Regency was not busy but there was one table where a group of men looked as if they were doing a business deal. Tony watched and heard them as he walked to the bar to tell the waiter that they were waiting for some service. The only waiter available was serving the group.

Tony listened inadvertently. His mind was still on what James had said. The waiter put the bottle and crystal glasses on a tray on their table. One of the men, important-looking and fat, looked at the bottle as the waiter laid it on the table and tutted.

"You call this whisky?" he read the label.

"Bag Pipers" made from molasses. I'd rather drink proper Scotch. Get me the real McCoy, waiter."

"Yes, sir," said the waiter, hastily taking the bottle off the tray.

"So you can get real Scotch here?" asked one of them with an American accent

"Sure Roy, it was always available on the black market. Now we can afford to get the best in the world."

Tony noticed his imperious wave to the waiter.

"The Scots want our Indian market. Lots of Scots' companies are here now to sell genuine whisky to the young millionaires who have more money than sense."

His pride in the new wealthy India showed.

When the waiter came over, Tony ordered a 'real' whisky each and they nursed their drinks. James's words were spent. He sat gloomily but seemed glad of Tony's presence. The peaty taste of the whisky was soothing. They both sighed at the day's events.

"Things will look better in the morning, James," he said and got up to bid him goodbye. Then on second thoughts he decided to see him to his room.

"You'll call me if you need me, right?" he asked James.

"I'm fine. Now that I've told Beth, I feel better, and talking to you helped too" said James. "Don't worry about me."

Tony headed back to the hotel. He said nothing to Tina or Margaret at first, "Just some business worries because of all this bombing," he said, "James is stressed out." But Margaret kept questioning him in the bedroom. He gave in finally, requesting her not to say anything to Brenda as he felt it was up to James to patch things up with her first.

"James is Beth's father! He's a dark horse that one," said Margaret.

Chapter 23

Tina and her parents were to leave for Glasgow in two days. The room was filled with suitcases in various stages of packing. Tony made a list of medicines that they might need for Tina. Margaret had written her thank you cards and was checking to make sure that she had included all the hospital junior staff, the embassy people and all of Tina's friends at the clinic and outside.

Althea had organised a send-off party for Tina and her parents. It was a low key affair with a simple meal at the Regency but it was a poignant one for Tina in many ways. Althea gave her a hand-made booklet with photos and had included in it some funny incidents that had taken place, using a comic sans font. The cover had a cartoon caricature picture of Tina and Andrew. Others gave her beautiful pieces of jewellery or silk scarves. Friendships that she had made in a short time now were something to treasure for life.

Parting with Andrew was the biggest wrench.

"Andrew you won't forget me, will you?" Tina implored.

"How could I? You are my life Tina. I'm going to visit you in Glasgow if you can't come back here."

"Andrew, will you promise me one thing?" asked Tina. Her tone was serious.

"Will you promise to look for E. A. Thomas for me?"

"Of course I will! I'll do my best. I know how much it means to you."

"Andrew, I don't know how I can live without you. This is awful," she cried.

"Hush, sweetheart. I'll find some way for us to be together. Maybe if I find her, you'll come back to Mumbai! Or I may even whisk you off to USA once I get into my Masters course there."

"Oh Andrew what if I can never see you again? I couldn't bear that."

"Hey, Tina, it's our last day together; let's make it a day to remember. Just leave it to me," he said and kissed her gently.

They stood at the altar of Mount Mary church in Bandra. They knelt and prayed together, a brief moment to give thanks for her lucky escape on that dreadful night of November 26th. Andrew lit a candle and prayed that they would meet again, soon. Tina was touched by his sincerity. When they came out on to the steps of the church they could see the Arabian Sea.

"God always gets the perfect spot, doesn't he?" Andrew said quietly.

They ate some bhel puri and then drove along Marine Drive.

The December breeze from the sea was cooling. They made a special effort to get their favourite spot on the beach and watched the waves ceaselessly moving in an age-old fashion. Nothing had changed in nature here. Andrew held her left hand and slipped a gold ring with a tiny ruby, her birthstone, onto her finger.

"This will keep me close to you always," he said kissing her.

"It's our unofficial engagement. We've had no time to organise one. You're mine; I love you, Tina Brown."

"Oh Andrew, it's beautiful, you shouldn't have."

Tears of joy moistened her eyelashes.

She looked at the ring, surprised at how it fitted her perfectly. They kissed and clung to each other wordlessly for a while, both wishing that they did not have to part so soon.

*

The airport was crowded. Once they neared the check-in counter Tina burst into tears, clung to Andrew and refused to leave him. Tony and Margaret tried their best to persuade her but she refused.

"Mum, dad, I'll have to come back as soon as my visa expires, please let me stay with Andrew. It's only a month, I want to be with him, please and I'm so much better now," she pleaded. Margaret held her tight.

"I can't go back without you…oh God I nearly died when I heard about the bomb."

"Look at me. I'm fine. Please let me stay," Tina appealed to Tony.

He took Margaret gently to one side and reasoned with her.

"She wants to be with Andrew, you can see that clearly," he said.

Margaret nodded. Tina hugged them both, gratefully and then they joined the tiny crowd that had assembled to wave them off. Rashmi, The Joshis, Althea, and David reassured Tony and Margaret that they would look after Tina. They left reluctantly, Margaret clinging to Tony. On the plane, Margaret looked out of the window.

"We've lost her, my Tina. I can't bear this," she cried to Tony

"Shush, she has Andrew there and you know Margaret that one day, she would leave with her young man so maybe we need to accept this. She'll be in Glasgow next month as soon as her visa is up," Tony comforted her.

Margaret wiped her tears. Only eighteen short years with a child that she had longed for all her life! The years had flown like a twinkle of her eye. She had undergone so much to have Tina and now she had to part with her.

All childhood is emigration.

A phrase that she had read somewhere came to her mind. She sighed.

Tina waved them goodbye then whispered to Andrew,

"See, I couldn't bear to leave you."

He patted her arm and held her close.

The next day Andrew and Tina drove straight to Thane. He had brought the piece of paper with the details of E.A. Thomas. The drive took them a good two hours. Luckily, despite the numerous new buildings that had sprouted in Thane, the old building with the same address was still standing.

They knocked on the door. There was no answer. On an impulse they knocked on the door next to it. An old woman opened the door, just a chink, and peered out.

"What do you want? I'm not buying anything today, jao, jao," she said, shooing them away, thinking they were salespeople.

"I'm sorry to disturb you Madame, but I'm looking for an E.A. Thomas," said Andrew.

She opened the door a bit wider and looked at him. The well-dressed young man could not be a salesman. He spoke with a foreign accent and addressed her respectfully. She was impressed, felt she could trust him. The girl beside him looked frail and quiet.

"I'm Andrew Saldana. I need to find her."

"The Thomas's? Oh they were a lovely family, here a long time ago. They moved out, no longer here."

"Do you have their address? I must see them," said Andrew.

She hesitated.

"It's really important. Please," he said.

"Are you related? Family?" she asked, the door getting opened wider with each question.

"Well I am kind of…," he blushed at telling a white lie. If that was the only way to get information, he told himself, he had to resort to that.

She looked him up and down. He seemed a decent person. She decided to help him. The girl beside him was quiet.

"I have an old address but they may have moved on. Come in. I'll find it for you."

She invited them in.

They saw her properly now that they were in the room. She was a frail woman, dressed in a cotton frock that seemed to be following a 1950's fashion. She wore thick glasses. Her hair was in a neat, short bob but was thin and some of her scalp could be seen. The room looked as if it was in a time warp from the 1950"s. There was a wicker seat to sit on and the blades of a ceiling fan moved languidly, hardly creating any movement in the air. Andrew noticed she had a Bakelite radio that was on the top of an old side board along with lots of photographs. There were piles of newspapers in a corner. Lacy headrests, some with greasy marks, were on the backs of old, wicker cushioned seats. There was also a tiny shrine with a picture of Jesus and a tea light burning in a small holder. Bright yellow plastic flowers, covered with dust, were in a tarnished silvery-looking vase. A picture of a tall man in a suit hung on the wall. A garland in sandalwood flowers adorned the photograph.

The old woman busied herself looking for the address in a small telephone address book. The pages rustled as she searched for the name. She continued talking as she searched.

"I was her very close friend, almost a mother to her. We attended the same church you know."

She looked up.

"Not in this book," she said, more to herself than Andrew.

There was a tiny drawer in the table under the shrine. She opened it carefully and rummaged through the drawers. An old bound notebook with a marbled design cover in blue with a black spine was what she was looking for. She held it up triumphantly.

"Here it is," she crowed, happy to have found it.

She sat down on a rocking chair that Andrew noticed was near the shrine. As she flicked the pages she seemed to be lost in her own world for a few moments. She mumbled, "Oh yes, these people too, not seen them in years," then "Ah, such a beautiful baptism that day," she said taking out a sepia photo and handing it to Andrew. He took it politely, wondering when she was going to give him the address.

"Elizabeth and George. A lovely young couple," she reminisced. "Such suffering to get a baby! They went through that IFV, IVF or what is it? You know, test tube baby thing."

Andrew nodded, "Yes, IVF," he said.

Tina stayed silent. The old lady looked at her.

"She gave birth to a beautiful baby boy named him after his grandfather. I baked a cake for his first birthday, I remember like it was yesterday, a cake shaped like a car. It took me ages to make it but it turned out beautiful."

"So when did they move?"

Andrew wanted to get her back to the present.

"Terrible! Terrible time for that poor girl! Just before the baby's second birthday George died." She shook her head. "He died at work, you know, at work, dreadful. But oh dear! Such suffering for a young girl." The old lady sucked on her false teeth, which Andrew noticed only now.

"How awful! So, did she go back to her parents or…"Andrew was interrupted.

"That poor girl had no one. Her mum had died just a year before. Sad, very sad. Like me, she had no one, just her step dad."

She wiped her face with a clean handkerchief.

Andrew waited for her to get her breath back. He could see that the story had taken its toll. She had obviously been close to the family.

"Elizabeth realised she could not stay here with George gone. Too many memories. She bought a small house and moved away, to Bandra. Here is the address." She handed him the book. He quickly took a note of it in a little book that he had brought with him and gave it back to her.

Andrew was about to ask her more questions but decided that he had tired her out already.

"Thank you so much Mrs…," he said.

"Mary, Mary Cummings," she said.

"Thank you Auntie Mary, you've been most helpful." he said.

"We'll take our leave now."

She gave them a big smile.

"Oh I didn't even offer you a glass of water. Wait! Let me get you at least a *Limca.*"

"No please, this is so helpful, we can't thank you enough. We must go now."

"If you see Elizabeth, please tell her I'm still here and would love to see her and her little boy again," said the old lady.

They sat in the car and looked at the address. Bandra was at least on the way back home.

"We'll take the EE highway," Andrew said to Tina. She nodded. "Thank God it is not in Colaba or the southern most tip of Mumbai. Are you okay, you've not said a thing?" he said glancing at Tina.

"I'm okay. Just nervous about this whole thing," she said softly.

He glanced at his watch. The crazy peak traffic time was imminent. The commuters and the people would be rushing home from work. The highway would be busy too. His mobile had pinged a few times. It was his mom.

"Andrew, I've not seen you for ages. Where are you?"

"Mom, I'm busy. I'll be late tonight. Don't wait up for me."

"Andrew I know you're upset that Tina has left, but…come home son."

"It's not that. I have a project for work. I'm busy. I'll call you when I'm free."

He switched off his phone. He did not want to tell her that Tina was still in Mumbai. He felt tense and irritated with his mom for no reason at all.

Finding E. A. Thomas had become his mission too now.

But it was not his day. The house was in darkness when they reached Bandra. The whole family were out celebrating their son's birthday. The red balloon on the doorstep had, "Happy Birthday Son" written in gold on it. They were disheartened and tired. Andrew left his business card and a note saying he would be grateful if they could call him and left. He drove Tina back to the Joshis.

"I'm sure we'll find her," he said, though his voice was low. Tina gave him a light kiss and went in. She was quiet, so unlike her. He could sense her tension and anxiety.

His mom was waiting up for him.

"Andrew, you look so tired. Have some dinner."

"In a minute," he said and went to his room.

She followed him.

He lay on his bed. The cool of the air-conditioning was what he needed. He wondered if they would find this E.A. Thomas. It meant so much to Tina. Now that her parents were away, she was more intent on fulfilling her quest.

His mom sat on his bed.

"Everything happens for a reason. Don't be upset. You're both young. Soon she'll forget you."

"For God's sake, leave me alone!" he exploded.

She saw the anger in his face and slunk out of the room.

Chapter 24

In Glasgow Brenda had been busy trying to get her life into order. She had decided to put her husband's junk from India into boxes and throw it out. She'd spent her life looking after him and this was how he repays her. It was a betrayal of the worst kind and she'd decided to take action. There was only one place for him and his things. The bin. She was interrupted by a phone call.

"Mum why did you call me in the middle of the night? Bobby was furious. What was the emergency? Thought you would be used to rowing with dad by now?"

"Typical of you Amy, you never support me."

Brenda started to cry.

"Stop, for God's sake, what's happened? Please tell me."

It took Brenda a while to stop crying then between sniffles and sobs she explained that James had had a "floozy in India" all those years ago.

"It was before you got married that he was in India. Why bring it up now?" Amy was bemused.

"You know how gullible he is? He's only got himself some harlot in India saying that she's his daughter and he's left me," she wailed.

"Pull yourself together. I'm sure Dad wouldn't have left you. Where would he go?"

"He… he said he was going back to India." Brenda sobbed.

"So you think he's going to live there! Mum! You're angry and not thinking right. Shall I call Auntie Margaret to come and help you?"

"Don't you dare! It's because of *her* daughter that all this carry on started."

"Poor Tina was injured in the bomb blast!"

"I know, I know but James would've come straight back from his work if not for that stupid, stupid girl."

"Remember you were all praise for her when she was wee and she saved me from…"

"Oh shut up Amy! She's not a bloody heroine. Look what she's done now, broken up our family."

"Calm down. I'll call you later when you can make some sense out of it all. I'm sure dad hasn't left you. I'll call him on his mobile now. Don't do anything rash. I'll call you back after I talk to him."

Brenda heard the click as Amy put the phone down. She sat down and calmed a bit. It felt good to have got her anger off her chest. She felt tired and forgot all about the boxes.

I can't let him get away with this nonsense, she thought to herself.

Amy called again.

"Look dad tells me he has not left you. He just needed to go back to finish some work in India. He'll be back soon."

"Will he now? I'll see that he gets what he deserves when he gets back. Don't you worry your pretty little head, Amy," she said.

"Well you sound more like your usual self but don't be harsh on dad. He must've said something in anger. He's the sweetest person."

"Amy, stop advising me. I know him better than you."

Brenda put the phone down.

She knew exactly what to do. She had spent the time planning her revenge. She got dressed and left for Glasgow with a list of places to go and people to see, starting with their lawyer. She rang for an appointment.

Brenda parked in Buchanan Galleries car park to get to her lawyer's office in the city centre. She was tempted by the shops, walked into John Lewis, and then decided that she really must get her life in order first. She strode into the office. The whiff of her Chanel perfume filled the room as she sat down in front of Graham Wilson-Smythe.

"What can I do for you Brenda?"

He smiled benignly.

"Everything," she said.

"I need to check all the papers, get the deeds for the house, the villa in Spain and the company."

Her face was flushed but she cast a challenging look at him, as if daring him to argue with her.

"It sounds drastic, what exactly for?"

He twirled his pen and placed it on the table as she glowered at him.

"I want every penny in my name. James's behaviour is appalling. I need you to change all the property over to me entirely."

She looked at him, the triumphant edge to her voice carried over strident and clear.

"Brenda, you're not thinking straight. It's not so straight forward or easy."

He shook his head.

"What do you mean? Surely everything is in our joint names."

She edged forward on her seat, tossed her head up and looked at him, the eyes smouldering with anger.

"Well, not everything for a start. James made a few changes when the chancellor imposed the inheritance tax."

His glasses slid down to the tip of his nose. She resented his patronising glance.

"Eh? He never said anything to me."

She twiddled her fingers, the rings on her left hand felt heavy and intrusive. She eased the skin around the rings as if they were hurting her.

"It was all for your benefit. You don't want a huge sum going to the chancellor, do you?"

"No, of course not. But you're confusing me now. Tell me exactly how I can clean him out."

He noticed her red nail varnish which matched the bright post-box red lipstick as she flicked a strand of hair from her eyes and tucked it behind her ear. The diamond solitaire in her ear twinkled.

"Let's take this step by step. The deeds of houses, the home in Glasgow and the one in Spain are in Amy's name."

"Jesus Christ! What do you mean?"

She jumped up from her chair.

"Remember when the accountant advised you, three years ago I think, about the inheritance tax. You must sign over the house at least seven years before either of your deaths, so you signed the house away to Amy. The company is entirely in James's name. You were never a partner, only a member of the board, an honorary one at that. Let me check. Sit down."

He called his PA and asked her to bring J. Campbell's file in.

Brenda sat in the chair, devastated at the realisation that her little plan might not work as she thought.

She was right.

She left the office dejected, walked to the bank, and withdrew all the money that she could lay her hands on and spent as much as she could. Ingram Street with the Italian Centre was the recipient of her shopping splurge. She got to the car laden with bags, her anger and frustration stuffed into designer bags, dresses that she'd never wear and shoes that were uncomfortable even when she tried them on but good to show off and add to her collection. The swell of anger changed to one of extreme exhaustion. She could turn to no one. She wanted to destroy James. Everything that she thought had been wonderful in their lives was now just a sham.

She drove back home, her mind scheming about ways of hurting James and not coming up with any plans that would really satisfy her. She reached her door. The absolute quiet of her home when she turned the key was eerie.

The phone started ringing as soon as she entered the house. A narrow strip of light came streaming from the safety lamp that switched on automatically when they were out. Everything felt strange. She had been home alone many times when James was away for his business trips but this was different. Her obsessive jealousy could not see past the fact that he had left for India in anger, claiming to go and see his daughter. To Brenda, Amy, James and herself were what she regarded as family, not even her son-in-law Bobby or her grandson whom she saw rarely. This tight knit threesome was her world, her security which nothing would break. In the dark of the house she felt as if she was waking up and the dream of her life was evaporating.

She let the phone ring, threw the bags on the floor and ran up the stairs and lay on her bed. Eyes wide open, glazed with uncertainty, she lay on the duvet and stared at the ceiling. She pulled a pillow out on which traces of James's aftershave lingered, she hugged it close to her.

I love him still, she thought, the line between love and hate blurring as she sat up and looked round the room, at their wedding photo, at the other one of James holding Amy and Brenda standing beside him, a proud mum.

I can't live without him. I need him. He's mine. I'll not let him go, she told herself. She got off the bed.

When Amy got her on the phone, at last, it was a different Brenda that she spoke to. Her mum's capriciousness did not surprise Amy. She was glad that her mother's anger had subsided and she sounded calm and collected.

"Mum, you sound so much better. Call me as soon as Dad gets back. Don't row with him again. I'm sure you misunderstood what he said. It was the shock of seeing Tina in hospital and the terrorism in India that must have unnerved him. Take care."
She rang off.

Brenda had days before James arrived back. She decided to tackle him in a different way. She would be all sweetness and light and make him promise that he'd forget that "bastard daughter" of his in India. She was going to make sure that her family was going to be strong and together again. James would never give her up, or Amy. She needed to be tactful, understanding and yet thwart any attempts that that girl from India might make to get hold of him or his affections. She knew her own strength.

Brenda bided her time and even called James and apologised and asked him to come back to Glasgow as soon as he could. She had the trump card. She *was* the trump card. She was his wife. No one was going to upset her life and family. Her family and her life were in her hands now. She would fight tooth and nail to keep what was hers.

Chapter 25

James arrived back home to find Brenda in high spirits. She had cooked a meal, had the house all tidied up and even told him that all his stuff from India had been neatly boxed and put away in his study. She hugged and kissed him and asked about his trip. She apologised profusely, saying that her behaviour before had been totally unreasonable.

"Will you forgive me James? I don't know what came over me. Must be because I love you so much, I couldn't take it all in."
He was trying to explain the circumstances to her but she put a stop to it.

"James, I'm so hurt about what happened between us, all my fault of course. Why don't we spend out first evening together, just be about ourselves. I love you James, you're my life you know."

She nestled in his arms and pressed herself into him. He responded as she had wanted. She cooked him a lovely meal that they ate by candlelight and he relaxed with his whisky, thankful that he had come home to his old Brenda again. However, as soon as they got into bed, the jetlag made him fall asleep. Brenda was disappointed. She had wanted to make love to her, patch up their misunderstanding and understand her need for him.
Next morning, James was relishing his full Scottish breakfast with two eggs, bacon, a square sausage, beans, tomatoes, mushrooms and fried bread.

"Good to be home," he said tucking into the huge helping. Brenda had just filled the tea pot with fresh tea when the phone rang.

It was Margaret.

"Could we come over and see James? There's so much to talk about. We want to know how Tina is coping."

"Of course, you're most welcome. You can come anytime. We're home all day," she said smiling at James.

"See you in an hour then."

Margaret rang off. She winked at Tony.

"Something's up, she's not her usual grumpy self."

They both laughed.

"You're too hard on her," said Tony.

"So would you be if she had been your sister."

"Thank God I've been spared that," said Tony. "It must be my good karma."

They laughed again and got ready to leave for Brenda's.

They arrived as Brenda and James were talking to Amy on Skype. They were watching their grandson run around and show off his new toy. Margaret and Tony joined in to say 'Hi' to Amy.

"I'd better be off then," Brenda said.

"Mum, wait! I've some really exciting news for you."

Amy brought a rolled up piece of paper and unfolded it.

"Well I did my bit of family tree here and guess what Bobby's family is so fascinating. Mum you'll never believe."

She held up the family tree for all to see on the computer.

"Look, Bobby's mum was an Inuit. Well at least that's her heritage. Isn't she gorgeous?"

"So that's where little Jamie gets his dark looks from," said Margaret.

"Yep, he sure is a true Canadian, like his dad," Amy said proudly, putting on a Canadian accent.

Brenda was very quiet. She swallowed hard. Her face went pale. She looked at the family tree and saw the chart showing Bobby's family's First Nations' forefathers clearly with their tribal names

243

and the dates of the marriages. Her heart was beating fast. Her face now turned a bright red as the blood gushed up from her neck upwards.

"Amy," she said after a pause, "I'll speak to you later. I need to look after Margaret and Tony."

"Of course mum, but I'm so proud and happy now that Auntie Margaret also knows. I mean isn't it great that Tina is Indian and we have another Indian in our family now."

Brenda was gripping the computer table, the whites of her knuckles showing. She managed a slight grin.

"Amy, sweetheart, as I said they want to talk to dad, so bye darling."

She switched the computer off as little Jamie and Amy waved a bye to all of them.

"Well how's that for news, eh?"

Tony slapped his knee. James was quiet. He glanced at Brenda.

"I'll make some tea," said Brenda and started towards the kitchen.

"I'll help," said Margaret and followed her.

They bustled about the kitchen in silence. James and Tony talked about the trip back, the airport strictures about not carrying liquids and the queues in the security section.

Brenda came back with the tea tray. Margaret brought some biscuits on a plate.

"James, how is Tina?   Tell me how she's coping. How's Andrew?"

"Give the man a chance," said Tony. "So many questions. Let's have some tea first."

"I'm sorry. You know that I'm anxious about Tina, especially since that dreadful attack in November. Is she okay James?"

"Fine. You know she's got Andrew with her for support. You both know she has made such good friends there, so nothing to worry about at all."

"She sounded a bit worried. I don't know if that's the right word, but I wondered if you noticed anything," Margaret insisted.

"Might as well tell you everything now, I suppose." James began.

"James!" Brenda warned, "I'm sure Margaret can talk to Tina if she's that worried."

"I wouldn't be here if I wasn't worried. What's it James? Please tell us. Should we ask her to come back? Has she broken up with Andrew or is there any health worry that she's not telling us about?"

James related the whole story to them. He started from his trip to Rishikesh, his love for Rita, the birth of Beth.

"Oh my God! Do we have to tell everyone?"

A strangled sound of disbelief came from Brenda. She stood up, paced up and down, shaking her head.

"James, we knew about this. Tony had told me all about it but this had to come from you, you understand," Margaret said gently.

James nodded. Brenda stormed out of the room. Margaret and Tony said their goodbyes quickly to let James deal with Brenda. They drove back in silence, lost in their own thoughts.

Chapter 26

The next day, Andrew got up, showered and switched on his iBook. It was well past midnight. There was new email in the spam box from someone he did not know. He saw the word Bandra and moved the email to his inbox and opened it immediately.

Hi Andrew,

Saw your note about E.A. Thomas. We bought this flat from Elizabeth ten years ago. We have no forwarding address. Sorry. Good luck with your search.

Shankar Roy

A blind end! Where next? How could you find one person in a city of nineteen million people? It was hopeless but at least he had tried, he told himself.

He walked over to the kitchen, warmed up the briyani that his mum had left for him and then made himself a strong cup of coffee. He stayed up, waiting for Tina's mobile call. The Xbox kept him amused. The mobile pinged.

She had text him:
Love you tons. Missing you.
Shd we try findg E.A. Th agn 2moro?
T xxxxx

Sure hun. He replied.

Their attempts at finding E. A. Thomas seemed to be in vain. After five days they decided to call it a day and enjoy the little time that they had left together.

The Arabian Sea was at its fiercest in Mumbai. The tide was in and the waves were huge, crashing onto the wall. Andrew and Tina sat on the wall off the walkway, looking at Mother Nature's strength. The full moon in the sky was casting a bright light on the darkening night. People always said that the tide was strong on full moon days. A myth, they said, but it often proved to be true.

"It's wonderful to be here with you, Andrew. I never thought I would be able to."

Tina nestled in his arms.

"I'm so glad you're here," he said crushing her in a bear hug. The ruby ring on her finger twinkled in the light as he lifted her hand to kiss it. She felt complete apart from one thing.

"I can't get her out of my mind. I've been thinking about the last address of E.A. Thomas," she said. "There must be some other way of tracing her. Should we try that old lady, Mary, again?" asked Tina.

"No I think she told us all she knew." Andrew's brow puckered.

Tina caught his arm

"What about the church? They must have some record of her wedding." She hesitated over the words, not sure if it was of any use.

"What a great idea, Tina! Let's visit the Catholic Church she was married in. It must have been a local one"

Andrew's voice could not hide his excitement. She looked up surprised at his reaction, still doubting her own assumption that things might still work out. He felt a renewed sense of urgency and started making plans about how to approach the church, who to contact. He told her that they should pursue the lead vigorously.

She loved his enthusiasm.

They set off the next morning after surfing the net for Catholic churches. St. Peters in Bandra was the nearest to her last address. The church was huge, able to hold a congregation of a thousand people. They looked with awe at the huge rows of pew and the amazing altar. As they expected, the church held meticulous records. The priest in the office, Father Ignatius, was helpful. Once he heard the reason for their search he agreed to open the files but suggested that if there was such a person he would not divulge the address till he had talked to her first.

"How many years ago did you say it was?" Tina asked.

"Let's see now," said Father Ignatius as he took the red ledger and turned the pages till he came to the letter T.

"E.A. Thomas, the name rings a bell but I'm not sure, let's see." He continued turning the pages of the old tome carefully.

"Yes, there was a Elizabeth Thomas, you are right, from *Thane*. She gave a donation for the restoration."

The priest laughed.

"Thomas, of course! I forgot she remarried and changed her name."

They exchanged glances. Tina had turned pale.

"Father, is there any way of finding out where she has moved to or when?" Andrew asked him.

"Moved? No, son the whole family is in Bandra. She still attends our church. Her married name is Fernandez. She lives quite close by. She's a very good person."

"Fernandez!" Both Tina and Andrew looked at each other. "In Bandra? Not Brian, Beth and their son David!" Andrew exclaimed.

"Christ, oh sorry father," he apologised and then turned towards Tina.

"Ah, so you know the family. Yes, her husband calls her Beth. Sorry I didn't remember her name was Thomas. It was such a long time ago."

Andrew was more concerned about Tina who had turned pale and was shaking.

"Are you all right my dear?" asked the priest as Andrew pulled up a chair for her. She nodded and sat down on it, holding the edge of the seat with her shaking hands.

When she had calmed down a bit, they thanked the priest and left hurriedly. The priest's puzzled expression followed them as they left the office. He hurried after them.

They sat on a pew in the huge hall as Tina had started shaking again.

"Beth, Mrs. Fernandez," Tina was saying softly, not quite believing what she had heard.

Father Ignatius sat down beside her.

"My child, this is a huge matter. You need time to collect your thoughts and approach this very carefully. A lot of lives are going to be affected. Come with me, let's talk about this more."

"Father, I'm so grateful to you but I really need to figure out what to do now. Please will you make sure you don't tell Beth anything till I see her? I promise I'll think carefully first."
Tina had found her voice but was worried about what she needed to do.

"I understand, child. Take your time and if you need to talk to me, I'm here to help," replied the priest.

He left them and made his way back to the office.

Tina was nervous; she held Andrew's hand tightly.

"Maybe I should just go there and tell her right away. Do you think it would be right to do that Andrew? I'm so confused."

"I don't know that there is a right way to do this," Andrew said gently. "It's wonderful that you were able to trace her against all odds."

"Andrew, I don't know what to do."

Tina bit her nails, something she hadn't done for years.

"You need to take it slowly. Why don't you wait another day or two? You've waited all your life."

"You're right Andrew," she whispered.

They left the church. The midday heat hit them when they came outside. The humidity was high. They felt the sweat seeping through their clothes. Andrew guided her into a restaurant's air-conditioned cool. He ordered coca-colas and they sat sipping the drinks. The bubbles rose as she sipped the drink through the straw. Tina's heart beat fast. Scenes of meeting Beth, the high tea in her house and the blood transfusion came flooding back to her. Beth's blood was coursing through her veins. She had bequeathed her life, not once but twice.

Tina spent the next day in her room, thinking about meeting Beth again. She finally summoned enough courage and rang her.

"Mrs. Fernandez, it's me Tina. Could I come and see you this afternoon? Are you free?"

"Tina, how nice to hear from you? Do you want to come this evening? David and Brian would be there and Andrew could come along. I could cook you something tasty."

"No thanks. I'd love to talk to you on your own if I may. Is two o'clock okay?"

"Sure, I'll bake some melting moments for you."

"Thanks, that's so kind of you. I'll see you. Bye."

Tina put the phone down and bit her nails again.

Andrew held her hand, pointing to her nails, ragged and chewed.

"Tina, you need to chill a bit. Are you sure you want to go by yourself? I could take some more time off work and come with you, if you want," Andrew offered.

"No thanks, this is something I must do on my own."

Tina was quite clear about that.

She took a taxi and arrived on the dot at two. Mrs. Fernandez opened the door. Sheba barked wildly, happy to see Tina again. Tina scooped her up, but her eyes were on Mrs. Fernandez. Her blue dress suited Beth. Flushed with the baking that she had just taken out from the oven, she looked younger today, fresh and happy.

"Come to the kitchen," she said, "I'm taking the biscuits out."

The heavenly smell of baking that came out of the oven teased Tina's senses in a delicious way.

Beth placed the biscuits on a cooling rack, and then took out some china plates for serving them.

"Let them cool a bit. How do you like your tea Tina? A tea bag dunked in the cup or the Indian chai with milk and sugar all added."

"I'd prefer just a cold drink, if you don't mind," said Tina.

"Yes, it must be hot outside. I'll get you some fresh juice."

Beth opened the fridge and got the jug of lime juice that was always prepared and ready. She poured the juice into two glasses and added some ice cubes. The tray with the glasses and the biscuits were carried over to the dining room.

"I know why you want to talk to me alone," said Beth winking at Tina.

"You want to ask me about young Andrew. Am I right? I can vouch for him."

"I know Andrew, I love him." Tina hesitated, blushing slightly, wondering how to start the topic.

"He's a really good young man. Both of you make a lovely pair."

Beth sipped her juice then took the plate of biscuits and offered it to Tina. She took a biscuit and put it on her plate.

"No, it's not about Andrew. It's actually, it's about something else."

Tina bit her nail, and then conscious of her habit, she hastily took her hand out of her mouth.

"These melting moments are not as good today. I usually add..." Beth chewed a piece and looked up at her. How appropriate, thought Tina, she cleared her throat.

"Mrs. Fernandez, Beth," Tina interrupted her. "David. When you had David?"

"Yes, what about David?"

Her eyebrows arched up.

"He was a test tube baby..."

Tine hesitated, her voice barely a whisper.

"Did someone tell you he was a test tube baby? Everyone knows, Tina. I've not kept it a secret if that's what you're worried about."

"I don't know how to..."

Tina bit her nail again.

"You know that I was working at the Patel Clinic."

"Yes, I know. In fact I even told David that's where his life began."

She smiled innocently.

"I... I'm... I found your records...I'm one of the embryos which you donated to the clinic."

There was a pause, a stunned silence, almost as if time stood still. Then the biscuit fell from Beth's hand. She smoothed her dress, disregarding the pieces of biscuit on the floor. They could both hear Sheba munching the biscuit pieces. The puppy looked up for more. Instinctively Tina picked up the puppy. Sheba squirmed in her arms, struggling to reach for the biscuits on the table.

"You mean…" Beth started then stopped.

"Sweet Jesus, forgive me."

She crossed herself.

"I…I'm… so sorry I didn't mean for any of this to happen," Tina's eyes filled with tears.

Sheba leaped out of her arms onto the table. She picked her up again and put her on the floor.

"My God, I don't know what to say."

Beth stood up smoothed her sky blue dress, and then sat down again. They glanced at each other, looking for some clue, something that might bind them together. There was an awkward silence broken only by the antics of the puppy. Each crunch of Sheba's stolen biscuit sounded louder.

Beth came round and gave Tina a hug. She held her at arms' length as if to look at her with new eyes. They held each other and cried. They sat across from each other again and Tina told her all she knew. There were awkward pauses, both trying to choose the right words but neither knew what the right words were. Suddenly the dam burst. They spoke for hours.

"The five embryos, yes I asked them to put in only the two male ones. Oh I'm so sorry," Beth apologised. "This is unreal. I never, never, thought about what would happen to the other eggs."

Beth's thoughts were confused as she tried to piece the bits together. Her mind darted back to the scene about the choice that she had made at the clinic. She on husband George's insistence chose two male eggs to be inserted.

Tina explained how she had been looking for an E. A. Thomas and told of the shock when she learnt that her married name was

Fernandez. They held each other's hands and noticed they shared identical fingers

Slowly, the incredible tale unravelled, their connection more intriguing as they found similarities. They both had a good head for figures, more inclined to science and maths than the arts. They giggled at their interest in Sudoku puzzles, a pastime that they both enjoyed. They talked and yet there were so many unanswered questions that racked both their minds, neither willing to ask the questions that mattered.

What would happen now? How would both sets of families react to this new relationship? And, Jimmy? Thought Beth.

It was too much to cope with. She had found her father only a few days ago and now she was confronted with a daughter she had never known had existed. History was repeating itself in some ways.

She smoothed her dress.

"There's so much to catch up with, so much to talk about…"

She stopped as she heard the sound of a car drawing up.

Footsteps at the door made Beth realise that they were sitting in the dark. The evening skies had started to darken and the room was gloomy. She got up and switched the lights on.

"Please give me time to explain to David and Brian," she said quickly. Tina nodded as Brian walked in.

"Smells good, more baking! No wonder I put on so much weight," said Brian, taking a biscuit from the plate.

"Nice to see you again Tina," he said, seeing her sitting upright on the chair.

"I'll make some tea," said Beth rushing to the kitchen.

Tina's mobile rang. It was Andrew. She was so relieved.

"Yeah, please come and pick me up," she said to him.

"Andrew is on his way," she announced to both of them. She added, "I'll help Mrs. Fernandez with the tea," and hurried into the kitchen.

The stilted conversation in the dining room was saved by Sheba. The puppy's antics to get more biscuits diverted their attention. Brian tired from his work noticed little.

Tina ran to the car when Andrew arrived. She waved goodbye to Brian and Beth and as soon as they were out of sight, she collapsed in a heap on the seat. He drove for a short while then parked the car.

"Are you okay, honey? How did she take it?"

Andrew waited for her answer.

"God, it was so difficult. I still can't believe I've told her." She sighed deeply, still perplexed about the fact that the momentous scene was over and yet she felt unsure about everything. She wiped away her tears.

"I don't know if I said the right things. I mean how do you broach such a subject? Oh God, Andrew I hope she doesn't hate me, and we've got so much more to say to each other."

He took her in his arms and nestled his face in her hair.

"Hey, this is awesome stuff. I mean, there's no right or wrong way, as long as you've connected with her. I think you need to wait now and maybe take some rest," he said gently.

Rest? Yes she was exhausted. The quest had taken its toll. She had looked forward to this moment for so many years and yet the whole thing had passed in a moment like a dream. It was like an old forgotten song that had suddenly burst into life and curled back again into the recesses of her mind. She wanted more. She wanted to shout and tell the world that she was Tina Thomas, Beth and George's daughter. The thought lasted momentarily and fused into other thoughts. Margaret and Tony were her mum and dad too.

The humid night helped little to assuage Tina's feelings of guilt, confusion and worry. Had she done the right thing? A cool shower helped and later she stood under the ceiling fan which whirled above her, its circular movements paralleling her thoughts. Mrs. Fernandez, she still could not think of her as Beth, and their talk, replayed in her mind. She also had texts from Margaret, her mum. She had to tell her. What was she going to say to her?

Tina picked the phone, and then put it down again several times. Her hesitation was short-lived as Margaret called her.

"Tina, how are you doing? We've not heard for a while from you,"

"I'm fine. Is dad okay?"

Tina's hand went to her lips, itching to bite one of her nails.

"Well, he's fine. I rang to ask what you'd like me to get you for Christmas."

Christmas! Tina had forgotten all about it. She had been so engrossed in her own world that she had not even bought any cards.

"I'll tell you later. There's something more important mum. I." Tina stopped, and then started again. "I've found her…the biological…my genetic…the lady who donated the embryo."

There was a pause and a deep sigh. She visualised her mum composing herself.

"My God! I'm surprised. How Tina? Where? I mean how did you find her?"

"Oh mum. You won't ever believe it."

"Who is she? What does she look like? I mean have you seen her?" Margaret's voice trembled with anxiety.

"It's Mrs. Fernandez, Beth, Uncle James's daughter."

Tina explained as quickly as she could about Father Ignatius and how they had found out that Beth's married name was

Fernandez. She heard her mum make a choking sound, then she exclaimed,

"What? No, that can't be! Oh My God! The oracle, the past in your future."

"What do you mean? You're not making any sense at all."

"Tina, this is incredible!" Margaret reminded her about the oracle of the leaves and the prophecy when she and Tony had visited India earlier.

"Oh that god man!" Tina exclaimed.

"Tell me more. What did Beth say? This must have been a terrible shock for her too," Margaret added.

Tina was thrilled that her mum had taken the whole thing in her stride.

"I need to see her again. I'm so confused but I'm so glad I've found her. I feel so loved, so wanted." Tina hesitated and then whispered, "I do love you mum, you know that."

"Tina, of course you do, my love. I wish I was with you."

Margaret's thoughts turned to the day she had given birth to Tina, the miraculous moment that had made her life complete. In her mind she thanked Beth, the young woman who had given her Tina.

*

Later that night, Beth couldn't shake off a recurring image of four boys and a girl from her mind. If Tina could find her after all these years, what about the other embryos? She thought to herself. She rested her eyes; images of a baby girl came to her like a vision and disappeared again. The baby girl was holding out her hands and smiling and then ran way. She woke up suddenly. She realised she'd had this dream before, and thought it was her mum's spirit looking down on her.

Chapter 27

In the reflection of the mirror, Tina looked for any resemblance to Beth, to David, to James. Her mind swirled. Were there any incipient behaviour traits that she had not noticed before? She and David had been conceived, at the same time! Conceived. Was that the right word she wondered? Images of cells dividing in Petri dishes, packets of blood dripping into her veins, baked goodies, and the puppy Sheba floated in her mind. She shuddered. There was so much to take in.

She kept questioning herself. What did she feel for Beth?
Images of Margaret and Tony transposed on Beth and Brian flitted across her mind. She was happy yet terrified. What had she unleashed?

This was what she had been pining for all her life. She had seen Beth in the flesh, no longer a fantasy. Beth seemed a good person. She had saved her life. But what did she mean now to Tina? She paced the room. She looked at the piece of paper that had led her to Beth. It had happened quicker than she had imagined. Her head throbbed.

What was Beth feeling? How would David react if and when he knew? There were more questions than answers.
Andrew knocked on the door.

"Tina, it's me," he said softly.

She opened the door and let him in. Safe in his arms she relaxed, cried a bit, and then wiped her tears.

"I'm confused, Andrew. I don't know if I did the right thing."

"Sure it was the right thing to do, babe."

Andrew's placatory tone was helpful.

"Maybe I should've kept it to myself. I mean, it's not just Beth, there's David and Brian too," worried Tina.

"Listen, she must be going through the same feelings as you, but remember she has just found out that you exist. That can't be easy."

Tina was quiet for a moment.

"She may even be wondering if there are more of her children somewhere in the world," he added.

"Oh gosh, I never thought of that. This is a nightmare."

Tina bit her nail.

Andrew took her hand gently from her mouth.

"Come on, let's have something to eat, take your mind away from it."

"I'm not hungry," she said.

"That can't be true. You've not eaten anything for hours now. I insist, come on!" he urged her and dragged her out of the room.

He made her a chocolate milkshake, chilled and frothy.

"Sorry, no marshmallows," he said, looking for a packet in the cupboard.

"Wow, this tastes so good," she said licking her lips.

"See, you've not eaten for so long that even my milkshake tastes good. I'm going to order a Dominos Pizza. Your usual toppings madam?" he joked, putting the tea towel over his arm and bowing slightly.

She giggled.

"Good to see that smile again," he said and lifted the phone to place an order.

For the next couple of days Tina was on tenterhooks. Would Beth call and want to see her again? Tina wanted to meet with her to apologise for intruding on her life. She had lifted the phone so many times to call and talk to her but had changed her mind at the last minute.

Andrew advised her to wait for Beth to make the next move.

The call came when she had almost given up hope.

"Do come and see me Tina. I must talk to you again."

The whole house was quiet when Tina walked in. Even Sheba was nowhere to be seen. The familiar smell of baking was missing.

"I'm so sorry. It was totally selfish of me to do this to you,"

Tina started with the apology.

Beth sighed and sat down heavily on the sofa.

"Yes, this has been an absolute shock. I've still not got to grips with finding my dad."

"I understand. I should've thought of you first, but…I've been looking for you all my life."

Tina's eyes darted about the room as the words were tumbling out. She found it hard to stifle her feelings.

"I had to tell David and Brian," Beth smoothed her skirt. Her nervousness showed too.

"How did David take it? Does…does he hate me?" Tina stuttered.

"No, he doesn't. Both were stunned of course. I think we're all coming to terms with It slowly. We're confused. We do love you Tina."

Beth looked at the picture of David in his school uniform. It was on the wall beside the photo of her parents.

The conversation was difficult. They were both at a loss to say how they felt.

"I'll make some tea," said Beth getting up from her sofa.

"No, please hear me out," said Tina. "I had this deep sense of wanting to see you, I hope you understand. Never for a moment did I think of how you would feel. I'm so sorry."

"Tina, I know what you mean. I wanted to find my dad all my life. That was a huge chunk missing from my life. Then James appears and within a few days before I could barely make sense of that, and then I learn about you. I mean it is so much to deal with. It's just that. I didn't even know you existed. I'm so sorry. Do you know what I'm saying?"

"I know exactly what you mean, Mrs. Fernandez. I had imagined this scene all my life but now I'm with you. I'm not sure what to say."

Tina dabbed at the sweat on her face with a tissue.

"I'm glad you've told me Tina. I really am. But where do we go from here? I mean your mum…Margaret." Beth hesitated.

"I love her," said Tina quickly. "I mean, she's everything…Oh God, I don't know what I'm saying."

She stood up and paced the room.

"Tina, of course you love her, she's your mum. I've just come into your life."

The awkwardness passed.

"Now that I know you and David, I'd like to keep in touch with you both if I may." Tina had said it at last. She felt herself lighten a little. She exhaled with relief.

"You've been special to us since you arrived in Mumbai, even more so now," Beth smiled. She relaxed too.

"I mean we must not lose touch with each other. I'll be back in Glasgow soon."

"Yes, I know. I don't know if there is a right way to go about this, but how about we make sure we call each other, or email each other?"

"Or even use Skype," added Tina.

"Of course," said Beth and she came over and gave her a hug.

They stood close, hearts beating together, breathing as one, a new connection forged in seconds.

Getting to know Beth and forging a link with her, fulfilled Tina in the way that she had hoped. Margaret was her mum but Beth would always be special. The shadowy figure that had filled her imagination was now a person who really existed. She was the piece of the jigsaw that had been missing in her life and now that she had found her, she would cherish her all her life. She felt complete. Her quest had come to an end and yet it felt like she'd been given a new beginning.

Christmas 2009

Almost a year had passed by, a year when Tina's life had changed irrevocably.

Back home with her parents, life seemed the same. That dull ache of uncertainty that had dogged her life had vanished, and now she could focus on her studies. David and she kept emailing each other. A new extended family filled her life with emotions that she had been unaware of. It was easier with David, a new sibling whom she felt close to. Beth was more complicated. It was a slow process, she was still feeling her way with her.

Her relationship with Andrew never wavered. Pictures of her and Andrew in Mumbai hung on the wall and her computer screen had his picture. Andrew had kept his promise of coming over for Christmas.

Tina looked out of the bedroom window at the snow lying in the garden, glistening in the vague sunshine. Her books for the university were piled high on her desk. Andrew got off the bed and put his arms around her.

"We'd have a foot high snow at holiday season", he said.

She laughed out loud.

"Holiday season, it is Christmas," she said giving him a peck on his cheek.

Tony and Margaret heard them moving about upstairs.

'She's happy," said Margaret.

Tony grunted a yes, as he cleared the table of the breakfast dishes.

"Andrew is good for her." Margaret added. She stayed at the table thinking. Her child, the miracle baby that she had to now share with someone she had never imagined would ever feature in their lives. Tina was theirs, but the Wilsons were an added dimension to her life. She thanked God that Beth was in India, far away.

Keisha, and Sean arrived on Christmas Eve for dinner. Keisha arrived, whooping with joy at the beautiful Christmas tree that Margaret, Tina and Tony had decorated in the lounge.

"You've topped it this year Mrs. W, utterly devastatingly gorgeous. Man, this is so good," she said in her loud voice then gave them all a kiss.

"Keisha, stop praising it to the skies! We all enjoyed decorating it, didn't we Tina?" Margaret commented and hurried away to get some mulled wine and nibbles for all.

Tina introduced Andrew to Keisha and Sean.

"Meeting you in the flesh at last Andrew," said Keisha and gave him a huge hug. "You've saved my best friend's life, her guardian angel that's you, thank you," she said graciously.

"He's, my life," said Tina squeezing his hand her eyes shining with love.

Keisha glanced at the cards and the one from Beth, David and Brian stood out, a beautiful picture of the The Basilica of Bom Jesus church in Goa.

"This is going to be the best Christmas ever," she declared hugging Sean and winking at Tina.

They all agreed as they raised a glass of mulled wine, and enjoyed the meal.

Late at night the Wilson's and Andrew sat in the lounge having a nightcap. They watched the snow fall gently outside, each one deep in their own thoughts.

*

In Mumbai, a woman switched her computer on and checked her emails. She read the one from James with great interest. A man she was learning to understand and forgive for his years of absence in her life.

She clicked open the next email.

Hi Beth,

Wish you all a very Happy Christmas. You and your family have a special place in our hearts. We hope to visit Mumbai one day. Give my love to David and Brian.

Love Tina x

A wide smile creased her face. She listened to the Christmas hymn that wafted over the internet connecting her to the other side of the world and her other life.